The Swamp Whisperer

**A Sidra Smart Mystery
Book Four**

Sylvia Dickey Smith

2019 White Bird Publications, LLC 3rd Edition

Copyright © 2012 by Sylvia Dickey Smith

Published in the United States
by White Bird Publications, LLC, Texas
http://www.whitebirdpublications.com

Paperback ISBN 978-1-63363-443-5
eBook ISBN 978-1-63363-444-2
Library of Congress Control Number 2019954627

PRINTED IN THE UNITED STATES OF AMERICA

To my dear friend, Penny LeLeux.
Her creative mind runs in fast forward.

Acknowledgements

Bruce Lockett knows more about the Atakapa Indians, the original inhabitants of Southeast Texas, than anyone I know. Bruce offered immense support and guided my research. His "field trip" to the shell mounds, and the tales he shared, fired my passion for this book.

Other books by Sylvia

Original Cyn

Sacred Lessons from Wilderness Wandering

A War of Her Own

Sidra Smart Mystery Series

Dance on His Grave
Deadly Sins, Deadly Secrets
Dead Wreckoning
The Painted Ladies

The Swamp Whisperer

**White Bird
Publications**

Chapter One

Boo Murphy snatched her fishing pole and her .22 rifle from behind the front door and stormed out. Dang it, she was going fishing.

Now.

"Don't need daylight to find my trotlines," she mumbled. "Traipsed these mosquito and alligator-infested bayous all my life. If can make my way in the middle of the night, I dang sure don't need to wait for sunrise."

The soft clump, clump, clump of her rubber boots echoed off of the early morning stillness as she made her way across the yard and down the path to the dock behind her house. Granddaddy had built the gray little shotgun house with the strongest Longleaf yellow pine he could find. It had taken everything Mother Nature could throw at it for a hundred years or more, and if she gave it the right attention, likely it could make another hundred.

Her pirogue waited, bobbing at water's edge. She'd built it some time ago, and in the typical Cajun-style—flat-bottomed, lightweight, and easy to maneuver. Since then, the small boat was like an extension of her home, for she spent as much time in one as she did the other. After stashing the gear, she climbed in and whistled for her dog, a brindle-colored mutt with long legs and floppy ears. Four years ago, he'd shown up on her doorstep smack in the middle of a hurricane. She'd had no idea where he came from, or what his name was, but he'd stayed, and she'd just called him Dawg.

Alert, waiting for her signal, he ran lickety-split down the pier, tongue and ears flapping behind him, toenails scrabbling across the weather-beaten wood. While still a good several feet away, he took a flying leap toward the boat and landed with a whoomp, back legs inside the pirogue, head, and front legs flaying and splashing in the greenish water on the other side. She'd never heard so much chuffing and snorting in her life. But after a quick, wet scramble, he'd reunited front and back inside the pirogue, regained his footing, and high-stepped it up to the bow where he assumed his position as front guard.

"Dang impatient dog," Boo mumbled, laughing at the silly mutt.

Once they were both settled, she used the long pole to punt the boat into deeper water, and then exchanged it for the paddle. By the time daylight peeked through the trees, they were well on their way up the Blue Elbow Swamp.

It was late September, and as usual in her part of the world, autumn's first chill was still weeks away. However, hurricane season wasn't, and there was something brewing off the Gulf Coast. No telling what direction it might take, but even if it did come her way, she still had time to get in a little fishing.

The dip and drip of her paddle in and out of the

murky water, Dawg's eager pant, and her own raspy breath were soon the only sounds she heard. They were also the only sounds she *wanted* to hear.

But when a mournful cry shattered the peaceful dawn and Boo saw a movement out of the corner of her eye, she yanked the paddle into the boat and grabbed her rifle. By then, whatever might have been there was long gone.

"I know I saw something, Dawg, and that scream sounded kinda like a panther. I ain't heard a big cat out here in so many years I thought they'd all died out."

Hackles raised and ears lifted, Dawg woofed and increased his vigilance.

Nope, she sure wasn't imagining things—not the way Dawg was acting.

Lifting her nose, Boo sniffed the air, turned her head and sniffed again, but all she smelt was the odor of fish, rotting vegetation, and cypress and pine needles after the night's fresh rain—that and musty Spanish moss, dangling from the trees looking like old men's curly gray beards.

The cak-cak-cak of a Cooper's hawk caused her to look up in time to see the raptor tip its speckled-brown wing at her and light in a treetop, but she heard no more screams.

"It must've been a panther, either that or maybe the…the…swamp ghost come to get us." She laughed at her own foolishness but shuddered all the same. Lord, she never thought she'd be glad to see a panther again, but the thought of a ghost sure didn't make her feel any better. She'd heard tales about the swamp ghost before. Didn't know if she believed them or not, even though she might've heard one herself a couple of times, but seeing it was a whole n'other thing.

Perhaps she'd imagined the scream, and the sense someone was there. But no, although Dawg held his position as front guard, he trembled all over. So much so, she feared he'd fall out of the boat and into the water.

"Don't feel bad, boy. You ain't the only one scared. They say folks what follow the sound of her crying ain't never been seen again, so we sure ain't heading that direction."

She didn't mention she wasn't positive which direction that was.

"But, then again, I heard the ghost is the spirit of a barren woman drawing folks to her 'cause she's lonesome. Then, soon as her ghostly hands touch them, they drop deader 'n a doornail."

The look on Dawg's face made her wish she hadn't told him that last part. Before she could take it back and tell him she was teasing, a cool breeze blew in, and along with it, a voice in the wind whispering, *all is not well.*

Boo looked around. "Who's there? What do you want?"

Whatever it was departed with the breeze, leaving behind the stillness of warm, muggy doldrums. The only sounds then were the pounding in her ears and Dawg's banging knees. He watched the shoreline with her as if he too waited for something to jump out and eat them.

A movement along the riverbank snatched her attention, but it was only a brown mink scampering across fallen tree branches, making its way home before it became another critter's breakfast.

"Boo Murphy, what's getting into you?" she admonished herself. "You've seen so many weird things in your lifetime you ain't easy to spook."

Imagining things—that's what she was doing—a sign of old age for sure, and she dang well wasn't giving in to that. "Come on, boy, let's forget it. Just act like we ain't heard nothing. Whatever it was, it's likely long gone now. Let's put it out of our minds and enjoy our day."

With that, Dawg whined his agreement and turned his attention to his task while she nudged slow and easy breaths in and out, slow and easy, in and out, forcing panic to release its vise around her chest.

Allowing the boat to drift, they wended their way around the bends, Boo reminding herself she had all day to get nowhere. Remnants of the earlier rainfall dripped from the trees and pitter-pattered into the greenish-brown water, leaving tiny swirls soon absorbed by the overpowering peace of still waters. She looked around, her voice barely above a whisper. "Lord a mercy, Dawg, ain't this the most beautiful sight you done ever seen? I never get tired of this place—even if the damp does make my joints ache." And they did ache, so much so that she and the arthritis she lived with were now on a first-name basis—Arthur, she called it.

Her thoughts floated to Mama, and the stories she'd tell Boo as she tucked her in between crisp, white, smelling-like-sunshine sheets. Stories about how long ago—maybe two thousand years, maybe longer than that—the Atakapa-Ishak Indians first settled along these rivers feeding into the Texas Gulf Coast. Savages some said. Others called them cannibals. She wondered at their disappearance with the coming of the white man. Reminded her of the Sodom and Gomorrah myth in the Bible, of how God destroyed the city because of the people's sinful ways. Maybe the God of the Atakapa-Ishak and the God people worshipped today were the same one—or at least cousins, like her and Sasha.

"Getting along with swamp critters is way easier than getting along with Sasha, ain't it, boy?"

Dawg chuffed and adjusted his stance.

"Yeah, I know. You ain't taking sides, but you know exactly what I mean, don't you? At least critters go about minding their own business, but kinfolk…humph."

It irritated her to no end how Sasha, her second cousin once removed, always tried bossing her around and making fun of how she talked to Dawg like he was somebody.

Well, dang it, he was.

The look of supreme pleasure on his face told her she wasn't the only one enjoying the morning. His tongue dangled down the side of his mouth like a dying man lying prone in a desert instead of a dog riding down the middle of a swamp filled with alligators, snakes, and, God forbid, ghosts. Every couple of minutes, he slurped in his tongue, excitement dancing in his eyes and in his butt. She figured his heart, like hers, thumped stronger and louder when they plied the swamps and bayous hunting, fishing, and looking for shell mounds, all the while, keeping one eye open for the Atakapa-Ishak—just in case.

They rounded a bend, and Andrine's place came into view. Her house, supported above the water by tall stilts, stood over an equally small piece of land smack in the middle of bayou country. A short path from a nearby dock led to a porch attached to the weather-beaten, dilapidated-looking shack.

Boo had known Andrine for years, and sometimes, when she saw Andrine on her porch or fishing off the dock in front of her house, she'd stop to chat. The woman supported herself on the services she rendered to people who needed what she offered. Never charged, just took what they could afford. She called herself a seer, read tarot cards, tapped into some energy way beyond what Boo could figure out.

Boo's cousin Sasha didn't like Andrine—said she dabbled in Voodoo.

"She ain't no more a Voodoo woman than me or you, is she, Dawg? I ain't never seen her cast spells, drink chicken blood or nothing like that."

But she did smell—something awful. Boo often thought of bringing Andrine a deodorant stick but feared she'd offend the women. Besides, underarm deodorant could only go so far. So Boo had just learned to breathe through her nose when she visited.

Sasha wasn't the only one who mistrusted Andrine.

Others in town didn't either. That's why, years ago, Andrine bought the little shack out here in the middle of the swamp, moved in and stayed. That way nobody could say a word about what she did—or what she smelled like.

Boo had feared the woman would starve to death, but enough folks knew where she'd moved and came to see her when they needed advice or help with a problem. Today, she was nowhere in sight, so Boo inhaled through her nose and paddled on.

In no time, Andrine slipped out of Boo's thoughts while catching fish slid in.

A while later, she arrived at her favorite fishing spot, her heart skipping a beat like it did every time she came. Disappointed to find her trotlines empty, she reset them, and then collected her bamboo pole, put the biggest, squiggliest worm on the hook and dropped it into the water, letting any and every other thought that crept into her mind slip right on out the other side. Meanwhile, Dawg took his first nap of the day, snoring to beat sixty.

But after a couple of hours without a single nibble, the idea of stewed squirrel for supper sounded better than wasting her time waiting for disinterested fish. She made her way across the canal to a tall, thick-kneed cypress. Rifle in hand, she swung her legs over the side of the boat and stepped into the boggy mire. "You stay here," she called to Dawg, now wide-awake. "I don't want you running around barking your fool head off scaring the squirrels before I can get a bead on them."

He whined his complaint but did as instructed.

Her boots squished and sucked as she trudged through the muck. When she reached solid ground, she trudged beneath a line of oaks, thankful the night's soft rain plastered the leaves into the mud. There was nothing worse than rustling leaves to scare away the squirrels— that is, except for maybe a dog that loved to chase them.

She eased along, quick eyes watching for the slightest movement. Before long, a fox squirrel barked at her and scampered to the other side of a tree.

"Dang it," she whispered. "Now, I'm sorry I made Dawg stay in the pirogue. We could've trapped that squirrel." She would have brought him, she reminded herself, if the ornery hound hadn't kept her awake half the night howling at that infernal train whistle. If she rewarded him, he never would learn that nighttime was for sleeping, not howling.

She slipped around the tree only to have the bushy-tailed critter scamper to the other side again. Minutes passed while the two seesawed from one side of the tree to the other. Then, remembering an old trick, she picked up a stick and tossed it, making a ruckus behind the critter. When he scampered to her side of the tree, she took quick aim and fired.

Dinner gave a soft thud when it hit the ground.

She collected the game, tucked it into the pouch of her hunting vest, and re-cocked her trusty single-shot rifle.

Half an hour later, she'd bagged two more of the clever little critters—enough for a good-size pot of stew for her and Sasha—and sloshed back to the boat.

Pleased to no end when he saw her approach, Dawg yipped and bounced around in the pirogue like she'd been gone a week and might never return. Once she climbed in, he resumed his place at the bow, eyes staring straight ahead. He'd whine every few minutes and look at her, then return to his task.

In a hushed, reverent whisper, she said, "Just think, boy, tens of thousands of years ago, the Atakapa Indians wandered this land. "Story also goes they was man-eaters, too. They not only killed people like us, but they cooked them and had them for dinner. Hear tell they smeared alligator fat on their skin to keep the mosquitoes from eating them alive. Folks think Andrine stinks, but I bet they stank to high heaven, too, don't you?" She slapped a couple of mosquitoes biting her neck. "On second thought, maybe Andrine uses alligator oil and for the same reason."

It wasn't that Dawg hadn't heard her stories before, but he always listened as if with new ears. And he never argued back like Sasha did. Sure would be nice if the men in her life had been and were all like that.

"Hear tell, the men hunted and killed giant sloths, wooly mammoths, and saber-toothed tigers. The women did everything else, like having and tending to babies, all the cleaning and skinning and cooking." She snorted. "Guess times ain't changed that much."

Goosebumps popped out on her arms, and she confessed, "You know what? Sometimes when I'm out here in the swamp, I kinda feel like I am one of them Indians. Then other days, I swear they're tracking me. One day, I thought I seen a half-dressed one standing on the shore, waving at me as I paddled by. A young Indian woman stood next to him holding her belly, big with child. I squeezed my eyes shut, and when I looked again, they was gone. Makes me wonder if they're still out here hiding from folks while keeping an eye on us all the time."

Dawg raised his hackles and woofed a couple of times while he watched the bank.

She paddled through a tunnel of low-hanging branches, and a twig tore at the sleeve of her dun-colored shirt. When she yanked her arm loose, a small piece of the material tore off and bounced into the tree along with the branch, but she paid it no never mind. Sasha hated the shirt anyway, said it reminded her of those filthy mud pies Boo used to make when she was a kid. For the life of her, Boo couldn't figure out why some people had so much trouble with dirt. "Heck," she said to Dawg, "the Bible says we was made from the dust of the earth anyway, so what's the big deal?"

They came upon an extra heavy growth of bald cypress and water tupelo, making it difficult to see ahead.

When she eased through a slip expecting open waterway, a mist curtain lay before her. Surprised, but no stranger to fog, she paddled straight toward it. Soon as she entered, however, the mist parted like Moses' Red Sea, leaving clear passage for her and her pirogue—that was, until a half-mile or so ahead, something else loomed.

"What in the world is that?" Heart pounding, Boo paddled faster, unable to take her eyes off of what lay before her, while her mind tried to believe it. She squinted, hoping to see someone—anyone—but not a single, solitary soul was in sight. Through the stand of oak and pine, however, she strained to make out the strange-looking hut made of dried palmetto branches. Its shape reminded her of an upside-down bowl, but with an opening on the side. Smoke curled from another hole in the top. Who would build something like that, she wondered, and then go and put a fire in it?

Chapter Two

Sidra Smart eyed the rearview mirror. Not a car in sight coming or going. They were on a remote stretch of New Mexico highway in the middle of the night somewhere between Las Cruces and Santa Fe, and Annie needed a bathroom now.

"I don't care if there's a bush to squat behind or not, Siddie. If you don't pull over and let me out right now, you might as well forget it."

"I pulling, I'm pulling." Sid wondered if she'd heard a knock under the hood as she eased the maroon Olds off the road and into a clump of weeds poking up through the asphalt, however, before she could bring it to a full stop, Annie, who was seventy-eight but wouldn't admit to more than sixty, was out and gone. In the bright moonlight, her neon yellow top shined as if in a spotlight as she high-stepped it across and around small bushes, yanked down her stretched-out black tights, and squatted.

Even though it was early October, the peak of a mountain off in the distance glistened with early snowfall. After the summer they'd had back home in Texas, breaking every drought and heat record, Sid was tempted to head up the slope and roll in what looked like cold drifts of the white stuff.

They'd left home a couple of days ago, spent the first night west of San Antonio and the second in El Paso—an easy one day drive from there to Santa Fe, however, a flat tire in the middle of nowhere and the extra hours it took to get it fixed cost them a lot of daylight. It almost cost Sid her sanity when Annie became hysterical at the delay, fearful she'd miss the wedding. She'd squeezed Sid's arm until she'd solicited a promise they'd get there before the wedding occurred, which gave them that day's travel time. Sid had accommodated Annie with the promise—for all the good that would do.

For the life of her, Sid wasn't sure why all the excitement over the wedding. It wasn't like it was the woman's first. The best Sid could tell, she had married and either divorced or outlived six husbands already. Still, she planned a traditional floor-length white gown with an eight-foot train.

Then there was Annie in a poufy bridesmaid dress.

But Annie had given her word to her friend. She'd be there and serve as a bridesmaid. Neither floodwaters nor brimstone would prevent her attendance.

However, having to fly just might—hence the road trip. Since Sid's vehicle was in the shop, they'd taken Annie's older model maroon Oldsmobile.

After the repaired-tire chore, they'd picked up KFC in some little podunk town and kept going.

The wedding was day after tomorrow morning, and if they missed it, Sid dreaded the drive home. Forced to live with her aunt in a ghost-active house was bad enough—add a major disappointment, and Sid just might not survive. That wasn't counting the fact that her Private Investigations office still occupied one corner of Annie's pre-Civil War house due to all kinds of construction delays on the new one.

The longer she waited for Annie, the more she realized the condition of her own bladder. She grabbed a handful of tissues and crossed to the opposite side of the narrow highway.

Halfway through—at the point that even if Jesus were to show up and tell her to stop everything and follow him, she'd have to disobey and take her chances— she noticed a pair of golden-looking eyes staring at her from inside a nearby creosote bush.

A mountain lion, a bobcat, cougar, a black bear?

What did she do now? Even if she ran straddle-legged, leaving a streaming wet trail behind her, she couldn't reach the car before whatever was in the bushes leapt out and grabbed her. In the midst of fright and indecision, the image of the scene broadcast on YouTube snickered through her thoughts.

The golden eyes moved through the shrubs, coming closer, but low to the ground, until a skin-and-bones dog crept out. It happened so fast, Sid had to finish and rearrange her clothes while she sweet-talked the dog. "You hungry, boy?" she said just to make sure he knew *she* was friendly—whether he was or not. "I've got leftovers in the car, and from the looks of you, you're not worried about whether or not the food is cold. Hold on, and I'll get you something to eat."

With the dog a few cautious steps behind her, Sid went to the car, reached into the red and white bucket in the back seat, and came up with a half-eaten drumstick. She extended her hand. "SPCA wouldn't like me giving you a chicken bone, but I figure if you've half-starved, a chicken bone's worth the risk. Here, boy, come on, it's yours for the taking."

The dog eyed her and the food with suspicion.

"What'd you say?" Annie asked.

"I'm talking to this dog that came up. Looks like he's starving to death."

Not taking his eyes off the meat, the dog went down on his belly and inched his way closer, sniffing as if to ensure he wasn't imagining things. When his nose tapped the bone, he jumped back as if he couldn't believe his luck—or thought it a nighttime mirage.

By then, Annie had walked around the car and stood near Sid, urging the dog to eat.

Decision made, the wild-haired dog snatched the food and took off around the open door, leapt into the car, and sprawled in the back seat as if he reclined on his own palace bed.

Annie laughed. "Looks like he's going with us."

Sid stood with her hands on her hips. "I don't believe this. We can't take him with us, Annie. For one thing, he's been out in the desert for no telling how long. He likely has all kinds of ticks and fleas and other parasites on him."

"You're right."

They both called and coaxed and pulled, but it was soon evident he'd found a good thing and knew it. He wasn't budging.

"We gotta go, Siddie. Maybe we can get him out at the next town and leave him on the doorstep of a vet's office."

"If we ever come to one." Sid climbed in behind the wheel and buckled her seat belt. Annie followed, and off they went, mangy cur dog and all.

"It's a cinch we can't take him home with us," Sid argued. "With your king cat Chesterfield and my dog Slider, there's no way."

A couple of hours later, and no civilization or daylight in sight, Sid gave in to Annie's pleadings to let her drive for a couple of hours so Sid could sleep.

"I'll wake you in two hours," Annie argued. "What can go wrong in that amount of time?"

Chapter Three

"Hullo—anybody there?" Boo called out and waited for an answer.

An alligator slithered off the bank and soon disappeared beneath the water.

She glanced at the darkening sky. "Rain's a coming sure as we sit here. I'm dying to check out that hut, but I'm wondering if we got time before it hits."

Dawg looked at her, disappointment clouding his face.

"I'm as nosy as you, boy. I been in these parts many a time, but I ain't never seen nothing like that." She pulled her collar up against the sudden rain now pelting them. Before turning to head home, she squirmed and stretched one last time to get a better look.

When it hit her what she'd found, she sat as still as if she'd been turned into a pillar of salt.

A couple of minutes passed before she found her voice, but when she did, she spoke in the softest of whispers—as if fearful the place would disappear if anyone heard her.

"An Atakapa-Ishak camp—yep, that's what it is all right, Dawg. I been dreaming about seeing something like this for so long, but now when I do, I can't believe my own eyes."

Dawg barked agreement.

Gawking, itching to get closer to shore, she picked up her pole and rammed it down into the murky swamp only to discover the pole couldn't touch bottom when, just a couple of minutes ago, she'd had no problem doing so.

A glance at the ever-darkening sky led her to recalculate how much time she had before the bottom dropped out. She came up short. As if that weren't bad enough, a bolt of lightning flashed across the sky like a warning from an angry God.

She pulled Dawg close and the two sheltered under her hunting vest, shivering, while she tuned her senses to the swamp and listened.

All is not well, the cold rain whispered. Boo looked around, expecting to see some ghostly figure floating across the swamp, but no one was there. This time, she knew she hadn't been imagining things—of that she was most convinced. She may be getting senile, but dang it, she heard what she heard, and by the way Dawg acted, he had, too.

"Something ain't quite right, boy, but I ain't got no idea what it is. Anyways, I think we better give it up for today. I just wish I could figure out what that voice is warning me about and what the devil it expects me to do about it."

Dawg's pitiful look said he certainly wasn't happy either going home or, in this weather, staying put.

"Don't look at me that way, boy. I know we need to get home before this storm hits, leastwise we'll likely be sleeping out here all night—that is if the rain don't drown us. Much as I love this place, I sure don't want to spend the night out here. Besides, I don't know about yours, but even an angel's butt must itch if she has to sit on these seats all night long—not that I'm saying I'm an angel, you understand…" Boo laughed at her own joke but got the idea Dawg wasn't amused.

The trip home seemed to take twice as long. Excitement built in her chest. If she didn't tell someone what she'd found, a bona fide, for-sure Atakapa brushwood hut, she'd explode for sure.

What puzzled her, however, was that the tribe walked the Texas and Louisiana coastal areas so long ago it wasn't possible one of their huts could still be standing—much less lived in. Either her imagination had run wild, or someone had built a hut just like the Indians. "It's been more'n two hundred years since any of them have even been seen around here," she mumbled.

Dawg high-stepped it across the seats to Boo and licked her square in the face. Without losing a beat, she wrapped her arm around his neck and kept talking. "But if it ain't Indians, who is it? Somebody's using that hut. I seen the smoke to prove it. Why on earth would anybody do such a thing out in the middle of nowhere? That's what I gotta find out."

Dawg barked his interest.

"Don't worry, I'll bring you along when I come back." She smiled at him and rubbed his head. "Besides, you're my protector, ain't you, boy?"

An hour or so later, she eased the boat alongside the dock behind her house, slung the bowline around a half-rotted pole and followed Dawg out. Halfway up the walk, she remembered her gun and the hunting vest full of squirrels. Hustling to the boat, she snatched them and headed across the hard-packed yard towards Sasha's small frame house catty-corner to Boo's.

The dwellings were similar to each other—small, unpainted clapboards anchored to the land by moss-covered, water-stained concrete blocks rooted deep into Orange County, determined never to leave, despite Hell, high water, and the occasional hurricane.

Mildew-finished, splinter-infested front steps led from the yard up to like-minded porches. The only difference between the two houses, however, was obvious. For nothing about Boo's place screamed of extravagance. Instead, serviceable was the operative word. Not a single flower had the strength to force its head through the soil around her place, while Sasha had the biggest, greenest thumb in the county.

When Boo saw Sasha in her flower garden, she danced a little jig, singing out, "Sasha, guess what I found. You won't never believe it."

Sasha stood, clippers in one garden-gloved hand, and a collection of multi-colored zinnias in the other. "Well then, why don't you just tell me, Miss Priss?"

"I seen a real Atakapa brushwood hut," Boo said, breathless, pointing behind her. "I paddled through this pea-soup fog, and on the other side, I come upon this island-looking place I ain't never seen before. And that's where I seen the hut. Really, I seen it. Swear to God."

"Shame on you—swearing to God. You know I don't like that. Besides, what fool thing you talking about now?" Sasha waved Boo off. "Tales about them heathen Indians once living around here ain't true, and you know it."

"Sort of like your Sodom and Gomorrah?"

"Yeah, like that…no, *not* like that." Sasha raised her voice. "You tricked me into agreeing with you. You know the Bible's true."

"That's right. I forgot them stories don't have to have really happened for folks to believe they did." Boo curved her lips into a smirk. "I'll have you know just because the Atakapa nation might not be in the Bible, don't make it no less true than Sodom and Gomorrah."

"I don't care what you say," Sasha said through

clenched teeth. "There's no such thing as a mystical island out there in the bayou. This is Texas, for God's sake, and Southeast Texas at that. Ain't nobody in this town gonna believe a word you say."

She leaned over a rose bush, then changed her mind, straightened her spine, and glared at Boo. "I'm fed up with you, Boo Murphy. You've dang well had your head up your butt your whole life. When are you going to grow up and act like a lady?"

She flapped a hand at Boo, then turned and high stepped it toward her house, calling, "Forget it. If you ain't turned into a lady by now, I reckon you ain't never gonna."

Boo thought Sasha might sit in one of the two rocking chairs on the front porch, but she changed directions at the last minute and stormed through the screen door.

Boo trailed after her. "But, Sasha, listen at me—"

"Ain't likely a woman on Medicare traipsing in the swamp all day, every day, will ever act like a lady. Boo Murphy, your pa would roll over in his grave. He always told you to *act like a lady* even though you ain't one. Good thing he's dead and gone."

"Pa might turn in his grave, but Mama dang sure wouldn't. Just listen, Sasha. I seen this, this…" Boo hesitated, took a step backward and then, disgusted, tossed the orange hunting vest at Sasha. It thudded on the floor near her feet. "Since you ain't gonna listen at me, I ain't gonna clean them squirrels for supper."

Boo and Sasha had shared chores for years. Boo hated to cook—although she had a reputation for duplicating Mama's mouth-watering biscuits—and Sasha hated to clean the game she loved to eat.

"I'm done being treated like I ain't got no more sense than God gave a goose. You can starve to death for all I care." Boo stomped her foot at Sasha, who, in turn, kicked at the vest.

"Okay, okay, I'll cook them," Sasha said, giving in. "But I dang sure ain't skinning them nasty things."

"Humph, they ain't so nasty when they're filling your big belly. Only way you'll listen to a thing I say is for me to do what you want doing first. Okay, I'll skin them, but then you gotta hear me out while you're cooking our supper."

She snatched the hunting vest and stormed out, smiling after her back was turned. She let the screen door slam behind her. Sasha hated it when she did that—drove her up the wall.

Boo pounded down the steps and crossed the yard to the old tree stump. Making quick work cleaning the lot, she marched inside and plopped the game into Sasha's sink. "I reckon now you'll listen at me."

While Sasha cooked the stew, Boo recounted her adventure, leaving out the cries of the swamp ghost. Instead, she started with the turn she'd made into the slip and how the fog rolled in and settled around the area, to how the bottom dropped out of the swamp just at that one spot, to the incoming storm driving them home—a storm that seemed to have passed them by—at least for now.

"Weatherman says we might get more though, there's a tropical storm stalled just off the gulf." Sasha sprinkled salt in the big aluminum pot, stirred, and then rested the big spoon on the counter. "If—I mean, when— you go back out there, maybe I should go with you. That way, I can prove you didn't see no such thing."

"Wait just a cotton-picking minute, you saying I'm lying?

Sasha raised her hand at Boo. "I ain't done speaking yet. Let me finish."

Boo sighed and settled in the kitchen chair. "Go on."

"As I was trying to say before I was so rudely interrupted, if I don't go and prove you didn't see nothing, you ain't never gonna shut up."

"Okay, let's go. I double-dog dare you." Boo

hurried to her feet.

Sasha tossed a dishtowel at Boo. "Pshaw. You know it's too late today, and with this storm coming in, we'd be a fool to try. Let's say if the weather's okay, we go tomorrow maybe around ten o'clock?"

"Heck no, we ain't waiting till noon. We head out at first light, or I ain't never hunting and fishing for you again." There, that's telling her, Boo thought, turning so Sasha wouldn't see her smirk.

"Have it your way." Sasha grabbed bowls from the cabinet and ladled stew for the two of them. "Oh, by the way, Durwood came looking for you today."

"That man bugs the pee-whining out of me."

"He's in l-o-v-e." Sasha's laugh indicated the impossibility of any man loving a woman who preferred the swamp more than she did looking pretty.

Boo ignored her. She'd heard that laugh before.

After they finished supper and did the dishes, Boo left to feed Dawg and then retired early, knowing she wouldn't sleep a wink.

The next sound she heard was the rooster outside her window saying *morning*.

Chapter Four

Boo sat at the kitchen table dunking a cold biscuit into a mug of warmed-over coffee when she glanced out the front window and saw Sasha walking up on the porch. At least the woman had enough sense to wear a long-sleeved shirt, denim overalls, and rubber boots. Knowing Sasha, Boo figured she'd come dressed in her Sunday best.

She headed to the screen door and shoved it open. "Morning, Your Highness. I'm surprised to see you up this early. Come on in. I'm almost ready."

"I come to say I'm thinking we better not go today. The weatherman—I mean weather*woman*—" Sasha rolled her eyes— "said the storm's regrouped and headed this way."

Boo shook her head. "I let a little bad weather scare me off yesterday, but it ain't going to today. Besides, if a storm does hit, it might blow the hut to kingdom come, then how could I prove what I saw. It'll be hours before the storm gets here. It ain't going to take us long. I swear I'll get you home before bad weather gets here."

"Well, all right, since you promised. You got a lot of faults, Boo Murphy, but breaking a promise ain't one of them. Give me a minute to *freshen up*." Sasha turned and marched to the bathroom, her boots bouncing off the bare floor.

Boo knew what *that* meant. Give Sasha time to *fix her face,* and they'd never get off. She called to Sasha's retreating back, "I'll be waiting at the boat—no more'n five minutes, you hear me?"

Outside, Boo whistled for Dawg, and the two went down to the pier and waited.

Ten minutes later, Sasha sauntered down to the boat, a hint of cherry lipstick on her lips, hair neatly coiled in a bun, a straw hat in her hand, and a cotton bag slung over her shoulder.

Boo watched her approach, then bowed with a flair fit for a goddess queen. "Anytime you're ready, Your Highness."

Dawg jumped in the boat and assumed his place as front guard while Sasha made ready to board. Despite living near the water, she had no experience whatsoever getting into a boat of any kind. Boo watched with glee as her persnickety cousin grabbed the dock post with one arm and shuffled her feet while trying to decide which foot went in first. The decision made—or half-made—Sasha stretched one leg toward the boat, but the other leg either didn't have a clue when to go or simply refused to follow.

Thrown off balance by the aborted attempt, Sasha gave a loud yelp as she swung around grabbing at empty air until her arms and legs latched around the post as if it were a long-lost lover. The action stopped her fall into the murky water but did nothing to help her get into the rocking pirogue.

"Sasha, we ain't taking that post with us no matter how tight you hang onto it." Boo suppressed a roar of laughter building in her gut. She knew if she didn't,

Sasha would hightail it to the house and never agree to go again, and then Boo could never prove that what she'd seen really existed.

After several more awkward attempts, they all got settled, Dawg in front, Sasha in the middle, and Boo in the rear. She stuck the paddle into the now-disturbed water while Sasha stuck her nose in the air.

"Now, if you *did* see this Atakapa hut—not saying you did, you understand—but, *if* you did, you know it's not some dang mystical place," Sasha called to Boo. "If it's there, somebody's just camping out—or did. You do know that, don't you? Sometimes you imagine things."

Dawg looked at them as if weary of putting up with the two crazies.

"Don't you cock that head at me, Dawg. This ain't my fault," Boo said, glaring at Sasha's stiff back. "And I'll have you know, Your Highness, I ain't imagining nothing—at least not this time."

Oh, it really pissed her off when Sasha acted like she was so much better and smarter than her. Lord, please help her find the hut. If she didn't, she'd never hear the end of it. In fact, if she didn't, she might never bring Sasha back to dry land—just leave her out there in the swamp with the other bigmouth 'gators.

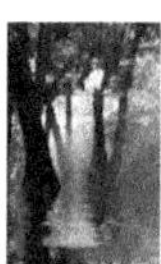

When they passed a spot Boo recognized from earlier that morning, she realized she'd gone in circles, but didn't dare admit it to Sasha. Instead, she said, "Its right around here somewhere. I know it is."

Sasha grunted acknowledgement, but her shoulders stayed hiked to her ears.

Disgusted with Sasha's attitude, but worried she hadn't found the hut, Boo increased her speed and soon came upon a patch of low hanging branches. Dawg scampered off his perch while Sasha ducked and yelled, "Christ Almighty, Boo, watch where you're going."

Boo grabbed the branches and shoved them over her head while easing the boat from underneath, smiling with the thought that if Sasha sat behind her, she'd let the branches go, and they'd slap Sasha right in the face.

Everything looked the same as yesterday—trees, moss, bends in the canal—however, no passage hidden behind fog, nor a single solitary hut. Boo began to doubt whether or not she'd seen what she'd thought. Maybe she had allowed her imagination to run wild again. Mama always said it was bigger'n Texas.

The morning grew into mid-day, and the hot, humid air left Boo struggling to breathe. In front of her, whiny-butt-Sasha wheezed too and complained about the mosquitoes feasting on her delicate white skin. Remnants of squashed insects remained on her neck, along with spots of dried blood.

"Hey, look." Sasha pointed to a bit of fabric dangling from a branch. "That's the same ugly color as that shirt you wore yesterday."

Boo looked where Sasha pointed and saw the torn piece of cloth from the day before. Relief washed over her. "Yep, it sure is. We're getting close." She paddled faster.

A few minutes later, she eased the pirogue around a bend, and there was the hut—grass and reed tied to a simple wooden frame. It looked as magical as a peacock spreading his magnificent tail feathers to court females, and indeed it had—her.

"Well, I'll swan." Sasha looked at Boo. "And here I didn't believe a word you said." She raised a hand and secured a tendril in her steel-gray bun. "Figured you was telling tales again like you did the time you said you'd seen a pirate ship. This time, you really did find something."

Boo *had* seen a pirate ship, but decided one victory

at a time was enough.

"There's something magical about this place, I tell you. My bones tell me it is." Boo glanced at the sky as she talked, swallowing a bad feeling about the darkening clouds. "I've got to paddle around to the other side—too many cypress knees sticking up here to get the boat close enough."

Excited, Sasha grabbed the edge of the boat and leaned over for a better look. The boat began to rock sideways.

Boo yelled, "Sit down. You're gonna flip us upside down."

Sasha tried to follow Boo's order but stumbled on her bag of makeup, clothes, and God knows what else she'd brought with her. Boo scrambled forward, snatching and grabbing but couldn't get a grip on Sasha or her bags as they tumbled out of the boat and into the muddy water.

The same high-pitched scream Boo heard the day before ripped through the air again. This time, Boo shoved it aside, fearful she might never see Sasha again.

"Sasha? Where are you? Help me, Dawg. We got to find her."

Dawg stuck his nose closer to the water, barking his head off.

When Sasha didn't surface right away, Boo snatched a rope, tied one end of it to the boat, and looped the other end around her waist. But before she could tie a knot, Sasha rose like a sputtering, spitting water nymph with silt and muck rolling off of her.

"Are you standing?" Boo hollered, remembering that yesterday her pole couldn't touch bottom.

"Yes, I'm standing, you nitwit, there's no sense in you screaming about it—won't help get me outta here any quicker."

Boo ignored Sasha's words, pretending to be busy with the rope around her waist.

"Where's my stuff?" Sasha raked mud and rotting vegetation off her face and arms while her hair maintained the look of mud-coated dreadlocks.

"Your *stuff*, as you call it, sunk to the bottom. Good riddance, I say." Boo tossed one end of the rope to Sasha, and together, the two pushed, shoved, yanked, twisted, and pulled until Sasha rolled across the edge of the boat and almost on top of a dog gone wild. Spooked, he raced around the pirogue as if the bottom were covered in red-hot coals, yipping with every step.

"Hush, Dawg," Sasha yelled. "Your infernal barking makes me want to cuss."

Oh, I wish she would cuss, Boo thought. For if Sasha cussed and God didn't strike her dead, then maybe there was hope for Boo.

Not so easily discouraged from celebrating the rescue, Dawg leapt in Sasha's lap and started licking all over her face.

"Get off me, you smelly mutt." Sasha shoved Dawg away and swiped at her mouth. In the process, she smeared what little cherry red lipstick still remained from earlier that morning.

Things couldn't get much worse, Boo decided, and then she spotted a leech on Sasha's neck. The woman had a hard enough time with mosquitoes. If she knew a leech sucked her blood, she'd mess her pants for sure—which meant Boo would have to take her home before they got to inspect the hut.

"Here, let me help you clean off some of that gunk." Boo sidled to Sasha and pretended to rearrange Sasha's nasty hair with one hand, while her other hand located the sucker at the small end of the leech. Trusting that the anesthetic leeches use to deaden the skin of their host did its job, Boo slid her fingernail to where the leech fed and pushed it sideways from Sasha's skin. Once she had the oral sucker loose, she quickly pulled loose the fat end, but when she did, the other end reattached to Sasha's neck.

Patience, patience.

Boo took a deep breath and repeated the steps. It worked that time. She tossed the leech into the water under pretext of taking extra effort to tuck a sprig of Sasha's hair under the remaining hairpins. Confident Sasha never suspected a thing, Boo smiled, pleased with her skills of deception. She didn't use them often, but sometimes a woman had to do what a woman had to do.

Still puzzled by the difference in water depth from the day before, Boo poled her way around the area and found nothing deeper than four feet. It didn't make sense, but mystical swamps often gave seemingly conflicting messages. Regardless, she had to inspect the brushwood hut. She nudged the boat further upland until she found a clearing, and paddled to shore. Dawg leapt to dry land. Boo followed him, and after that, dripping-wet Sasha.

Boo knew if she couldn't find a way to get Sasha cleaned up, and fast, she'd harp until Boo took her home. She already gave an occasional low whine. Now wasn't the time to go—not until Boo satisfied her curiosity with a closer inspection of what she'd seen.

"Come on, there's a path. Let's go see if we can find a place to get this mud off of you and get your clothes washed." She took Sasha by the arm and looked for Dawg, who'd already taken off on his own adventure.

"Stay in whistling distance," she called as he ran ahead of them. He barked his response and kept going.

Boo gave dripping wet, silent, sad-looking Sasha little choice but to follow her as she trudged up a narrow shell path canopied by the overhang of oak and pine trees. Spanish moss brushed their faces as they walked underneath.

The way opened to a trail winding alongside shell middens with fresh-looking, empty clamshells scattered on top of decaying ones. Nearby, the remains of an old battery or gun placement and a rusty cannonball lay half-buried in the dirt. Further down, someone had built a stone platform for boats to tie up. Since then, the river had evidently risen several times depositing sand and silt halfway up.

Sasha whined and limped along, stinking to high heaven.

"We've been going uphill and look, the trail turns here." Excitement built inside Boo, and she grabbed Sasha's hand as they cleared the trees and stepped onto a wide green field. "My guess is it's around this next stand of trees."

Instead of a brushwood hut, however, they saw a large house perched atop four ten or twelve-foot high piles driven directly into the ground. At one time, the place had been yellow, but most of the paint had peeled off in patches. A large, covered porch clung to the upper level as if it didn't hold on tight enough, the next strong wind might blow it away. On the ground underneath the house, trash lay in haphazard heaps.

"Well, call it what you will, but this house ain't a brushwood hut, that's for sure." Sasha looked at Boo, accusations flashing in her eyes.

"Don't be silly. I ain't blind. It must be on the other side of the island. We'll find it. In the meantime, come on. Let's see if these people can help us get you cleaned up."

"If they ain't home, I don't have the energy to climb all them steps for nothing. First, you go see if anybody's there."

Boo didn't argue, for she knew which side her bread was buttered on. It was *take care of*

Sasha, or go home before Boo was ready.

She took care of Sasha.

Chapter Five

Boo studied the situation for a couple of minutes, looking for options she might have missed. Finding none, she made her decision. She propped her shotgun on the stairs and looked at Sasha. "You rest. I'm going upstairs to see if anybody's home." She almost swallowed her tongue when Sasha obliged.

Boo brushed her hands down the front of her overalls, hoping she didn't look like the old swamp woman come to visit, and started up the outside stairs hoping they didn't collapse under her. She reached the porch, rounded a dilapidated wicker settee, tripped on a loose board, and knocked over a dried potted plant. She waited, wondering if the commotion would bring a reaction from inside the house.

A set of French doors creaked open. Was someone inside, peeking out to see who or what made all the noise? Certain someone was coming when the white lace curtains billowed out and flapped in the breeze, Boo listened for footsteps.

Hearing none, she waited a couple of minutes, then called out and knocked on the doorframe.

No one came.

She rapped again, harder, and then again. She peeked through the window, hoping she'd see someone—anyone.

Nothing.

She waited, holding her breath until disappointment finally crowded the last bit of oxygen out of her lungs. Resigned to calling it a day, she schlepped down the stairs to tell Sasha, who sat on the bottom rung, legs splayed out in front, hands in her lap, palms up. Her eyes were closed. Tears streamed down her face and dripped off her chin.

The sight tugged at Boo's heart, and she intended to tell Sasha they were going home—honestly, she did—but those weren't the words that came out of her mouth.

"Come on." she grabbed her shotgun, and with her other hand, lifted Sasha by the arm and started up the steps.

"Why? Where we going?"

"Upstairs. The owner won't mind. After all, we need to get you cleaned up. It's just the way swamp hospitality works. Come on. Let's put you in the bathtub."

Without saying a word, Boo prayed to whoever might be listening, and might also have the power and patience to overlook her behavior. *Lord, please don't make my nose grow any longer. I promise you I won't never stretch the truth like that again.*

Halfway up the stairs, Sasha paused, looked down at her mud-coated overalls, and pulled the wet denim away from her skin. "What good's it going to do me to get my body clean. I'll have to put these filthy clothes on again. I'm not doing that, Boo. I'm not getting in these clothes until they're washed. I need you to take me home. Now."

"Never you worry, honey. I'll scrub them clean and hang them out in the sun. They'll be dry in no time."

"What sun? The sky is getting darker by the minute. I told you the weatherwoman said a storm was coming."

Boo thought fast. "Well, the lady inside said she had a clothes dryer. I hate them contraptions, but on a day like today, I'll sure use one."

Boo guided Sasha across the porch to the open French doors.

Instead of entering, Sasha cemented her feet to the porch and put a vice grip on Boo's forearm. "You're not going to knock? We're not just going in, are we?"

"That's what the nice woman said to do, to go on in and make ourselves to home." A god-awful itch on the end of Boo's nose caused a quick renegotiation of her promise not to lie again, offering, instead, that this would be the last time.

Once inside, Boo saw they were in a large square room. Shelves filled with books of various sizes and bindings lined the walls. Loose papers scattered across an old oak desk rustled in the breeze coming in through the open door. Directly across from where they stood, an opening led to what appeared to be a hallway.

Sasha looked around. "Where's the owner? She ought to be here to show us where to go and what to use? I don't know about this…" Mudpack and panic created deep ruts across Sasha's forehead and down her cheeks, making her look a hundred, if a day.

Boo took a mental note to ensure Sasha avoided mirrors until clean; otherwise the woman would have a coronary. Boo forced patience in her voice as she made up yet another lie. "The woman said she had to go out back to batten down her chicken coops from the coming storm and for us to—"

They both jumped when a blue vase suddenly toppled to the floor and crashed at their feet.

"—make ourselves to home," Boo said, staring at

the broken porcelain, confused as to what made it fall. Shrugging off the question, she grabbed Sasha's hand. "Come on, the bathroom's around here someplace." She led the way across the office and down the wide hallway where faded old-world-looking tapestries hung from high ceilings. Boo didn't know much about tapestries, but she knew enough to know these looked expensive. The middle of the swamp, with all its heat and humidity, seemed a risky place to hang such valuable art.

Without warning, the realization of what she was doing sent a shiver of guilt through Boo's chest. She'd never trespassed someone's land before, let alone gone into some stranger's house and made herself to home. Not only were they inside, but they were about to use the owner's bathroom. The thought of getting caught almost made her grab Sasha and run. That, plus Sasha's constant whining about not seeing a chicken yard outside and about being in a stranger's house without them being there.

The bedraggled pair shuffled down the hall until they found an open door. Inside, a claw-foot bathtub sat under a small high window covered by a roll-up shade. Dried out bars of soap filled a metal basket on the side of the tub, along with an old scrub brush with a long wooden handle. If anyone lived here now, Boo decided, they sure must be dirty, because it looked like no one had bathed in that tub for a long time. On the wall, however, a tankless gas hot water heater looked ready and waiting—meaning there must be a propane tank outside. She peered through a small opening on the front of the heater while saying a prayer that the gas tank wasn't empty.

There wasn't a flame.

She'd lit this kind of heater before, and thankfully a book of matches lay on a small table near the heater. She started the process of lighting the pilot and sighed with relief when a tiny flame popped up. Sasha had problem enough taking a bath in a strange tub; Boo couldn't imagine how she'd act sitting in a tub of cold water.

On second thought, she could imagine—and it wasn't a pretty picture.

Soon, hot water poured out of the tub faucet. It took a couple of minutes to rinse out a thick layer of dust, and then she put in the stopper.

"Okay, Miss Sasha, let's get you cleaned up," she said and pulled a chipper smile.

Despite Sasha's pleadings that they wait for the woman to come and approve Sasha's cleanup, Boo nudged her down on the toilet lid, pulled off her boots, and started unfastening the muddy overalls.

Sasha slapped Boo's hands away. "Stop, dang it. I can at least undress myself." She unfastened the buckles, peeled off the wet clothes, and, shivering, stepped into the hot water.

"You take your time. I'll go see if I can find clean clothes for you." Boo turned and started out the door.

"Wait," Sasha called, her voice near panic. "Where's my lipstick? I didn't lose it in the bayou, did I? Look in my left front pocket, will you?"

Weary, stressed, and almost out of patience, Boo bucked up and reminded herself of her assignment to take care of Sasha.

She crossed the room and gingerly put her hand down into Sasha's nasty, stinking pants pocket. Relieved to find the lipstick still there, she pulled it out and slapped it on the lavatory. "Here's your *bleeping* lipstick, Your Highness. When you finish, draw another tub of hot water and put these filthy clothes in to soak. I'll scrub them later."

Boo left Sasha and wandered through the house while the raindrops beat a staccato rhythm on the roof. Feeling like a thief with a conscience, she peeked into three of the four bedrooms, surprised to find them all empty except for dust bunnies and cobwebs. Willing there to be dry clothes in the last bedroom, she cracked the door. The odor of stale sweat, dirt, and rust assaulted her. Hairs on the back of her neck stood straight up.

Sasha's needs vaporized as Boo pushed the door open and peered inside. It took a minute for her eyes to adjust to the dimly lit room, but when they did, she made out a large rectangular workbench in the center with a rolled and tied piece of tanned deer hide laying alongside a tattered old book, it's cover cracked and peeling. Curiosity led her into what she soon realized looked more like a mining shack than a bedroom. A pickax lay on the floor, along with a coiled rope propped against a cot. A large shovel, muddy boots, and panning equipment lay scattered around the room. Dried mud caked the legs of a cot, giving the impression someone pulled it from a boggy mire and brought it inside to dry.

The room gave her the heebie-jeebies. Who in the world would store this kind of stuff in a bedroom instead of outside in a barn? She shuffled to a set of windows and looked out—or tried to. It seemed someone had smeared Vaseline on the panes and left it to dry.

The small piece of leather atop the workbench kept pulling her attention. What was it? Why was it there? Maybe it wouldn't hurt if she looked at it. After all, no one but Sasha knew she was in the house, much less in the room. She'd take a peek and put it back like she found it.

Without giving herself time to change her mind, she snatched the piece of leather and unrolled it with stiff arthritic fingers. Black lines drawn on the inside caught her attention. What was it? She ran her finger along the maze, tracing a winding path until it reached a dead end. Choosing another line, she followed it past drawings of rocks, bushes, and other types of landmarks, one of which might have been a river or something, until the line ended in front of a large rock formation and what looked to be crosshairs.

Crosshairs?

Of a rifle scope?

No, dummy. An X. She'd found a dang treasure map.

Excited as all get out, Boo stared at the map, trying to decipher directions and landmarks. Instead, a squeaking sound caught her attention. When a mouse skittered across the floor toward her, reflex crammed the map in her pocket. Boo wasn't scared of much and never had been afraid of mice—that is until the time one ran up her leg and she couldn't get it out of her pants fast enough. The resulting *Saint Vitas Dance* couldn't have been a pretty sight. The poor mouse finally died of fright before it was over.

Not this one. He kept coming.

She stomped and yelled, hoping to alert the mouse of the danger that loomed up her pants leg.

Halfway across the room, it got the message and stopped mid-skitter. It wriggled its nose and locked eyes with Boo as if to ask, who are you and why are you in my house.

It took every ounce of strength Boo had not to blink. The mouse didn't blink, either.

As if she weren't concerned enough, the low, pulsating beat of a drum added to her discomfort until she realized it was her heart pounding in her ears.

Finally, the mouse blinked, turned, and darted under a filthy black tarp in the corner.

Relief washed over Boo, but it didn't last, for the tarp started moving. At first, she discounted it, thinking the mouse must have run into something that shifted.

But when the tarp picked up and moved across the room, dragging anything and everything in its wake, it scared the living daylights out of her.

Reaction, however, soon exchanged places with action. She took a quick step between the moving tarpaulin and the door, grabbed the fleeing cover, and yanked.

A beautiful, wild-eyed girl, maybe thirteen, tried to dart around Boo.

"Whoa, whoa, what's this?" Boo asked.

The girl was dressed in tanned animal skin, and her black hair looked coated in grease. The wind chose that moment to distract Boo as it whistled through the house banging doors and rattling hinges. The girl tried to take advantage of the distraction, but Boo recovered soon enough to stop her. "Settle down," she said, stepping in front of the girl. "This ain't the time to run outside, if that's where you're headed. Bad weather's coming in something fierce. What's your name?"

The girl lifted her chin and stared Boo in the eye.

"Mine's Boo, and I suspect you don't belong in this house no more'n I do. What say we make nice to each other? Looks like we might hold-up here till after this storm passes, and that ain't likely soon."

The girl hadn't said a word, but a woman's demanding voice from behind Boo did. "Who are you? What are you doing in this house?"

Startled, Boo spun around.

The wild-eyed girl took advantage of the distraction and fled around the dark-skinned woman in the doorway. She looked to be in her early thirties, wore a blue print dress, white socks, and athletic shoes. A crescent moon-shaped scar beneath her left eye marred an otherwise perfect complexion.

"Pardon me. Is this your house?" Boo asked. "If it is, I'm mighty sorry if we..."

The woman simply turned to leave.

"Wait," Boo called. "Don't go. I want to talk to you. Whose house is this? Where's the owners? What's all this stuff in here?"

A scream echoed through the house—undeniably Sasha's—calling Boo's name.

Chapter Six

Head down, arms swinging, Boo hurried toward Sasha's screams as fast as her arthritic hips allowed. When she reached the bathroom, Sasha stood in a puddle of water, wide-eyed and stark naked except for a dingy, threadbare towel clenched in front of her.

"Boo, you won't believe what I just saw."

In no mood to play guessing games, Boo let out a long, loud sigh. "If I won't believe it, then how come I got to guess? Dang it, Sasha, just tell me what you seen."

"A ghost! I saw a real live ghost right there where you're standing."

"Ghost? What kind of a ghost?"

"It looked like a woman wearing a long filmy dress. Her hair looked like it was coated in some kind of oil or… I didn't see her for long before she faded… She didn't stay long, just… Sasha shivered.

Boo wasn't sure if the idea of oily hair was what repulsed Sasha, or thinking she saw an apparition. Knowing Sasha, it was likely both.

"Don't sound like a ghost to me, sounds like you just

dozed off."

"No, Boo, I could…could…see right through…" Sasha's eyes rolled back in her head. The towel fell to the floor.

"Sasha!" Boo grabbed Sasha's elbow just as her knees buckled. "My lord, Sasha, here sit on the toilet and put your head down between your knees."

"I don't… think it'll… go down that far." Sasha said, trying all the same.

Boo suppressed a roar of laughter, for she understood Sasha's dilemma. She wasn't sure if her head would go between her knees anymore, either. She gingerly patted Sasha on the shoulder. "Catch your breath, Hon," she stammered. "You'll be all right in a minute."

"I never believed in ghosts before, but if they don't exist, what was I seeing?" Sasha looked up at Boo, her face now drained of all color.

"Like I said, maybe you just dozed off."

"I was as wide awake as I am right now sitting here looking at you. I swear I was."

"Then, I don't know. I ain't never seen a ghost before neither." Boo looked around the room, remembering the screams she'd heard earlier in the bayou. Maybe she hadn't seen a ghost, but she dang sure might've heard one.

When Sasha recovered enough to notice her bone-white legs splayed out in front of her, she looked down at her naked, jiggly belly. Horror of another kind crossed her face. She snatched the towel from the floor and covered what private parts she could. She glared at Boo's empty hands. "You were going to find me some dry clothes. Where are they? I can't go around like this all day."

Boo's mind raced. How in the world did she fight her way out of this plastic bag of a situation? She sure couldn't tell the truth, which was that she'd been so interested in checking the house, she'd forgotten all about either Sasha or dry clothes. "Well, I, uh… I had them in my hands...I must've dropped them when you screamed. Hang on, I'll be right back."

She bustled down the hall to the miner's-shack room where she vaguely remembered a khaki shirt and pants dumped on the floor. She grabbed them and hurried to the bathroom.

When Sasha saw them hanging from Boo's hands, panic crept into her face all over again. "I ain't never worn men's clothes before, and I sure ain't starting now. Besides, they been worn and put up dirty."

"For Christ's sake, Sasha, they're *dry*. Put them on till we can find you something better." She shoved the garments into Sasha's arms. "Look, the pants already got a belt in the loops like they was waiting for you. There's a clean pair of socks stuck in the pants pocket. Come on. I got something to show you."

Sasha cringed, but pulled up the pants, buttoned the shirt and stuck her feet into the over-sized white socks. "Wait. I got to straighten my hair and put on some more lipstick." She grabbed the tube from the lavatory where Boo put it earlier and looked at herself in the mirror.

Time ticked away while Boo crossed her arms and patted her foot, her thoughts taking her to the woman and girl. Were they were still in the house? Would she run into them again? If so, how'd she explain their trespassing?

"That's about the best I can do with what I got," Sasha said, at last moving away from the mirror. "Okay. Now. What'd you want to show me? And ain't the owner come yet? I still think we ought to find out who owns this house before we go wandering around anymore than we already have."

A scuffle from down the hall startled Boo. Likely the owner had come home, and he'd run into the other two. "If that's the man that owns this place, wait until he finds out we're here," she said, grinning at Sasha.

Sasha didn't return her smile. Instead, her eyes stretched wide. "Yeah, and that I've made myself to home so much I took a bath in their tub."

"Come on, let's go. We just might have some explaining to do."

Rain pounded the tin roof while wind howled around the windowsills as they made their way down the hall.

"Weather's getting worse," Boo said. "If they left, they must've got caught in it."

Sasha grabbed Boo by the forearm and squeezed. "They? You mean the owner? Who else is here?"

Boo shrugged but said nothing. Something told her not to mention the woman and the girl—at least, not yet.

"You gone slap crazy, Boo Murphy. If it wasn't for this storm, I'd make you take me home right this minute."

"Like you're one to talk—seeing ghosts in the bathroom and thinking they're real."

Sasha peered around as if expecting another specter at any minute, but said nothing in her defense.

"Here's the room I wanted to show you." Boo stopped in front of the mining shack-bedroom. "When you screamed, I was standing here talking to a woman and a girl. But where'd they go? There was also an old journal on the workbench, here, and a small map... Oh, wait, now I remember, a mouse ran at me and..." She dug in her pocket and came up with a corner of the map. "Well, I'll be danged, here it is. I must've put it in my pocket when I saw the mouse. There was a book or something, too. That's what I wanted to look at."

"You mean you put something in your pocket what didn't belong to you? I'm ashamed of you, Boo Murphy."

"I ain't taken it nowhere. I didn't even know I did till just now. There was this old-looking book on the bench, too. Sure wanted to take a look at it." Boo said, stepping into the room.

Sasha followed and moved around Boo to look. "What else is in here, and what else did you take what don't belong to you? I swear. I gotta watch you like you was a little kid."

Feeling the pressure of Sasha's accusation, she explained how she'd found the room, how the girl had been hiding under the tarp, and how she ran, only to have the girl's mama—she guessed, her mama—show up in the doorway. And then Sasha screamed, and Boo went running.

"Sounds like those two don't belong here anymore than we do. That's scary." Sasha's voice rose to a fever pitch as she looked around her. "Where are they?"

While Sasha stepped closer to the workbench, Boo fidgeted, wondering how she'd explain their intrusion to the owner, if indeed he showed up. True, swamp hospitality existed, but maybe she'd stretched it just a bit.

"Whose feet are those down there?" Sasha cried, jerking Boo's thoughts back to attention.

"What feet? Where?"

Sasha pointed to a pair of muddy boots sticking out from behind the workbench. "Those feet right there."

Boo followed Sasha's finger pointing to the floor, saw the muddy boots, and hurried around the bench to inspect.

A swarthy man dressed in prospector-looking clothes lay face down. Underneath him, lay the woman Boo had seen earlier. "Oh, my lord," Boo said, somewhat embarrassed, thinking she'd caught the two in a compromising situation. Then, just as quick, realized the man looked either unconscious or dead, and the woman wasn't.

"Help me get him off me," the woman begged, pushing

at the dead-weight man twice her size.

"Come on." Boo motioned to Sasha. The two helped shove the man off and on his back. Wide-open, vacant eyes stared at the ceiling.

Now free, the woman scrambled up, holding onto the table leg for support. "I think he's dead, but I...I didn't kill him. At least I didn't mean to. I don't think I.... He accused me of taking..."

Was the map what the man looked for? Had he thought the woman had taken it instead of Boo? The piece of leather in Boo's pocket felt heavier when she realized her taking it might have led to... She reached for the map, but before she could pull it out of her pocket, the woman grabbed Boo's shirt and started sinking to the floor.

So weary of fainting women, she could spit, Boo caught the woman by the arm—the arm with a small hawk tattooed on the inside of her wrist—and guided her out into the hallway.

Sasha trailed along, helping as she could.

Only when they got out into the light, did Boo see the woman's bloody nose and scratches on her neck and arms. The map forgotten, Boo said, "Someone's worked you over real good, ma'am. Come on," she said. "Let's go find the kitchen and get you cleaned up. Maybe there's a box of tea or something. I reckon we could all use a cup."

The three went through the house, closing windows against the blowing rain on their way to the kitchen. Faded, green chintz curtains hung at the window above the sink. Atop the yellow Formica countertop lay knives, cooking utensils, and a banged-up aluminum pot. As elsewhere in the house, dust covered everything halfway horizontal. The last person in the kitchen must've left in a hurry, for a can of beans lay on its side, open enough for a mouse to empty its contents. Dried tracks led from the can and down to the floor.

A large, round pedestal table sat in the middle of the room. Sasha and the woman, who told them her name was Mili, pulled out chairs and sat. Meanwhile, Boo scrounged in the cabinet and came up with a box of teabags, found a teakettle, and put water on to boil.

"I'm surprised that rusty tank in the backyard has enough propane in it to light a fire," Sasha said, sarcasm filling her voice. "If I ever get home, you'll never get me in this swamp again. I'll tell you that for sure." She sighed, propped her elbows on the table, and rested her chin in her hands.

"Okay, Mili. We don't belong here, but something tells me you don't neither. Tell us who that man is, how'd he die, who are you, and what're you both doing here." Boo patted the kettle to track the temperature of the water. "Soon as this storm blows over, one of us has to get the sheriff. I reckon it'll be me, and I can explain why we're here, but what do I tell him about you?" And what, she wondered, did she tell him about the missing journal and the map in her pocket.

Something smelled about the whole thing. Right now, she'd wait until then to tell anyone else, and as soon as she could, she'd warn Sasha to keep her mouth shut.

"You can go see the sheriff, all right, but only after you drop me home." Sasha stared straight ahead. "I should've known not to get in that pirogue with you. I swear Boo, you attract trouble like I attract flies." She slapped at one buzzing her face.

Mili's cheeks had gone from colorless to bright pink. She intertwined her fingers on the table and sat motionless.

"I was surprised when I got to the room, and you were still there," Boo said. "I figured both you and the girl would be long gone. By the way, where's your daughter?

"My daughter?" Mili sounded surprised. "I don't have a child. What girl are you talking about?"

"The same one in the room there with me when you came in."

"I didn't see a girl."

"The girl under the tarp, she—"

"All I remember is you running when she screamed at you," Mili said, indicated Sasha.

"Next thing I knew, someone came from behind and grabbed my throat. I thought it was you, returned to catch me by surprise. Didn't know it was him until after we struggled. Then, we fell to the floor. I must've passed out because the next thing I remember was your voices."

The teakettle whistled. Boo rinsed white cups and saucers that she collected from the cabinet and poured hot water on the tea bags tucked in each. "At least we got a reason to be in this house, but so far, you ain't told us nothing about you. Now, I want to know who you are, why you're here, and what's that got to do with the dead guy in the other room?"

"Well…as I said, my name is Mili, and…well, it's a long story."

"With this storm getting worse, looks like we got plenty of time." Boo shuddered. The house did, too. She couldn't tell if the howling wind was what caused it to shake, or if the force came from inside. At one point, she'd have sworn the house breathed.

Mili appeared to notice it too, for she tensed, shifted in her chair, and gave a furtive glance around the room. A lock of hair, black as a new-moon midnight, fell across eyes the same color. She shoved it off her face and looked like she might dart out the door any minute.

"You scared of us, or that ghost I seen?" Sasha asked, checking over her shoulder.

Mili pulled her lips into a thin, straight line, but said nothing.

"She's scared, all right." The cups rattled in their saucers as Boo put the steaming tea in front of the other two and returned to the cabinet for hers. "But it ain't us who's got her spooked." She glanced at Mili. "Maybe someone's after you. Or maybe it's this house. Heck, it'd spook a dead man." Boo couldn't help but glance down the hall toward the room where the dead man grew colder by the minute. And how Mili had not seen the little girl.

That was if she told the truth.

The big-face clock on the wall ticked while the three sipped their tea.

Sasha broke the silence. "What I want to know is, what do we do with that dead body? 'Specially in the middle of a hurricane."

"Right now, we don't do nothing." Boo swirled the teabag around in her cup. "Ain't a phone here, so there's no one to tell till the storm's over. That is if we still have a pirogue to get home in. I tied it the best I could, but with this wind, I'm a feared it'll be gone to the happy hunting ground of pirogues and paddles by then." Eyebrows hiked in question, she looked at Mili again. "So?"

"What? I can't tell you much, but…" Mili's chair squeaked as she shifted her weight.

"But what? You're driving me crazy." Boo stood, shoved her chair under the table, and paced the room. "What's so dang important you can't spit it out?"

"You don't understand."

"*What* don't I understand? That's what I'm asking you. You don't explain who you are pretty quick, I'm gonna…" Boo threw her hands up in a helpless gesture.

"Okay," Mili said. "I'll tell you this. I'm one of a handful of surviving Atakapa. Actually, we call ourselves Ishak, meaning *the people*. Others call us Atakapa—*man-eaters*."

Sasha roused, startled. "Did they eat people? Do you?"

"We don't—not very often, that is." A smile played around Mili's mouth. "Only as a last resort."

Sasha gulped.

Boo started to tell Sasha that Mili was teasing her,

but some days Boo felt more ornery than others. This day hadn't started out as such, but it sure was there by now.

When she realized Mili continued talking, Boo tuned in again.

"…some of us, half-breeds, really—not even half—survive. But we're trying to rebuild our race and our culture."

Boo sat again, and leaned back in the chair, lifting the front legs off the floor. "Well okay, then, now we're getting someplace. Why'd the man attack you?"

"Evidently, he thought I'd taken something."

"Like what? Maybe that journal I seen on the workbench?"

"What journal?"

"Okay, don't gimme that. How come all of a sudden you're playing dumb? You know what I'm talking about. You saw it there on the table same as me."

Mili looked away.

"You think he took it before he attacked you?"

"If so, why would he have accused me?"

"You tell me. I ain't seen nobody else in this house. Have you?"

"Maybe it's that—" Sasha started, until Boo cut her off with a hard stare and a mouthed no. It wasn't like either one of them to steal anything, but there were too many unanswered questions about Mili, the dead man, and what he thought she'd taken, and why.

A lull in the wind came at the same time an uncomfortable pause edged its way into the conversation. The room, now quieter than it had been since they entered, echoed a soft sound like someone snoring.

"Shh," Boo said, her finger to her lips. She tiptoed to the pantry door and peeked inside. Dawg lay sprawled on the floor, sound asleep. Nearby lay a bag that, at one time, held doggie nuggets. It was now ripped open and empty. Boo eased the door closed, leaving a crack so he could get out when he awakened from his gluttony-induced sleep.

"It's Dawg, sleeping. He ate his belly full first, though." Boo chuckled as she rejoined the other two at the table. "Okay, here's the deal. Pussyfooting around never has been my strong suit. I don't think you killed that guy, but you need to tell us what's going on."

"I wish I knew." Mili looked as confused as Boo felt. "Whatever it was, I don't see how he could have taken it since he's dead. Of course, he could've hidden it, and then had a heart attack or stroke while he was trying to strangle me."

"How could he hide it? Didn't you say he came in right after I left to find Sasha?"

"Well…" she stalled. "Not right in. I'd been in the room a few minutes before he grabbed me from behind."

Boo wasn't buying it. "So what were you looking for?"

"I saw the journal when I walked into the room the first time, but I didn't see a map—and I don't know what happened to the journal."

Mili fidgeted, sipped her tea while glancing at the backdoor that led to a screened-in porch, as if she feared someone might be watching, listening.

Boo threw her hands up in frustration. "Just say it, Mili. What?"

"Leave her alone, Boo, it ain't important." Sasha rested her hand on Mili's shoulder. "Can't you tell she don't know nothing? Bless her heart. Look at her. You got her all fidgety and half scared out of her wits."

Mili gave Sasha a sidewise smile and then cut her eyes to Boo. "Maybe it was a map to some lost silver mine or something."

Chapter Seven

Dawn was breaking over the mountain range when Sid roused from a deep sleep. A god-awful smell filled her nostrils, and some weird jazz-fusion blasted her ears. She lowered the volume on the CD player. "What's that awful smell?"

"It's that dog in the back seat." Annie bounced and swayed as if the music still blared. "I don't know what he ate before you fed him the fried chicken, but he's been breaking wind for the last half hour. I wanted to pull over and try to get him out, but I didn't want to wake you."

Sid glanced behind her. The mutt slept in the same position as her Chesapeake Bay retriever, Slider—on his back, all four legs sticking up, his head hanging off the edge of the seat, and his tongue dangling out the side of his mouth. Red and white shreds of what had once been a bucket of chicken lay scattered everywhere. An exhausted dog if she'd ever seen one. She lacked the heart to wake him, too. A contented snore resonated from the animal, along with the occasional other sound that smelled to high heaven.

"How long did I sleep? Did you stop and get gas? If you did, I slept through it." Sid grabbed her cell phone to check the time and saw she'd gotten a phone call from Durwood—when she did have service. Not a bar showed at the moment—not even enough to check her voice mail.

She stared at the reddening sky ahead of them. "Where are we?"

"I'm not right sure. I haven't seen a sign in a while. Hoping one comes up pretty soon. Sure wish we'd have gotten that GPS you ordered before we headed out west, and—"

"West! That's what wrong, Annie. Santa Fe is *west* of Texas, yes, but the sun comes up in the east."

"Yeah, sure. I know that." Annie swelled with offense. "What's your point?"

"My point is, there's the sun—straight ahead. We're going the wrong way."

"We couldn't be. I only made one turn... Maybe two...

Sid pointed toward the windshield. "Is that the sun or not?"

"Yes," Annie stretched the word out as long as she could. "But if that's the sun, and we're heading that direction, that means we're not heading to Santa Fe.

"Wherever we are, we're in the middle of a big fat nothing. Look, front back, both sides—barren. Sid squinted as they approached a road sign. "Eight miles to Yeso—isn't that a ghost town?

"Beats me." Annie shrugged. She never had believed the original owner of her pre Civil War house haunted it.

Sid believed. On occasion, the vaporous woman stood at the end of Sid's bed. Slider believed it too—for every time *Kate* appeared, his hackles went on high alert.

"Seems we have little choice but to go east a little

longer. Ghost town or not, I'm hoping they have a gas station, and it's open this early. With no idea how far we'll have to backtrack, we better not take a chance." She'd taken chance enough—letting Annie drive while she slept—but she kept her mouth shut about that. No sense in starting an argument. She'd always sworn she'd prefer living in a bed of red ants before moving in with Annie, but all in all, it worked tolerably well—except for times like this.

They drove the last few miles on fumes, and the town came in sight just as the engine sputtered and died.

"Perfect timing," Sid said. "An abandoned town. If it isn't haunted, I'll be surprised."

"Not totally. Look, there's a post office right off the highway." Annie pointed to a building with a U.S. flag flapping in the hot desert wind.

"Yeah, but it's closed. Too bad, I'd have stopped and chatted with them—see if they need a dog."

Annie let the car coast to a stop in front of a two-story box-shaped brick building that had at one time been painted white. Now, it peeled off in patches. "Built in 1909, the sign says."

"Annie, if we can't find a gas station, we're not going to make the wedding."

Tumbleweeds blew across the road, and a dust devil followed close behind.

"I don't see a soul, but some folks must live around here," Sid looked from one side of the road to the other, "or they wouldn't still have a post office. We'll scout around."

The dog in back roused and looked out the windows, closed his eyes as if to continue his nap, then his eyes flew open again. He leapt to his feet and pawed on the window, desperate to get out.

"Looks like he sees something familiar. Guess we're not going to have him with us much longer."

Annie laughed. "Unless he's like me and desperate

for a potty stop. Wonder what Chesterfield would say if we have to take that mutt home."

"Don't even think it. We are *not* taking him with us. Can you imagine us pulling up to a wedding with that thing in the back seat?" Sid got out and opened the rear door. The instant she did, the dog took off in a dead run.

She shielded her eyes from the sun and watched his progress through the deserted town. When she didn't see anyone, she said, "I'll be back. I'm going to walk around a little bit—see if anyone's here."

She crossed the road and headed down the same dusty side street the dog took, looking for a gas station, a hotel, any place where she could ask for help. Spindly dry weeds sprouted here and there. Lopsided buildings had given up the ghost and let gravity have its way with them.

As she rounded first one building and then another, all was quiet—abandoned—except for an old codger in a pair of nondescript, dusty pants and shirt, unshaven for years. He rolled on the ground with the dog they'd brought, laughing and rubbing his crippled-looking hands in the scruff of dog's neck. Sid swore the dog laughed as well, licking the man's face.

"Where you been, boy? I been looking everywhere for you."

"So the dog's yours?"

Startled at Sid's voice, he looked over, and then scrambled to his feet. "Sure is. Lost him out in the desert a week or so ago when we was out hunting. Figured I'd never see him again. Broke my heart." He wiped away a tear. "You bring 'im?"

"Not exactly. It's more like he brought us. Found him wandering in the desert half-dead. He got in our car, and we couldn't get him out. Glad to find his home, even if by accident.

"Much obliged to you, ma'am. A man don't like losing his dog." He scrubbed his fingers in the fur atop the animal's head. "Sure did miss 'im. By the way, what brought you to this place? Hope you're not looking for car parts. If you are, you're outta luck. Ain't nothing working in this town but ghosts."

"That's what I was afraid you'd say." She smiled at him. "Actually, it isn't a car part, it's gasoline. We made a wrong turn sometime back and…"

"Ever once in a while, somebody comes through here. I reckon you could stand by the side of the road and wait." He swatted away a fly that landed on his mustache. "Maybe they'd let you siphon out a couple of gallons to get you to Fort Sumner. They got gas stations there."

"Wow. And how often does that happen—someone driving through, I mean?"

"Oh, sometimes as often as once a day."

Sid choked. "So…since we're one…"

"Yep, you could well be it for the day."

"And how far are we from Santa Fe? Would you know that?"

"Couple of hours."

"That's a relief. So, if someone came by first thing in the morning, we could still get to Santa Fe by ten?"

"Might." He spat in the dust, pulled out a pocketknife, and started whittling on a piece of what looked like driftwood, then added, "might not…"

Sid laughed—not funny—nervous.

"I better go back to the car and watch. Thank you for your help."

He tipped his forehead in a salute and continued whittling. "I'll be around if you need me."

The dog trailed along behind Sid as if thankful for her help and willing to return the favor.

Annie stood in the middle of the road waving down a yellow pickup truck about the same shade as her top. The shirtless driver, an Indian man with a long black ponytail hanging down his back, his bare arm propped on the door, looked at them as if he wasn't sure he believed his eyes.

"Is that your dog, ma'am? If it is, you really should feed him better."

Sid looked at Annie, and the two exploded into laughter.

After they explained how they came upon him, or he them, and went on to explain their plight, the man collected a can of gasoline from the bed of his pickup and sauntered to their car.

However, once he emptied the gas into Annie's tank, the vehicle still wouldn't start.

"Could be the timing belt," he suggested, and opened the hood, and stuck his head inside. After fiddling around, he came up and shook his head. "Can't tell for sure, but from looking at your camshaft and valves, I'd say that's what it is. Know when you last had it replaced?"

Sid looked at Annie.

"Timing belt?" Annie looked puzzled. "I didn't know it had one."

The man shook his head. "Ma'am, an old car like this, with these hot temperatures, your timing belt is going to degrade. Plus, it looks like your engine's been throwing oil. That makes it worse."

By the look on Annie's face, Sid knew she wasn't surprised.

"You noticing more exhaust coming from your vehicle than normal? When a timing belt starts going bad, the timing with the pistons and valves is off, and this makes your car shake."

"It was making a funny noise last night."

He shot a knowing look at Sid.

"When I get to Fort Sumner, I'll send a tow truck out to get your car."

"A tow truck? How long will that take? I have to get to Santa Fe by ten o'clock tomorrow morning." Annie's pitch elevated up three levels. "You know I'm her bridesmaid."

"No, ma'am. I didn't know that."

Poor guy. He tried so hard to be polite. He looked relieved to crawl back into his truck and drive off.

Sid and Annie took up their spots, one watching east, one watching west, and waited.

And waited.

The sun dropped behind the mountain range while Sid and Annie watched for a tow truck that didn't come.

Chapter Eight

"Don't be ridiculous," Sasha said. "There's no silver mine around here."

"Hold on, Sasha." Boo held her palm out to her cousin. "Shh. Listen to what Mili has to say."

Mili looked from Sasha to Boo, and back again before she continued. "The story goes like this. There was a cave somewhere near here that had a vein of silver running through it. The little history that's been written about the Atakapa confirms that. When the early Spanish explorers came ashore, the Atakapa, a gentle, peace-loving clan, gave them a warm welcome. Soon, however, the greedy explorers realized the Indians knew the source of the silver and asked them where they got it. Innocent and trusting, the Atakapa showed them the mine."

"Let me guess. Spanish explorers took all the silver they could carry." Boo shook her head in disgust.

Sasha scooted her chair closer to Mili. "So, where's this mine supposed to be?"

"No one knows for sure, but lots of folks sure would like to. Rumor is, its somewhere in Wild Azalea Canyon, close to what's now called Bon Weir."

The wind and rain pounded the roof. Boo saw something fly by the window and glanced out in time to see a piece of tin fly across the yard. The house shook as though threatening to collapse at any moment—or throw them all outside into the storm.

When Sasha let out a squeal, Boo knew she'd better come up with something for Sasha to do to keep her mind off the storm—that and the fact she sat in a stranger's house, bathed in a stranger's tub, wore a stranger's clothes, and drank a stranger's... Tea—that was it! "Anybody ready for another cup of tea?" Boo looked at Sasha and asked, "Hon, would you see if the water's still hot?"

"What? Oh yeah." Trance-like, Sasha stumbled to the stove and patted the kettle. Without a word, she brought it back to the table and refilled their cups.

Boo dunked her still-wet teabag and inhaled deeply. "Smells good," she said, cutting a quick glance up at Sasha. "This damp air chills my bones."

By the time Sasha returned the kettle to the stove and retook her seat, the lines across her forehead weren't as deep, and her mouth wasn't as tight. Boo breathed a sigh of relief, ready now to focus on Mili, who kept looking back. Dealing with two shaky women was almost more than Boo cared to handle, but something was going on, and Boo was determined to get to the bottom of it— or die trying.

"It's okay," she said. "Now, go on with the story about the silver mine. So the Indians knew about it and, innocent enough, told the Spanish explorers, who I just imagine, hauled off all the silver they could carry."

"That's about the size of it." Mili scraped her chair across the linoleum floor, stood, and paced the room. "I hope you'll keep this confidential—about the mine and all. We don't need a bunch of treasure seekers stomping around."

"We ain't gonna tell no one," Boo assured Mili. "I'm tickled pink to hear it. Lord knows, the Atakapa people what's left need a break. And if this storm don't let up soon, looks like we'll all be spending the night here anyways, so there ain't no one to tell."

"Speak for yourself." Sasha shoved her chair back and jumped to her feet. "Storm or no storm, I can't get away from here fast enough. Get me home, and I ain't never going anywhere with you again."

The first thing on Boo's list wasn't taking Sasha home, but she let the comment ride. Better to deal with that when the time came.

Which it did a few minutes later when the wind died down, and the rain slowed. "Okay, looks like the storm's passed. Let's go." Sasha gathered the cups and saucers, went to the sink and started the cleanup.

"Not so fast, Your Highness. You know well as I do, there's another side to these storms."

"Well, that body in the next room's giving me the creeps." Sasha shuddered. "At least go find something to cover it up. He really ain't looking too good."

"Well, I reckon he ain't. He's dead. Come on. Let's go cover him up with something." She led the other two to the dead man. Sure enough, he looked deader than he had a few minutes earlier. Boo grabbed the tarp in the corner and covered him while Sasha and Mili gawked.

"You satisfied now?" Boo crammed her fists against her hips and glared at Sasha, who nodded and walked out of the room. The other two followed her into the hall.

"One thing I ain't figured out yet, Mili. Do you live here?"

"Why?"

"'Cause I ain't seen another boat when we tied up. I'm wondering how you got here."

Mili cleared her throat.

"Well, do ya?"

"I guess you could say so, yes."

"Say what? That you come in a boat, or live here? Good lord dog, woman, you sure can be infuriating."

"The house belongs to me."

"Which house? This one?" The warmth of embarrassment flooded Boo's cheeks. Here she'd been in this woman's house without permission and treating her like she was the intruder.

"*This* house?" Sasha's eyes looked as big as dinner plates. "You mean we've been trespassing, and you ain't said a word about it? You acted like you didn't know the house when we ransacked the kitchen looking for teabags."

Mili looked at the floor.

"Well, like you said, I guess you got your reasons." Boo knew more than one way to skin a squirrel and switched topics. "Say, can you show us around this island?" If she didn't find that hut they'd seen earlier, Boo felt like she'd go insane.

"I...no... If I do, I'll..." Mili's voice grew soft, almost unintelligible. "I'll get in trouble."

"Trouble? What kind? From who?"

Mili glanced back toward the door like she thought someone might be listening.

Boo looked too, but neither saw nor heard a soul. Then, she noticed Sasha almost dead on her feet. "You're tired, Sasha. Let's go to the kitchen, and I'll get you another cup of tea"

"No, I'm about done for the day. Y'all can talk till the cows come home begging to be milked," she said. "I'm going to lay down somewhere." She shuffled from the dead-man room and headed down the hall.

Not eager for Sasha to bug her about going home, Boo didn't say a word. Let her sleep, she thought. Made her life easier.

Boo followed Mili into the hallway and through the

house. Mili acted uneasy, but Boo got the idea it was about something more than the storm and the damage it was doing to the house. The way Mili paced, one would think she had a death sentence hanging over her head with all appeals lost. She held herself so tight it looked like she'd built a wall around herself ten feet high and just as thick.

After a few minutes of getting nowhere, Boo walked away from Mili and strolled the house. She pretended to look at pictures on the wall or whatnots on bookshelves, but all the while kept an eye on Mili.

Soon, she realized the storm must indeed have passed. Maybe it hadn't been a hurricane after all, just one of those god-awful rainstorms common in this area. So, when she heard Mili walk out the backdoor, Boo hurried to the window and peeked out to see her cross a water-soaked field and disappear into a stand of trees.

"Dang it, honey, you just think you're getting away from me," Boo whispered. She headed to the front room where she'd left her rifle, grabbed it, and dashed out the backdoor. Hopefully, she could reach the tree line before Mili got too far into the woods.

She hurried across the field, frustrated that arthritis—*Arthur,* as she called it—slowed her pace. Storms always made the pain worse. She eased around puddles when she could and through them when she couldn't, thankful once again she'd worn rubber boots.

"Lord a mercy, I hope Sasha don't wake up while I'm gone." Boo splashed through an extra deep puddle. "She'll have a hissy fit if she discovers I left her there alone, but there ain't no way she'd take off in the boat by herself. Ain't got the guts."

Energized by the rain, swarms of mosquitoes buzzed her head. She batted them away and stepped onto a path that led further into the woods—hopefully, the same one Mili took. The trail curved through trees and brush so thick, even if Mili wasn't far away, Boo might not see her.

Boo had no proof Mili killed the man up at the house. But she had no proof she hadn't, either. Something about the whole thing didn't sit right in Boo's mind. If he'd been murdered for the map, that must mean it held valuable information. Maybe there really was a silver mine, and if so, she wasn't sure she trusted the intentions of those she'd met so far. One ran away, one died, and here the third one was trying to pull a disappearing act. She'd stay quiet about having the map until she had a better grasp of what was going on.

She rounded a bend in time to catch sight of the tail of Mili's blue dress before it disappeared around another turn in the path. Boo knew she shouldn't go any farther, that she should wake Sasha, try to find the pirogue, head home, and call the sheriff. But just as the thought entered her brain, rustling leaves on her left made her swing around and peer through the underbrush, thankful she'd brought the shotgun. She pointed it in the direction of the sound, expecting a bigmouth gator or a wild hog to come through the woods.

She waited.

Nothing came.

"Who's there?" she called.

A twig cracked.

Must be a critter, she thought, admonishing herself for being so skittish. She'd never been one who wouldn't jump off the deep end, and she sure wasn't scared of her own shadow—like Sasha. Boo felt a twinge of guilt for not having left a note telling Sasha she'd be back soon, to stay put, but doggone it, she hadn't had time.

Boo moved deeper into the woods. A baby fox jumped out and scampered off like his mama caught him in some kind of mischief. She laughed and watched until it darted from sight. When she turned to proceed, she came face to face with Mili standing in the middle of the road with her hands on her hips. "Why are you following me, and why are you carrying a shotgun?"

Boo stopped short.

"I said why are you here. You have to go."

"It's a free trail. I can go wherever I want to."

Mili's expression eased. "Please don't follow me. It isn't safe."

"What do you mean, it ain't safe?"

"Just what I said."

"What's the danger?"

"Go take care of your cousin. I can handle this by myself."

"Handle what?" Irritation coated Boo's voice.

Mili refused to implicate herself. Instead, she said, "Just go. I'll meet you there later."

Boo glanced at the long lazy shadows, her curiosity so whetted there was no way she could leave. Sasha would have to fend for herself a little longer.

"Okay, don't say I didn't warn you." Mili commenced down the path. A few minutes later, she stopped again.

"Why'd you stop? Where you going?" Boo pushed.

A rustle in the leaves didn't startle Boo this time, but when the musky smell of dank earth and leaves joined that of intense man, she whirled around and glared into two black eyes staring into hers. His straight black hair shined as if it had been smeared with oil. He wasn't tall, but thick, muscular arms and thighs made him look like Mr. America. His skin was the color of burnished copper. He held a spear in his hand and a frown on his face. His clothing consisted of a loincloth—a *small* loincloth.

Chapter Nine

Her cheeks burning like fire, either from embarrassment or an old memory—or both, Boo escaped looking at the man in the loincloth by turning to Mili.

"I warned you," Mili said, laughter creeping into her voice.

"You mean to tell me you know this bare-ass man?"

Mili's hand flew to her mouth, but that didn't stop the snicker. She said something to the man that sounded like gobbledygook.

"Who is this?" Boo repeated. "Is he why you didn't want me to follow you?"

"Lucky for you he's my brother, otherwise you'd be—"

"Lunch, I suppose."

"Boo, this is not a joke." Frustration coated Mili's voice.

"So he's an Indian like you?"
Mili nodded.

She forced herself to look at him again but insisted her eyes stay focused on his when they wanted to stray lower. "Atakapa?"

He stepped closer—only inches away. The smell of him grew so strong she had to open her mouth to breathe. "What the heck you got on, alligator oil? You smell gawd-awful."

He didn't blink.

Neither did Boo.

"She sure is stubborn," he said, breaking eye contact to look at Mili.

As soon as Boo did the same, he grabbed her arm and yanked her so close the smell of his breath made her sick to her stomach. "Take your filthy hands off me!"

"Come on, sis, let's me and you take a trip." He snatched Boo's gun from her hand, shoved her around and forward.

"Don't hurt her, she's a harmless, nosy old woman," Mili said.

"Nosy, maybe, but I get the idea she's anything but harmless." He motioned Mili to continue down the trail from which she'd come, took Boo by the arm, and nudged her forward.

After walking for several minutes, they stepped into a clearing and continued on. The man's pressure on Boo's arm grew uncomfortable.

"Lemme go. I don't need you hanging on my arm."

"Lady, you want to see what's up, and you're going to see. The thing is, once you do, I'll have to kill you."

"Tarek, don't tell her that. You know we're not going to kill anyone."

"No, I don't know that. I'm not as sure as you are."

"What?" Boo looked from sister to brother. "What are you two talking about? And where are we going?" She pulled her arm loose, but Tarek—at least she had a name for him now—grabbed it again.

"Keep going," he ordered.

"When we get there, I guess I'll know what this is all about since it looks like you two ain't going to tell me nothing. Must be something big for all this secrecy. I get that your name's Tarek, but why are you dressed like one of them savages?"

"'Cause I *am* a savage. I eat people." He growled at her—then roared with laughter.

Boo swore under her breath. If he thought he scared her, he had another think coming. "I'll tell you right now, ain't no savage gonna scare me. Eat me if you want, but you gonna lose a few teeth if you do. I'm as tough as they come. Feel this muscle." She tried raising her free arm to demonstrate but tripped on a rock. His grip kept her from falling.

The sun dropped lower in the sky as they found their way, and soon they stepped into a camp of some kind. Her mouth flew open. She took a wide stance and stared at what lay before her. Men and women, all dressed similarly to Tarek, busied themselves like bees around a beehive. Some repaired and rebuilt palmetto-thatched beehive-shaped grass houses alongside wattle-and-daub buildings, while native-looking women stitched clothing out of feathers, hides, bark, and cloth, along with furs from what looked to be deer, bear, bison, and smaller game animals. Other men and women crafted necklaces, bracelets, armbands, rings, and ear and nose plugs out of shells, pearls, and—copper?

Naked children ran barefoot on muddy grounds. Older women squatted in a circle spreading wet corn to dry. A pregnant woman held her belly with one arm and an infant in the other. She laid the baby on a woven grass mat and pulled over a red clay pot. A swarm of mosquitoes buzzed around them. She waved them off, stuck her fingers in the pot, and rubbed some kind of oil on the baby's skin.

Holy swamp fox, Boo thought, I must've gone through one of them time machines I seen on TV. She glanced at Mili, who stood grinning at her.

"I figured this would catch your attention," Mili said.

Pots sat on hard-packed ground beside a large campfire in the middle of the compound. The potshards she'd collected through the years when she hunted and fished could have come from an identical pot.

Empty oyster and clamshells lay in huge mounds alongside the river. A chief, or at least some guy playing chief, stood nearby. His face was painted red and he wore an earth-red cloth draped across one shoulder, and a brown sash tied around the middle. Rustic woven straw sandals covered his feet. He looked up when they approached and met them halfway. He spoke to Mili and Tarek in the same gobbledygook talk as had Tarek, and then motioned that they follow him.

He headed to a cluster of huts, each looking like upside-down bowls made from dried brush, big enough for maybe four or five people. Smoke curled from openings in the tops of each. When they reached one opening of the largest hut, the chief stepped aside and indicated Boo go in first. Figuring she better not argue, or she might end up in one of his pots, she stooped and entered. Surprised when he didn't follow her in, a surge of panic squeezed her chest.

Soon as she stepped through the opening, the smell of unwashed bodies and smoke hit her in the face. It took a minute for her eyes to adjust to the dim light, but gradually she made out animal skins spread on the damp earth floor. A couple of rough-hewn stools were off to the side.

Mili and Tarek, along with two other men, singled-filed in a few minutes later. The first was a tall, slender middle-aged man with a scruffy beard, brown ponytail, and icy blue eyes that made Boo shudder. Then, she admonished herself for being so darned judgmental, like goody-two-shoes Sasha. Crisp blue jeans and tan shirt added to his air of authority over the half-dressed natives.

"Sit," Tarek ordered.

"No offense, but it takes too long to get these legs bent that far. I'm pretty stove up as it is. If it's okay with you, I'll stand a little longer."

"Suit yourself."

"If you don't mind me asking, who are these other two men, and what is this place?"

"Name's Peabody," the pony-tailed man said. "And he's Mouton." He motioned behind him, and the other guy stepped out and nodded at Boo.

Mouton—bald-headed and brown-eyed—wore the native garb of the Indians, but stood taller than the others.

"All the people you see out here," Peabody said, "are descendants of the Sunset people of the Atakapa-Ishak tribe."

Boo looked from Mouton, back to Peabody. "Sunset? What in the world's Sunset?"

"The Sabine River divided their tribes. Those on the east side of the river were known as the Sunrise. Those on the west were referred to as the Sunset tribe—for obvious reasons."

"There is more of them left than there is of us," Mouton chimed in. "We've lost almost all our heritage because… Well, let's just say we're doing this experiment to see if we can correct...I mean, recreate it."

"What do you mean, recreate?"

Peabody ducked his head and glanced up at Mouton before he spoke. "We live here much the same way as did the ancients."

"Does that mean you're gonna eat me for supper? Cause if'n you do—"

"Not if you behave." A twinkle of humor warmed Peabody's cold eyes.

Boo held Peabody's gaze. "How long y'all been here?"

"A year, this month."

"A year? How do you live? Does someone bring you food?"

"We catch it or grow it. We don't want anyone to know about us, or else the media would descend on us like a pack of wolves. We're not ready for that yet."

"What do you mean—yet?"

"Mili is Atakapa," Mouton said. "But what you likely don't know is she's Doctor Mili Samples, a cultural anthropologist. She and Professor Peabody here are conducting research. They've replicated an Atakapa camp as closely as they could make it."

"So how do you fit in, and why bring me here under armed guard?"

"You sure are nosy, ma'am. However, if you must know, one of our warriors saw you on the bank yesterday morning and knew you'd seen the hut."

His words sounded friendly, but something about his gaze made Boo uncomfortable.

Peabody chimed in. "We've been keeping an eye on you for some time, because…" He looked at Mouton and his words faded mid-sentence.

Fear about leaving Sasha by herself poked Boo's consciousness. She debated whether to mention it or not, then realized they'd been watching her and Sasha the whole time anyway. "You know, my cousin's at the house by herself. I better get back."

"She's doing fine," Peabody said, his voice gruff and no-nonsense.

"How do you know?"

"We have our ways—our eyes—I should say. We'll make sure she's fine. In a few minutes, we'll escort you to the house, and you can take your sister home."

"Cousin," Boo corrected. "I guess you already know there's a dead man in the house. She'll go berserk if she spends the night alone with him."

"Trust me; she's doing fine. She got something to eat from canned food in the pantry. Our spy put a few

things in it a few days ago."
"Your spy?"
"Your dead man."

Chapter Ten

Flabbergasted, Boo said, "You mean to tell me the dead man was like a scarecrow perched in a cornfield?"

"That's about it." Mouton flicked dirt from underneath his fingernail with the blade of a red Swiss Army Knife.

His attitude convinced Boo he didn't care if the dead man still stood in the *cornfield* or lay in the dirt turning into compost. She fanned her face with her hand. What in the world had her curiosity gotten her into this time?

"His job was to make sure no one found us. Looks like he failed at that because here you are." His face came close to cracking a smile, but he quickly pulled it to serious.

"So as not to ruin the experiment—yeah, I get it." Something niggled in her mind, and she searched for the source of the elusive discomfort. What was it that didn't sit right? It had something to do with Mili. She glanced at the woman, at the scratches down her arms and the bruises forming on her neck. That was it.

"If the dead man was your spy, then why'd he attack Mili?" Soon as the words came out of her mouth, Boo regretted them.

"That attack is none of your business." Mouton moved to the other side of Boo and changed the subject. "Seems you know these bayous and rivers pretty darn well."

"Nobody knows the swamps and bayous around here like me. I can go faster and know the easiest ways to get there. Should. Been plying these backwaters longer than you been a living, sonny."

"Won't argue with you there, ma'am," Peabody said. "We know the ways of our people, but regardless of how hard we work, we don't have anyone around here who knows the ins and outs of the swamps like you."

Boo looked from Mouton to Peabody. "How the heck do you know what or how much I know?"

Mouton cleared his throat. "As we said, we've watched you."

"Watched how? When?"

Peabody cleared his throat. "Sorry if we've intruded on your privacy."

Okay, enough was enough. "Privacy spivacy, who's the dead man, and who killed him?"

"His name is—was—Rafe Nations," Peabody said. "Actually, he's the one who saw you yesterday when you spotted the hut. We figured you'd return today, but we didn't expect you'd bring your sister."

"Humph. She ain't my sister. She's my second cousin—and once removed, at that." She rubbed her chin. "So who killed Dead Man?"

"My guess is no one did. He's had a bad heart for years."

"But why'd he attack Mili?"

Mili glanced at Peabody then looked at Boo. "Like I said, Boo. He thought I'd stolen something."

Boo sucked through her teeth. "What's that all about?"

Mili glanced at Peabody before she answered. "Truth is, he'd been coming on to me for some time. I didn't want to cause any trouble with the man. Just thought if I ignored him, he'd let it go. He didn't."

"Ain't no woman should put up with such nonsense, if'n you ask me." Boo turned to Peabody. "But somebody here needs to report his death to the sheriff. You plan to do that?"

"Don't you worry. We'll take care of that. Now, let's get you back to the house so you and your sister can go home."

"I don't need any help getting to the house. And second, I'm not sure how long I'll stay here," Boo said, ignoring the second reference to Sasha being her sister.

He scooted the other stool closer and sat across from her, hands on his thighs, back stiff, face serious. "I suggest you take our advice."

"Which is what?"

"Leave."

"'Fraid I can't do that, sonny." She noticed the man cringe when she called him sonny, but heck fire a mighty, he couldn't get straight that her and Sasha was cousins. "I can't take any advice from people I ain't got a clue what they're up to. I may look senile, but—"

"Ma'am," he said, sneering, "you don't look senile. All this secrecy—as you call it—has to do with the timing of the project."

"It ain't nothing against the law, is it?"

"Everything we do is completely up and above board. Actually, our work is sponsored by a grant from the states of Louisiana and Texas—a cooperative agreement. Mili and I are professors at Lamar University in Beaumont. We must demand, however, that you not tell anyone what we're doing. Tarek will escort you to the house. Now that the storm's passed, you can take your sister home and forget what you've seen here. Hopefully, your boat is still in good enough shape to travel. My guess is you haven't checked it yet."

Boo shook her head. "Not yet. Got too busy trailing Mili."

"If you find it is damaged, let us know. We are happy to help you get it repaired." He stood and added, "And don't forget to make excuses with your sister, so she won't know where you've been and what you've seen."

Boo leaned toward Peabody, glared in his eyes, and spoke through gritted teeth. "I'm gonna tell you this one more time, *sonny*. Sasha *ain't* my dang sister. She's my second cousin once removed."

"I apologize, Miss Murphy. I'll try to remember that."

A look of chastisement convinced her of his seriousness. "All right, now we understand each other, but there's something else. How do I know you're who you say you are? You got ID or something?"

He and Mili pulled out their university identity cards and held them out to Boo. Peabody went so far as to reach into a folder on a small table and got his driver's license.

Boo squinted at the documents. With her reading glasses in the bureau drawer at home, she could barely make out their photos, let alone the words, but she wasn't going to let him know that. "Looks like you're legit, okay. But what I want to know is, since I figure you live around here someplace, how come you don't know nothing about all these bayous and swamps?"

"Ma'am, when you've spent the last thirty years with your nose in books, you have a lot of book learning, but you don't have much street smarts...or maybe I should say swamp smarts."

"Then where you from—like where's your mammy and pappy live?" That fact always told Boo a lot about the person she was dealing with. Anybody from the big cities, she didn't trust one iota. They always had the almighty dollar sign as their god. Local folks liked money all right, but their town and its people stood taller than the dollar.

"I was born in a small Midwestern town, but my folks have both been dead and gone for years now."

"Well, it sounds all up and above board, but..." Something about the whole thing didn't set right with Boo. When she'd gotten here, she'd planned on showing them the map—giving it to them if that seemed the thing to do. But now? Maybe not. Maybe she'd wait a bit—maybe even check it out herself. She stood to go. "I better get back to the house and check on Sasha."

"Good." Peabody looked at Mouton, who shrugged and walked out of the hut, leaving the whole thing in Peabody's hands.

"Boo, let me warn you again, don't tell anyone about all this, okay?"

"Is that a warning or a threat?"

"Take it anyway you want, just don't tell your sister what you've seen here."

"That does it. I'm done." Boo huffed out her chest and started for the doorway.

"Cousin, second cousin...once removed. I'm sorry," Peabody said.

Boo recognized *begrudge* in a man's voice when she heard it.

"Mili, have Tarek take this young woman to the house so she and her sis, uh, cousin can go home." He turned to Boo. "Hopefully, the storm hasn't caused too much damage to your boat or clogged the waterways."

"I'm a big girl. I don't need Tarek or anybody else to walk me back. I can find my way just fine. But we ain't going home tonight. I figure Sasha ain't gonna be too happy spending the night in the same house with Dead Man, but it's too close to sundown, and who knows what kind of storm damage we'll meet. We'll head home first thing in the morning." She turned to leave, then stopped and looked at Peabody. "You said you're gonna call the sheriff, or you want me to when I get home?"

Peabody and Mili exchanged glances.

"We'll contact the authorities and let them know. Don't know how long it'll take them to get here, though. Likely won't be until after you leave in the morning."

Although he didn't add the word *hopefully* to the end of his sentence, Boo heard it all the same.

Tarek stepped in as if bidden from afar, took her by the elbow, and tugged. "Come on, Boo, I'll walk you home."

"I said I don't need no help."

"Come on, humor me. Walk with me. It isn't often I get to accompany a woman brave enough to stand up to me."

Boo laughed. "Keeps you humble, eh?" Giving in seemed the wiser thing to do. She pulled loose from his grasp, but walked out of the camp with him.

"You ain't as bad as I first thought you were, Tarek," Boo said as they walked along the trail.

"No, ma'am." He smiled at her.

"Say, you ever heard a panther scream out here, or heard other sounds in the wind?"

Tarek looked at her and smiled. "Does that mean you have?"

"I reckon. Something like that."

"Haven't heard a panther scream, but there's a legend among our people that tells of a young woman named Parahaia, a high priestess who lived in this area—one of the sunset people."

Boo's heart pounded. Now she was getting somewhere. "Go on."

"Well, let me see—as I recall, the legend is that Parahaia had powers above everyone else in the tribe. She controlled the weather—the animals. But one thing she couldn't control was the Yellow Fever brought here by the explorers. Her beautiful daughter, Ikunya, came down with the sickness, along with many others in the tribe."

"Yeah, the fever killed a lot of the settlers too—even the confederate soldiers fighting at Sabine Pass during the war," Boo said.

They walked in silence for a couple of minutes before Tarek continued. "Parahaia is said to have had a talisman that could heal Ikunya and the others, but because the tribe believed it had power, the Spaniards stole it, believing it would weaken the will of the people, thereby freeing them to take all the silver they could carry from a mine discovered by the tribe. In the end, Ikunya died, along with many of the others."

"Somehow I knew that was where the story was headed." Boo kicked a rock out of her way as they walked.

Tarek continued, his words full of quiet reverence. "Grief-stricken, Parahaia spent the rest of her days on this earth unsuccessfully searching for the talisman. On her deathbed, she is said to have sworn she'd never give up looking for it and vowed she'd forever watch over the swamps and bayous of the sunset people."

"Wow. That's quite a story," Boo said. What she didn't say was that she didn't believe a word of the fairy tale.

When they reached the edge of the woods, Tarek bade her goodbye, and Boo headed across the field toward the house. With just enough time to check on the pirogue before the sun dropped below the horizon, she hurried down to the water and found it still in good enough condition except for several inches of water in the bottom. She spent the next half hour or so bailing it out.

Drag-ass by the time she reached the house, she could barely put one foot in front of the other.

Sasha stood at the kitchen sink washing dishes. "Finally!" she said when Boo walked in. "I wondered where you'd traipsed off to and if you'd ever return. Now, let's get out of here."

"For heaven's sake, Sasha, it's nighttime. You know we can't leave in the dark, 'specially after a storm like that." Then she remembered, Sasha didn't know. She'd never been in the bayous, storm or no storm. "It'd be foolishness to start out now. No telling what we'd come across. We'll head out at first light. I already checked the boat. It's got a few more dents in it, but looks like it ain't gonna leak."

"You don't expect me to sleep in this house with a dead man, do you? Can't we pull him out in the backyard or something?"

"Now, Sasha, you know we can't do that. The critters will be fighting over him all night long. You sure won't be able to sleep then. We gotta make the best of this."

"Well, I stayed here this long, I guess I can make one more night, but I ain't sleeping by myself. Sasha shoved a plate at Boo. "Here, I kept some food for you."

After Boo had eaten and they cleaned the dishes, she headed to the bathroom laughing at the thought of two old biddies sleeping in the same strange bed of the same strange house with a strange dead man on the floor in the other strange room.

She filled the tub and lay in the hot water, cupping her *girls* in her hands. At one point in her life they'd filled a double D cup and brought all kinds of attention from the boys. 'Course she didn't pay them no mind. Climbing trees had been a whole lot more fun than letting the neighborhood boys cop a feel. Now, she could fold the shriveled flaps and stuff them in an A—that is, when she wore a bra at all. She lathered with a bar of soap, massaging the loose skin on her stomach. It ain't wrinkles, she thought, snickering. I just got too dang much skin.

She scooted further down in hot water, weary and not a little confused about the goings-on of the day. She must've dozed off when a deep, resonant voice whispered in her ear, "I need your help."

Creepy, skin-tingling sensations came and went and came again. Her eyes flew open.

A vaporous-looking dark-haired woman floated just above the bathwater, her long dress tipping the surface.

Boo covered her bosom. "Are you for real, or is it just my turn to sit in the tub and dream?"

The ghostly looking woman didn't speak again, but Boo swore the big dark eyes stared straight into her soul. She blinked twice to be sure the figure was really there, and when she did, it disappeared. Sasha said she'd seen a ghost. Was it the same one? If so, why had the specter asked for Boo's help earlier while she plied the waters, and hadn't asked for Sasha's?

On second thought, she reckoned that made sense.

She'd heard of haunted houses before, but bathrooms? Either she was seeing things, or her brain had gone around the bend.

"Guess I just didn't want Sasha to get ahead of me." She laughed, chalking it up to one weird day.

Finished with her bath, she pulled on the white cotton nightgown Sasha had found in one of the drawers, stuck her feet in her boots, and, somewhat refreshed, opened the bathroom door.

The see-through woman stood in the hall waiting. She motioned Boo to follow her.

"Where?" Boo asked—or did she think it? Heat flushed her cheeks at the silly idea of talking to a ghost. But when it turned and glided down the hall, Boo followed her like a schoolgirl slipping off from her mama to go smoke cigarettes with her friend.

She watched as the figure exited the open doorway, crossed the porch, and floated down the steps and into the cool night air.

Boo hurried to catch up.

"Dang it, how am I supposed to keep up if you go that fast?" she mumbled, following the glowing trail of footprints across the yard.

They led up to and then stopped at a large shell mound.

Why had she led her here? If she was a ghost, she ought to know Boo had seen dozens of shell mounds on her trips into the swamp.

Boo kicked at the mound then jumped when something rolled down and bounced off her foot. She stared at it a second, contemplating whether bending to pick it up would be worth the pain it would cause her back and hips.

But of course, her curiosity was stronger than her stiff back.

The piece felt cold and hard as metal. The moon peeked from behind a cloud while she rubbed, and soon, a shiny-looking vein running through it glistened up at her. Maybe something washed ashore, something that broke off of an old ship, maybe. She shoved it down in the pocket of her nightgown to inspect when she got inside.

Finding the object had taken her mind off of the figure that led her here in the first place. She looked around, but the ghostly woman had disappeared, along with the glowing footprints.

Weariness pulling on her again, Boo dragged herself in the direction of the house only to realize she'd been led further off the trail than she realized.

In the distance, a coyote howled at the big yellow moon hanging heavy in a night sky filled with a million trillion stars. Bullfrogs begged for more rain while a pack of wolves raced across her path a few yards in front.

"The world sure is a mighty pretty place," she whispered. For the first time in a while, she recalled the lighthouse keeper. The man who had touched a passion in her she never knew existed. Anytime she caught wind of the Gulf of Mexico, its fresh, salty smell jerked her right back to those days. She'd loved the feel of his beard, and the tenderness of his touch despite rough, calloused hands. Why had they stopped seeing each other? Oh yeah, he'd wanted her move to the lighthouse. She'd wanted him to move to the swamps. Neither gave in and in time, they grew apart. Durwood wanted to marry her, too. Hell, if she'd ever wanted to be married, it would've been to the lighthouse keeper. Durwood barked up the wrong tree.

But at least he loved the swamps and bayous—not as much as she did, but…

Moonlight—especially a full moon—always brought out the romantic in her. A woman had to remember these things, especially one her age, or else she'd dry up and blow away—either that or get married. She shook off those thoughts in a hurry.

Chapter Eleven

By the time Boo got to the house, Sasha had crawled in bed, pulled the sheet over her head, and sounded like a fast-moving freight train barreling down the tracks.

"Good thing Dawg's sleeping on the porch," Boo mumbled, "else he'd be howling his head off." She crawled in beside Sasha and gave her a nudge. "Turn over, toots, you're snoring."

Her next conscious thought was about the irresistible smell of bacon frying. She opened her eyes to discover the room filled with daylight and the other side of the bed empty.

Nightgown billowing, she hurried to the kitchen where Sasha stood at the stove cooking. "That ain't bacon I smell, is it?" Then, "Where in the world did you get bacon?"

Sasha barely looked up. "Smells good, don't it? I'm so hungry my stomach thinks my throat's cut. I come in here to put on the tea kettle, and there it was on the counter, a whole pound of bacon along with them eggs." She pointed to a small basket. "I figure Mili brought them. Don't know who else would've. Do you?"

"No clue," unless, Peabody had hired another spy, but she sure didn't intend to tell Sasha that.

After a quick meal, they cleaned the kitchen and then headed to the bedroom and did the same.

While Boo was away the day before, Sasha somehow got her clothes cleaned—halfway, at least— and now the two women dressed in silence. All the while, Boo's mind stayed sidetracked by haunting memories of the night before. She tucked the small piece of ore she'd found in her pocket, and it banged against her leg like a ten-ton weight.

At long last, the three, Boo, Sasha, and Dawg, trailed down to the boat, excited to be heading home. "Here, Dawg, you get in first and then you, Sasha. By the way, you think you can manage not to fall out of the boat this time?" Boo ducked her head to hide a smirk.

"I'm going to act like I didn't hear that." Sasha tilted her nose in the air as she climbed in behind Dawg.

They wended their way through canals damaged by the storm. Uprooted trees, broken branches, silt, and muck stretched way above the waterline. The pain of the bayou's destruction settled in Boo's gut as if she'd been the one ripped and shredded into a thousand pieces.

Back home, when they docked, Sasha hurried out of the pirogue and stomped to her house without a word or a backward look. She didn't have to. Boo knew how she felt—thrilled to be home and determined never to let anyone talk her into leaving again. She needn't worry. Folks in Hell would have their own icebox before Boo took her out again.

Boo put things away, then spent the rest of the day going about her daily chores, all the while thinking of Peabody. Intrigued by their experiment, she'd like to learn more about it and the tribal life they were creating.

But on the other hand, why'd she feel so uneasy about the whole project?

By suppertime, and still in no mood for Sasha's company, Boo decided to stay home and eat alone. She'd cook a pan of biscuits and fry that venison sausage Durwood gave her last week.

He must've read her thoughts, for while the biscuits baked, his black, rattletrap truck pulled to a stop out front, his bumper dragging the ground and smoke billowing out of the exhaust.

"Just like him to smell my biscuits cooking and come running." Boo suppressed a smile.

She peeked through the front window and watched him climb out of the truck dressed in what looked like a new pair of overalls, a red plaid shirt, and his spit-and-polish black shoes. That man sure knew how to court. He never came to see her that he didn't wear his dress shoes, buffed to a high shine. Like he never left the Army after German surrendered in '45.

When he headed toward the front steps, she jerked away from the window and headed back to the kitchen.

He rapped once, called her name, and opened the door. "You home, honey? It's me, Durwood."

She stepped to the doorway between the kitchen and the sitting room, a dishtowel in her hands and flour on her face, thrown there to prove she wasn't watching out the window. "Yeah, I'm home, but don't call me honey. I told you 'bout that. I ain't nobody's honey." She spiffed and turned her shoulder to him.

He limped over, reached around, and pecked her on the cheek. "You are, too. You just don't know it yet. That or you won't admit it to nobody. Let me guess. You're cooking that venison sausage I brought you. Bet you're making biscuits, too." He rubbed his belly. "Mmmm, my favorite. Got any Steen's syrup to go with it?"

"I reckon."

"I knew it. I knew it for sure. I smelt that sausage

and biscuits cooking before I ever left my place." He stepped outside her back door and fetched his rusty coffee can he used as a spittoon.

"If you want to set your feet under my table, you'll have to get rid of that dang chawin' tobacco."

He did and returned the can to the back step.

Boo opened the oven and pulled out a pan of crispy, golden brown biscuits. "Looks like I'll have another set of feet under my table tonight."

Durwood eased behind her and rested his hands on her shoulders. She started to shrug them off, but couldn't bring herself to hurt the old man's feelings. Besides, she wouldn't admit it to him, but she kind of liked his touch.

"So can I set the table, honey?"

Gawd, that man knew how to infuriate her.

"You know where the plates and silverware's kept."

He gave a satisfied little chuckle and marched to the safe where she kept her few dishes. Her place was small, and she didn't need much in the way of kitchenware, especially since she mostly ate at Sasha's.

"Oh, I forgot. I brought you a dozen fresh eggs. My hens are laying right nicely. Let me go fetch them outta the truck. I was so excited to see you, I plumb forgot."

When he returned with a paper bag loaded with big brown eggs, Boo pulled out four and fried them in the grease left from the sausage. After filling their plates, she set them on the table along with the pan of steaming biscuits.

"I came by yesterday but didn't catch you or Sasha home. What you two women been doing? I know Sasha might've been shopping—but I dang sure know you ain't." He split open a biscuit, buttered it, and then covered it in rich, dark syrup.

"You ain't never gonna believe what we did." Boo filled her plate and started eating while she recounted recent events—leaving out, of course, the woman who showed up while she lay soaking in the bathtub.

Durwood sat holding his fork in midair, stunned. "You're jawing me, Boo."

"I swear on a stack of Bibles."

"Pshaw, you never put much stock in the good book anyways. Why should that matter?"

"I do, too. Just don't believe it all really happened like folks want to believe it did. Okay, then, I swear on my mama's grave. There—you know how I feel about Mama."

"Then it's true? Lord, deliver me." Durwood wiped the sweat off his top lip. "You mean to tell me—"

"That's what I mean, all right. There's Atakapa Indians living out there like they did thousands of years ago—well, close to it. They ain't as dirty and don't stink as bad as you'd think. But don't you tell nobody. I ain't supposed to say nothing about it."

When Durwood didn't say anything, she said, "I'd like to sneak out there and learn more about what they're doing. I know that swamp like I know the back of my hand—and they don't. They should—you understand. Them're Indians, but they don't—not like me, anyway." Boo's chest swelled and she straighten her spine.

"But you ain't, are you?"

"Thought I might." She suppressed the smile that welled up from her insides. She hadn't told Durwood of Peabody's warning to forget what she'd seen and whether she did or not weren't none of his business.

A chance to learn more about the Atakapa tempted her, but something about the group out there *playing* Indian bothered her. She couldn't quite put her finger on it yet, but she would—at the right time. When Durwood ever went home, she'd call Sid and ask her what she thought about the situation. Maybe she could check on whether or not Peabody and Mili were telling the truth or not. They sounded like they were, something about the whole thing sure sounded fishy to her. Research, she could understand, but one thing she couldn't. Why would anyone want to live like that anymore?

Durwood jerked her attention by declaring, "No, you ain't."

"Ain't what?"

"You ain't going back out there and mettle into the goings on of them people. You don't know a thing about 'em. Besides, we're getting old. We can't take that kind of living no more."

"We may be old, but I sure ain't sitting on my laurels and waiting for Gabriel to come take me anytime he decides to blow his dang horn."

"Then, I'm going with you."

"Oh, no, you're not."

Dang it. Wouldn't you know he'd call her bluff?

"Besides, I was just messing with you. I ain't going out there and live like that with them people. Me and Dawg's staying right here, so you don't have to worry none."

A look of relief washed over Durwood. He let out a big sigh. "Thank the good Lord. I was beginning to think you'd lost your marbles."

"Ain't got many of them left, but I plan to keep what I got."

After supper, he helped with the cleanup, she let him kiss her on the cheek, and then he headed home. The subject of her going back hadn't come up again, which pleased Boo to no end. One thing she didn't need, and that was some old man meddling in her business.

Chapter Twelve

Soon after Durwood left, Boo went to the phone and dialed Sid. After several rings, the call went into her answering machine saying to please leave a message, and she'd return the call soon as she could.

"Sid, I don't like bothering you, but there's the situation… You see, it's like this… I found this Atakapa tribe out in the swamp, and I ain't right sure they're telling me the truth."

She paused, wondering how much to leave on a voice mail.

"If'n you could, I sure would like you to check and see if you can find out if they're who they say they are. I'm hoping you can swall me back pretty quick because something smells mighty fishy. Call me."

Certain that Sid would return her call the next morning, she pulled a well-worn book about the early Indians off the shelf and made her way to the bedroom. She rested the book on the bedside table, took her nightgown off the hook behind the door, and changed clothes.

Regardless of how weary she felt, she never crawled in bed without fluffing the feather bed nice and high, just like Mama taught her. She did so now, then propped the pillows against the old iron bedstead and climbed in. The bedsprings creaked, making her think of Mama and how she'd sit on the bed and read bedtime stories to Boo.

After a few squiggles and squirms, she settled in, put her cheaters on, and opened the book. She read again how the Atakapa womenfolk didn't count for much. How they'd strap their babies to a board and carry them on their backs, how they did all the work around camp while the men hunted for food. How they rubbed smelly alligator oil on their skin, their young'ns too, to keep away mosquitoes.

When her eyelids grew thick and heavy, she snapped the book shut, returned it to the table, and switched off the lamp.

Sometime later, her eyes popped open. Startled, she checked the clock. Two? She must've fallen asleep soon as the light went out. But what woke her?

Moonlight filtered through the white eyelet curtains and made weird shadows dance across the room. She blinked and looked again. The shadows now looked more like fog, which soon grew larger until a vaporous feminine figure appeared to come through the wall and rested her hand on the foot of the iron bedstead.

Boo squeezed her eyes shut. Maybe when she opened them, the woman would be gone, and the hair on her arms would lie down.

It wasn't that the figure's mouth moved, but somehow Boo heard—*I need your help—our people need your help*, then, *but be careful*. As the woman returned through the wall, she left behind a word—or was it her name—floating in the room. *Parahaia*.

Boo flipped and flopped on the hot, sticky sheets

trying to figure out what in the world the figure wanted her to do. Help her? Do what? Why'd the woman—*Parahaia*—think Boo could do anything about whatever might be going on out there? And what was she talking about when she said *our people*, and why'd Boo feel like she was included in the word *our*?

A rustle and a low growl outside her window told her Dawg had felt the energy inside the house as well, which didn't make her feel any better.

"It's okay, boy, whatever it was is gone. Go to sleep," she called toward the open window. Her words must have worked, for when the infernal three a.m. train passed, he didn't make a sound.

Daylight barely peeked through the curtains when Boo opened her eyes and stretched tight, achy muscles. Given what she and Sasha had been through the last couple of days, no wonder she felt as stiff as a corpse left out in the cold.

That thought made her wonder about Dead Man.

Well, maybe she didn't feel quite that stiff—or cold.

She dressed, ate breakfast, and went outside to give Dawg her leftovers and freshen his water dish, reminding herself to give him a pat on the head for not howling at the train the night before.

"Dawg?" She called a couple of times.

"Now where'd that dog get off to so early in the morning?"

When he didn't come running, she guessed he'd gone off on an early hunt.

Sasha stood working in her yard. Boo waved, snickering at how the woman wore her Sunday best even when she tended her garden. Only thing different than church clothes was the hat, a broad-brimmed floppy straw instead of the white hat with turquoise feathers in the brim. Boo hated that hat. Made her look like a dang peacock.

Sasha's late husband hated roses, so the first thing she did after he died was to plant Knockout Roses all along the front porch. Just to spite him, Boo figured, although Sasha never admitted it. They bloomed profusely now, with bright red flowers covering each bush. Sasha straightened her gloves, picked up a pair of shears from a basket, and took great care to clip the bushes at the right place to make them bloom more.

"Morning, Sasha. I figured you to sleep late this morning, after the last few days we had."

"I tried to, but when the train roared by, I kept waiting for Dawg to do his howling at the whistle. I want him to learn not to do that."

"People in hell want ice water, too. That don't mean they're gonna get it."

Sasha rolled her eyes.

"You can't complain about him howling at the train last night, though. He mustn't been tired too, 'cause I didn't hear him bark once."

"That's just my point. He's got me so used to hearing him, I kept lying there waiting for it." Sasha dumped a clipping into a trash basket at her feet.

"Speaking of the hound, you seen him this morning?"

"No. Thank goodness."

Boo looked around. "He's never gone far this early in the morning." Without another word, she turned and started calling and peering underneath and behind the house, all to no avail. The ground underneath her window looked like there'd been a scuffle. Dawg's water bucket lay turned upside down, leaving the earth around it still muddy. Footprints—large bare footprints—led off toward the water.

Heart pounding in her ears, she followed the trail to

the dock. She stooped over, collected a piece of mud stuck on the edge of the pier, and rubbed it between her fingers. Reddish brown hair—Dawg's.

He wasn't here, and it looked like someone took him. But that made no sense. Why would they do that?

The realization knocked the wind out of her. Her knees buckled. She grabbed the rough dock post and slid down until she sat, legs akimbo, her breath quick, short puffs. She stared at the rough-hewn gray wood, and then at the empty clamshells circling the post.

What the…

She collected one of the shells, breaking the symmetry. "I know this weren't here yesterday when we got home. Somebody put them here like this," she whispered, "and that somebody took Dawg, and they're fixing to get hurt."

Chapter Thirteen

Boo held onto the post and struggled to her feet, her mind running fast-forward and then to instant replay while her heart tried to keep up. Fingering the shell from the circle, she stumbled to where Sasha was pruning those blasted roses again.

"Somebody *took* Dawg!" Boo thrust the shell out to Sasha. "Here, look at this."

"It's just a clamshell, Boo. What's that got to do with Dawg?"

"Come look." She grabbed Sasha's hand and pulled her to the dock.

"See? That one empty spot right there," she pointed, "that's where I took this one from. And looky here. That's Dawg's hair for sure."

"Huh."

Boo returned the shell to its original place in the circle. "I've gotta go to that house on stilts. I got this feeling something, or someone out there knows where

Dawg is."

"Don't be ridiculous! How in the world would he have gotten there? He's not that good at swimming. Fact is, the mangy mutt's good for only one thing, keeping me awake every night while the train goes by."

"That ain't very nice, Sasha. You know Dawg's like my own kin." Boo paced the dock, Peabody's warning to tell nobody what she'd seen echoing in her head

"Just forget about it, Boo. He's likely off chasing squirrels or something. He'll find his way home. Dogs always do."

"He ain't out chasing critters. Look at where they scuffled there under the window and this hair on the edge of the dock and tell me you still think that's what he's doing."

Sasha threw up her hands. "I'm sorry. I wish I knew what to tell you."

"So, just forget him? That what you saying?"

Sasha stared at the shells circled around the pole. "What's that there?"

Boo's gaze followed Sasha's to another smear. Boo swiped it and smelled. Something about the primitive, oily odor wasn't Dawg.

"There's these folks I saw out at this camp near the house. If they come and took my dog, they ain't seen hell's fury yet." Boo pounded her fist into the palm of her other hand. "You just don't take a woman's dog."

Sasha snorted a sarcastic laugh. "That's for sure, especially yours. Well, don't expect me to go with you. I won't be putting my feet in that pirogue for a long time— if ever."

Boo straightened. "Kind of figured you wouldn't be wanting to. But you know me. If'n I could, I'd live out in the swamp. Feels more like home than here. That is, till them people came in and—"

"What people? Mili? That reminds me, we still need to call the sheriff and report that body." Sasha looked up through her eyelashes. "Knowing you, if you go out there, you'll raise the man from the dead and make him go fishing with you." Her shoulders shook with laughter at what Boo didn't consider funny.

Sasha put her hands on her hips and looked out at the water. "Well, as I said, have at it. You'll not get me on the boat again."

"Well, I'll swan. I just knew you'd want to go with me." Boo smirked.

Disbelief spread across Sasha's face until she looked at Boo's grin. "You're pulling my leg."

"Yeah, I figured you wouldn't go but—"

"You got that right. You'll play heck ever getting me out there again."

"Well, I'm going." Boo looked up at her house. "Might's well pack a bag and be ready for it to take a few days 'cause I just might have to spend some time out there before I find Dawg."

"I'm calling the sheriff about the dead man. If we don't, we're likely to get in trouble if they find out we were out there and didn't report it," Sasha said.

"Never mind. I'll call it in. That way you won't have to stop working on your roses." Boo was afraid if the sheriff got involved, he'd get focused on the dead man and not Dawg.

The first thing she did when she went back inside was to check her voice mail. When she saw that Sid hadn't called, she dialed her cell phone again.

Once more, her voice mail answered.

"This is Boo, she said without preamble. "These people have took my dog, and I need you to help me find him. Either that or you're gonna have to help my lawyer prove I had a good reason to kill them what took him. You best call me back real soon," and slammed the phone back on the receiver.

She packed a canvas bag with extra clothes, a toothbrush, a roll of toilet paper, two packages of crackers and peanut butter, and an old tin can full of kitchen matches, and last, collected her shotgun and an extra box of ammo—just in case. If these people would hurt Dawg, they just might try to hurt her, too.

But they'd have to do it before she hurt them.

Her mind on Dawg, she stomped outside, surprised to see Sasha standing in front of the house waiting.

"Okay, before you head off half-cocked, let's sit and talk a minute." She grabbed Boo by the elbow and led the way across the yard to the rockers on her front porch.

"Here. Sit."

Boo wasn't used to getting or taking orders from Sasha, but something about the expression on Sasha's face made Boo do as instructed.

For the first few minutes, neither of them spoke, rather sat and rocked. Boo had never seen Sasha like this before, and it unnerved her.

The morning had grown hot and muggy. Sasha picked up a couple of flappy funeral parlor fans and handed one to Boo, who inspected the pink and yellow flowers on one side and the funeral parlor logo on the other.

"Don't just look at that fan, missy," Sasha said. "Use it. You look like you're about to faint."

"I ain't gonna faint," Boo said, "but I'm sure madder 'n hell at the sumbitch who took my dog." Tears filled her eyes and threatened to spill over the brim. She wiped them away with her sleeve.

"I'm worried about you, Boo."

The tender words made it tougher for Boo to control the tears. Then Sasha rested her hand on Boo's arm and said, "Okay, honey, tell me again why you think someone took Dawg?"

"Dang it, Sasha, stop being so nice to me," Boo sputtered between her attempt not to cry and the tears that insisted on running down her cheeks.

Sasha sat and rocked. "You ornery old coot. You

don't want nobody to know you got a heart beating warm blood." Sasha paused, then said. "You ain't so tough, honey."

"Not when it comes to Dawg—"

"I know. I know. Now, dry them eyes and start at the beginning. What happened out there?"

Boo spilt the beans about the Atakapa camp, what they said they were doing, how not to include Sasha in the information.

Sasha sat with her mouth open.

"Say something, dang it. You don't believe me? You do? What?"

Sasha got up and stomped across the porch, opened the screen door, and let it slam behind her. Boo heard the icebox open and close and dishes rattle, then the sound of footsteps leading outside.

Sasha returned carrying two large, sweaty glasses of ice tea. She shoved one at Boo. "I thought you'd outgrown making up them Indian stories, Boo. Your mama would be so embarrassed of you."

The two sat and rocked, both of them swelled up like old toad frogs after a day of catching flies.

"The only way I know to get you out of this nonsense, young lady, is to call your bluff. I know I said I'd never, but as bad as I hate to, I'm going out there with you so I can prove to you that camp is only a figment of your imagination. I swear. You're like some kid playing make believe."

Boo shook her head in resignation. "I'll take what I can get. How long before you're ready to go?"

"Give me thirty minutes." Sasha headed inside.

"Make it fifteen, and this time you better pack a change of clothes," Boo called to Sasha's retreating back. "I'll meet you at the boat. You be there in fifteen, or I'm going without you." Boo rested her glass on the porch and headed down to the dock. On the way, she recalled Peabody had warned her about telling Sasha they were out there. But the way she figured it, those folks gave up any right to privacy.

You just don't take a woman's dog.

Worried sick, and missing Dawg something awful, she climbed in the boat, stored her bag, and then bailed out a little water that seeped in overnight.

She never went on this kind of journey without Dawg, for he filled in the spaces of her knowledge about the swamp. In her mind's eye, she saw him standing on the dock begging to go with her.

"You might's well join me, Dawg. I know you ain't gonna be happy if you don't get to go," she invited. Dawg barked twice, jumped in, took his usual seat up front, and waited. But soon, he disappeared—everywhere except in Boo's heart.

Fifteen minutes later, or reasonably close to it, lipsticked Sasha traipsed down the path, tossed in four bags of stuff, and repeated the same method of entry she had the first time, straddle-legged, clinging to the dock post so as not to take a dunking.

"One of these days you'll get the hang of it," Boo said, unsuccessfully suppressing a snicker. But proud of herself for resisting the urge to comment about Sasha bringing enough clothes to outfit an Army regiment. Give the woman a little credit. She was trying.

Very trying.

The trip through the swamp seemed like it took forever, and at one point, Boo felt certain she'd seen *feu follet* but didn't dare tell Sasha.

Boo wasn't Cajun, but she'd plied the swamp enough times to see the dance-lightning more times than she wanted, for it always carried a warning. Some claimed the will-o-the-wisp was souls escaped from purgatory come back to earth to get prayers for their delivery to the next place. Even her own Irish ancestors used to believe the feu follet were elves and fairies holding their dances at night over marshy places.

Others called it swamp gas.

One thing she knew for sure. It always predicted something evil about to happen—that or a death. Boo remembered as a kid sitting on the front porch with the old folks late at night after the day's heat cooled off. Her ears always perked up when they talked in hushed whispers. For she knew they were talking about things never mentioned aloud or in the light of day. Things like feu follet, and how it showed the way to pirate Jean Lafitte's buried treasures.

Lessons learned the hard way had taught her not to follow the dancing light. She got lost every time she did. But what never failed, was the lesson her old Cajun neighbor taught her one day when the two fished. "Stick the blade of a pocketknife in the ground," he'd said in a hushed voice. "That way, you cut the spell." She'd returned and found the knife the next day, and sure enough, there'd been blood on it, and no one died— leastwise, that she knew.

Whatever it was, and however it worked, it showing up today wasn't a good sign.

Sasha didn't say a word the whole way, sat up front with her back stiff, shoulders set. The certainty she'd prove Boo wrong danced off the top of Sasha's head like her own feu follet.

It took longer to reach the island because Boo went another route to avoid the Indian who had seen them the other day. The storm had left behind so much damage Boo wasn't sure she would recognize it again and thought she'd missed it, but when she rounded a bend, and the mist appeared straight ahead, she felt the muscles in her neck relax.

Moving closer, she motioned Sasha to take their bags and get out, whispering, "Shh, make as little noise as you can. We don't want them to know we're here." Which received a disgusted look from Sasha, but she at least did as she was told—this time.

Boo pulled the pirogue ashore and took care to conceal it with brush blown down from the storm.

They tromped past the half-covered concrete dock, the half-buried armament, and on around the trail till they saw the house on stilts.

The closer they got, the stronger grew the stench of something awful.

"You smell that?" Boo asked.

Sasha wrinkled her nose. "I sure do. What is it? Smells like something dead. You don't think that dead man's still inside, do you?"

"My guess is we'll find him still there."

A quick trip up the steps and a silent response to their knock on the door told them the house sat just as empty as it had when they'd come a couple of days ago— or as she'd thought it was.

They entered and, despite the heat and foul odors, Boo closed and locked the door behind them.

First, they dumped their bags, then checked the Dead-Man room, relieved to see the body had been removed. Evidently, the coroner ruled natural causes because there wasn't crime scene tape around the door. Made Boo wonder if Peabody had contacted the sheriff like he said he'd do, and if not, had he been the one who moved the body.

That's when it hit her—the smell downstairs under the house—surely, no one would be stupid enough to keep the corpse there, not in this heat.

After a quick bathroom stop, Boo advised Sasha to wait while she checked out the campsite, then she'd come get her so she could see it. Better a lie than for Sasha to see what Boo feared she'd find under the tarp.

Sasha put up no argument. "Good, I'm tired. I think I'll take a nap till you finish."

Relieved, Boo headed downstairs and went straight to the pile of junk covered with the tarp. Hand covering her nose and mouth, she lifted the cover.

Rafe Nation's body was there all right, along with what looked like ten zillon maggots, click-clacking their way through his flesh.

Alongside him lay Mili, nose gone, and eyes already empty sockets. It had to be Mili, for she had that same hawk tattoo on her arm—what was left of it, that is. But why was she dressed in the same kind of clothing as the Atakapa women at camp?

Boo forced her breakfast down and dropped the tarp. The feu follet she'd seen earlier was evidently the restless spirits of these two wandering the swamp trying to figure out what in the world happened to them.

"Sasha, Sasha?" She hurried upstairs again and bustled to the bedroom where Sasha had said she'd be napping. The bed had been turned down, but Sasha wasn't in it. A trail of blood across the floor looked like someone had been dragged across it to the window, now open, with a breeze ruffling the musty curtains. Her heart stuck midway up her throat, Boo rushed to the window, calling "Where are you, Sasha? What happened?"

But when she stuck her head out and looked below, she saw Sasha on the ground, and blood, everywhere. At first, Boo thought she might be dead, but then she moved her legs and tried to raise her head.

Boo stuck her head out the window. "Sasha, wait. Don't move," she called. "I'm coming…"

An overwhelming grief ripped through Boo's gut. She'd never fainted before, but now, a threatening blackness crept in. She grabbed the window ledge with young tanned hands she didn't recognize. Winds howled through her mind, like she was traveling at a rapid rate, but to where? Her knees surrendered to the confusion, and she eased to the floor before the fast-encroaching icy darkness pushed everything else out of her mind and pulled her into a dark blue vortex.

For the first time in her life, the swamp wasn't calling her, which left her with little choice but to follow the trail inland and take a chance that she might pass the slagheap of silver ore where her people lay dying. But why were they dying? The silver ore must be tainted with the white man's blood. Her people never had what the white man called Yellow Fever until after they landed in their big sailing vessels.

She walked into the village feeling somewhat dazed but didn't understand why this place embraced her with such familiarity. A woman sat grinding corn with a big, well-worn stone and pestle, while another tanned a deer hide. Their skin was filthy, but their matted hair glistened like fresh oil had been rubbed on it. Each person wore a simple piece of leather wrapped around them and tied at the waist.

A third woman squatted at the river pounding on her laundry with a smaller rock. Beside her lay wet pieces she'd evidently finished washing.

Two boys played with sticks and a rock, knocking it back and forth.

Boo saw a young woman, her belly swollen with child, waving Boo over and calling out, "Parahaia, Ka has been looking everywhere for you."

"Pardon me?"

"Our father's patience is wearing thin. He came to me and said, 'Taka, tell Parahaia that Ka cares not how many shark she has harpooned, or how many brave enemy she has slain in combat. If she doesn't show up in time for the ceremony, it will be her flesh I dry and feed to the pregnant females.'" The woman, evidently named Taka, rubbed her belly.

"Sorry, my name's Boo. I don't know what you're

talking about."

Taka reached for Boo's hand and yanked her down the trail behind her. But when Boo looked at the union of her hand in Taka's, much like siblings joined in care for each other, Boo didn't recognize her own arm and hand.

Gone were the bulging veins, wrinkled skin, and age spots of an old woman.

She still felt the pressure of her hand clasped by the young woman, but Boo's extremity was now the brown arm and hand of a strong, sinewy young woman.

Chapter Fourteen

Stunned, Boo allowed herself to be led through the village by the young woman. They rounded the fire pit and kept going—to where, Boo hadn't a clue. Never before had she feared tricks the swamp sometimes fooled around with her mind, but for the first time in her life, she hoped it played tricks now. If not, she'd paddled her way into the loony bin.

Surely, the people she passed were the same ones she'd seen a couple of days earlier—civilized folks dressed in costume, playing like they were their own Atakapa ancestors. But what kind of gibberish were they speaking, and why did it sound so familiar? And what was that God awful smell?

"Whoa, wait a minute," she said, dragging her feet. "What's going on?"

Taka glanced at her. "We've no time, Parahaia. Father will be quite angry if we don't hurry."

Boo faked a pant to buy time. "Hurry? I'm not sure

I can walk at this point, let alone run."

"What is it? Why are you breathing so hard, sister?"

"I don't know who you think I am, but I ain't your sister."

"Do not be silly. Of course, you are," Taka replied. "Come along now. Our father, Ka, was elated when he heard you were here in time for the ceremony. He sent me to fetch you to his hut."

"What on earth are you doing coming here again?" Peabody's voice, calling from behind her, seemed to clear the fog diluting Boo's thoughts.

"I told you to stay away—forget you'd been here."

She wobbled a bit, then shook her head, scattering the last wispy remnants. "I… What just happened? What kind of language was them people speaking…and what the heck was that awful smell?"

"What smell?" Peabody raised his eyebrows and looked around, sniffing. "I don't smell anything unusual. And as far as what happened, nothing other than Mili brought you here to see me. The only words I've heard anyone speaking are English. We wish we had a better foundation of what the Atakapa spoke, but so far, we haven't learned enough words to keep a conversation going. It's so guttural—"

"You can say that again, but how come it sounded like I'd heard it before?"

Concern clouded Peabody's face. "Boo, I don't have any idea what you're talking about."

"And Mili, here… I saw her… she's—"

Mili or Taka, or whoever the woman was, interrupted Boo. She spoke softly, her words full of concern. "Come on, Boo, you know me."

"But I saw… I know I saw…" Boo stopped mid-sentence. Something odd was going on. Better she shut her mouth. Let them think she'd gone off her rocker. For all she knew, maybe she had. She looked at the hand holding hers, relieved to see it was no longer Taka, but

Mili, who stood beside her living and breathing as sure as Boo did.

"You saw what, Boo?" Peabody raised one eyebrow as he took a step closer.

"Never mind. Just the dreams of a crazy old woman, I guess."

If that wasn't Mili under the tarp covered with maggots, then who was it? And why did the woman have the same hawk tattoo on her arm as Mili?

From that, her thoughts ran to the most important questions eating at her insides, like, who took Dawg, and did they have Sasha? She had to hold out hope the two lived, else she'd lose her own will to keep putting one foot in front of the other. She'd use the old honey instead of vinegar approach when she asked. Otherwise, she might not get either one of them back.

"You didn't tell anyone about us, did you?"

"You asked me not to, so I didn't," tell anybody except Sasha and Durwood—she thought, finishing the story in truth, if only in her mind.

"So why'd you come back?'

"Can I ask you a question first? I don't have any idea what an Atakapa campsite should look like, but a couple minutes ago, it not only sounded different, but it also looked different than it does right now, or even yesterday."

A confused expression crossed Peabody's face. "What do you mean, different? How?"

"More like I'd think the real Atakapa might look. Makes me think these people really are cannibals. Do they really eat people's flesh?"

"Not today, but likely they did in the past. Only their enemies, though. That way, the enemy couldn't return from the other side. If they ate them, they conquered them forever."

Peabody looked at the ground, hesitated a minute, then looked back at Boo. "You haven't by perchance seen a piece of deerskin lying around up there at the house, have you?"

Boo wasn't good at lying, which is why she made it a point to tell the truth most of the time. Except maybe for those times when she stretched it a bit. She reckoned today was just going to be one of those days.

"Seen something that looked like that up at the house, but then Mili showed up. When I found her with that guy on top of her, it wasn't in the room."

Peabody didn't say a word, but he scrutinized her every move. She forced her lips into a tight line so they wouldn't twitch. She must have been successful, for his shoulders relaxed, and he gave her a little smile.

"I didn't figure you did, but I just had to ask. Now, tell me. Why did you come back?"

"As I said yesterday, I just like the swamps. I spend every day out here that I can. Just stopping by to say hi and no hard feelings."

"That's right nice of you. How long you going to be here?" Peabody glanced around, as if impatient for her to move on so he could go about his business—whatever that was.

"Oh, I won't be here long."

A man with a black-painted face walked up. When Peabody called his name, Boo almost *lost it* for a second time that day. The contents of her stomach came up into her throat, but she swallowed hard, willing it down.

"Ka, this is the woman we told you about. She's just offered to keep an eye out for the map." Peabody bowed in respect as he spoke as if Ka were the real chief today instead of thousands of years ago—like the one Taka talked about earlier.

"Your honor—or high chief—not sure what I should call you…" Boo bowed as low as her stiff body allowed.

"Ka will do fine, Boo Murphy."

Boo hesitated, still unsure whether or not to mention Dawg and Sasha's disappearances and that she suspected

Peabody had something to do with it. That was the reason she'd returned.

The same confusing questions continued to whirl behind her eyes. Questions like, why had the young woman called Boo Parahaia? And why had the spirit woman at the foot of Boo's bed claimed her name was Parahaia? Based on what she'd read about the ancient tribe, the name had something to do with harpooning a big fish in the mouth. That seemed an odd name for an Atakapa woman. The men were the ones who did the hunting and fishing, and the women did everything but.

"Sit," Ka said, indicating the ground, "and I will tell you the story of our ancestors."

Boo laughed. "I might be able to get down, but it'd take the whole tribe to get me on my feet again. Maybe you better just tell me what's on your mind."

Ka stared off in the distance as if recalling facts deep in his psyche. When he spoke, his words were filled with great reverence. He paused from time to time, as if for emphasis. "We are the Atakapa-Ishak people. A number of tribes made up the great nation present in these parts for thousands—maybe tens of thousands of years. A long time ago, our tribes were made up of coastal and inter-water river groups known as Bedia, Patiri, Akokisa, Deadose, Atakapa, and Opelousas. Our domain included the area now known as the Colorado River of Texas all the way to Vermillion Bay of Louisiana, plus, some hundred miles inland to where Lufkin, Texas now sits. Tied together by our language and by marriage, we were each independent tribes."

Boo squirmed, eager to get on with looking for her missing loved ones.

"Be patient, my daughter."

"Daughter? I'm not your—"

"Shhh. Hush now. It is important that you know."

The chief's soft words, rather than sounding offensive, seemed to imply something Boo couldn't quite wrap her thoughts around. Her best course of action, she decided, was to again bide her time, hoping something would soon make sense.

"We lived along the coast and inland waterways of Texas and Louisiana. When the first explorers came, they found our people with a simple lifestyle of hunting, fishing, and food gathering—much like you see here today. They didn't find what they looked for—gold, silver, and precious jewels—so for the most part, they bypassed our ancestors, who only knew hardship and how to overcome it."

Ka stood, walked off a short distance, and stared out over the campsite. Boo couldn't help but feel great sadness from the man, but also a strong sense of pride. When he returned to her side, grief coated his words.

"The early Europeans thought our ancestors were savages whose customs and cultures pushed the limits of *civilized people*—whatever that is."

"Which sorta makes you wonder," Boo said, kicking a clod of dirt, "who says what's normal or not."

"Exactly. Remember, it was the Europeans who came to conquer them. Before that, Atakapa had lived in this area for thousands of years. Some say there's evidence some of them had been in the area for ten to twenty thousand years. What we know today is just the last five hundred years or so. But one of these days, our clans will all come together and claim what we've lost— regardless of the cost." He steepled his fingers and looked at Boo.

Uh oh, that sounded like trouble might be brewing.

"Also, my dear, if you find something out here that you don't understand, I beg you not to disturb it."

"Like what?"

"Oh, some type of talisman or something. You know, stuff like that. If you do, just leave it there. Hide it if you can."

Whatever it was that told Boo to shut up, she

decided to take its advice.

Don't let them see you sweat, that same voice, now resident in her gut said. *Something's going on here you don't yet know. Watch, listen, pay attention, but don't reveal what you learn. Let them think you're going along, believing every word.*

"You see," Ka said, interrupting her thoughts, "our forefathers believed in a spirit god that lived everywhere. We don't call our religion a name, because it is above naming. We don't have church services. We don't have a religion, per se. We incorporate our beliefs into our daily life. We live what we believe. We believe in the afterlife all right—but not the way you do. Our shaman— or high chief—is really the one who keeps us safe. Whatever he does when he's up on that shell mound doing his magic, we know something mysterious is happening. That he knows something we don't. Of course, in our hearts, and his, we know he doesn't, but that doesn't stop any of us from acting like he does."

"How do you act when someone steals your dog, and you can't find your…" Dammit, the question popped out of her mouth without first checking with her brain.

"Excuse me?"

"Nothing—pay me no never mind. I just couldn't find my—"

"Your what? Couldn't find what? Your dog?"

Boo felt his strong and steady eyes before she looked up to confirm the fact. But when she did, a look of consternation had frozen his face.

"Never mind, I reckon he's just gone off on a hunt or—" Boo stopped mid-sentence, fearful she'd give away too much of what had happened. If Peabody was involved, it might be in her best interest to play dumb with everybody. She just hoped it wasn't too late.

Boo looked around the camp. "This place makes me feel like I stepped back two thousand years."

"We have tried to recreate that atmosphere and live

as close to how we think they lived as we can. Otherwise, we'll never connect with our forefathers again."

"What do you expect to get from all this?" Boo's question sounded more combative than she'd intended but hoped he didn't notice.

"Like I said before, we want to build a tribe using the old ways as a model for other Indians who may have lost the sense of who they are. We want to tap into our past, know the confidence of our forefathers so we can survive and thrive." He bowed. "You honor me by listening. Thank you."

Boo returned his thank you like Mama always taught her.

As Ka turned and strolled off, Peabody strolled over and patted Boo's shoulder. "Don't let him get to you. He's a little extreme—always goes over the top in anything he does. We're not that fanatical. We do hope to regain what we've lost, however, and that includes our native tongue."

She looked at the camp and said, "You tell me you think these women are going to be comfortable living this life? Looks mighty tough, compared to standards today."

"Some of them may leave, all right. And that's okay. Those who want to stay, can."

Peabody and the shaman both sounded sincere, but Boo still wasn't convinced whether or not she was indeed going crazy or whether she'd already arrived.

Mili stepped up and spoke to Peabody. "I've taken care of everything, sir. We're ready."

"Good. So you called the sheriff, and he came and got the body? Did he ask any questions?"

"The normal ones. I told him I'd come in and sign a statement. One of the detectives said that likely Rafe died of a heart attack while we struggled."

Boo tucked away what she suspected was a bald-faced lie, knowing she'd have to bring it out one of these days, and also knowing now wasn't the time. "So did you tell him about me and Sasha being there?"

"No, I kept it simple. Said I was the only one in the house. No sense in getting you two messed up in the situation."

"Not rightly sure that was the best thing to do, but what's done's done."

Boo needed time to think and made the only excuse she could think of, and that was to go relieve herself. She wandered off into the woods, found a secluded corner, and took care of business.

Strong voices from the camp convinced her to return on silent feet. She stepped behind a bush and watched as Mili unfolded a small camp table, laid out what looked to be the journal Boo had seen on the worktable in the dead-man room. Mili and Peabody leaned in to take a look.

Soon, Mouton, the man she'd met that first day in the hut, walked up from out of nowhere.

It was all Boo could do not to stomp right up and demand they tell her where they got the journal—the one no one admitted they had. She wondered if they suspected she had the map. Evidently not, or she'd likely be dead by now. They didn't have to kidnap Sasha and Dawg—they could just kill Boo outright, take the map, and be done with it.

But, she reminded herself, they might suspect she did it—but they weren't sure, and if she did, they didn't know where she'd stashed it. Best she keep that secret.

As she stood watching, that same voice she'd heard before, cautioned her to stay quiet and just listen.

She did.

Peabody looked at Mouton. "We know the Indians continued to take out silver under the slavery of the Spanish until they rebelled. Supposedly, the mine had a cave-in years ago. When the Indians died out, no one knew where the mine had been. Except, rumors always told of a map the Atakapa hid away, but no one could find. I talked to the son of an old-timer some five years ago who was in his eighties at that time. He had a copy of a story written by a Mr. Combs that was printed in the *Beaumont Enterprise* many years ago. The article included a map, but it was so old we couldn't make it out. Next thing I heard was that someone had broken into his house and stole the article."

Mouton pulled a piece of yellowed newsprint out of his pocket. "You mean this?"

Peabody's mouth dropped open. "So it was you! Why didn't you tell me you had it?"

"Didn't figure it made any difference since it is too faint to read." He folded the article and stuck it in his pocket. "Rumor has it, the mine sits on property owned by Temple Inland."

Peabody picked up the conversation. "Now, the question is, does she have the map? And if so, maybe she'll lead us to it."

Boo had enough. She threw back her shoulders and stepped into the clearing. "Is that the same journal I saw on the table up at the house?

Peabody stared at Boo, who glared at Mili, who refused to look Boo in the eye.

Mouton stood as if chiseled from granite. But after a long silence, he picked up the journal and plopped it on the table facing Boo. "Here, Miss Murphy, take it. Wipe away the dust, and a treasure will appear before your eyes."

"Humph, I ain't that easy to fool. You got something up your sleeve, or you wouldn't be showing me that now."

He shoved it closer to her. "No tricks."

Curiosity got the best of Boo. She snatched the faded-green journal and cradled it in her hands. A hint of a name had been scrawled in the bottom right-hand corner. She squinted to make it out. *A. Phillips.* Taking great care with the brittle, yellowed pages, she opened it and scanned a left-hand column of men's names, each in a different handwriting. Next to each name, someone else had recorded his date of death, which ranged over a number of the years—decades, even. Only one name did not include a date of death—A. Phillips.

"What's this all about?" Boo looked up to see the eyes of the other three—Mouton, Peabody, and Mili—focused on her.

Chapter Fifteen

Puzzled by the book with the names of men and their dates of death, Boo stood staring at the three—Mouton, Peabody, and Mili—who stared at her.

"I'll ask you one more time," Boo said. "What's this book, why's it here, and what's it got to do with what you're doing rebuilding the Atakapa tribe?"

Mouton spoke first, his voice carrying an air of authority. "When World War I broke out, many men from East Texas joined the forces to fight the Germans. A large group of these men signed up and went overseas together. When the war ended, they were in a French town. They made a pact that they would each take a bottle of French wine home with them. In memory of all of those who served, they would meet each year to remember their fallen comrades. As a part of the meeting, they would recall the sacrifices each made, until only one man was left. When that happened, he would open his bottle of wine and make a toast to all his comrades who had fallen before him. The final veteran from that group was from Vidor, the town between Orange and Beaumont."

Her patience wearing thin, Boo sighed and said, "I was born and raised in this area. I reckon I know where Vidor is. Get on with the story."

Mouton, Peabody, and Mili grinned at each other.

She knew they laughed at her, but she'd stopped caring what other people thought a long time ago. Now critters? That was a different matter all together.

Peabody picked up the telling. "Anyway—we don't know what happened to all these bottles of wine. But this journal in itself is priceless. WWI collectors will pay big dollars for it."

He paused while she inspected the find, then continued. "If you flip to the back page, you'll see one of these fellows made a note. Seems he'd heard rumors of a lost Confederate treasure of 39 kegs of Mexican silver dollars that the Sunset People found and hid in their silver mines."

"So let me get this straight," Boo said, beginning to see the full picture. "I thought you were here to rebuild a great nation. Now it's beginning to sound like you guys are just plain old treasure hunters." She spat on the ground. "Ain't got no use for such."

Mouton held his hand out to Boo. "Whoa! Wait just a cotton-picking minute, lady. You know a better way to help these people? Seems to me finding a lost silver mine is right up there at the top of the money makers—right alongside casinos."

Boo's eyes ripped him top to bottom, then settled on his eyes. Was it the milky brown irises, or the yellowed whites that made her skin itch? "Saying you find this treasure, how you plan to use it to help these people."

"Forgive my rudeness, Mrs.—"

"It's plain old Boo. Ain't got time or tolerance for titles that tell you if I got a man or not."

"Just courtesy, ma'am. I meant no offense."

Boo strolled to a bush, broke off a twig, and chewed it into a toothpick. She didn't believe Mouton any more than she figured he believed himself. "These folks can live out here like this for a while, but soon they'll die off in the elements like their ancestors."

"Not that any of this is any of your business, but if those in Texas government had any sense, they'd let them build casinos like Louisiana did." Peabody shuffled and kicked the ground with the toe of his boot.

Boo snorted. "That ain't likely to happen. Too many of them holier-than-thou around here believe gambling's a sin. That, and they think it's their job to control how poor people spend their money—the bastards. Just the other day, I heard this lobbyist on the news say gambling shouldn't be legal in Texas because poor people would gamble away their money, and they couldn't afford it. Can you believe that? Government controlling how anybody spends their money goes against our American rights, dang it." She pounded her fist on the table.

Mouton jingled a handful of coins. "Whatever."

Mouton cut a glance at Peabody, who laughed and said, "She talks so much I hear the swamp even talks back to her."

"I'll talk back to the old biddie, all right." Mouton balled his hand into a fist.

That did it. Boo could bite her tongue no longer. "Just goes to shows you don't know nothing about nothing. The swamp likes balance. Someone or something comes in and messes things up, then bad things start happening. Mother Nature needs the bayous and its critters—helps keep things balanced." She crossed her arms.

No one spoke for several seconds until Peabody broke the silence. "So are things out here balanced or not?"

"Something stinks. I'm just trying to figure out what

or who it is."

The others laughed.

Boo didn't crack a smile.

Peabody cleared his throat. "You'll know once we find the mines. Then these folks will have all kinds of resources to help them get re-established as a nation. It will convince the federal government that they have indigenous rights never afforded them."

Boo harrumphed. "What makes you think finding the mines will make a hen's tooth of difference to the U.S. Government? The Atakapa ain't never got their rightful due. Stories of the tribes that walked the Trail of Tears gut-wrenched decent white folks into doing something for the few that survived. Problem is, the government never felt guilty about the Atakapa 'cause they didn't have to walk the Trail 'cause weren't enough of them to cause a problem and for the most part, they was peaceful."

Mili, who had been standing quietly, letting the men carry the conversation, stepped forward at that point and took Boo's arm. "These folks' ancestors were the true founding fathers of Texas and Louisiana. Some believe they descended from the group that migrated across the Bearing Straight eons ago. Ever since the Europeans first set foot on this land, the life of the Atakapa people have been run by others. It's time they were in charge of their own world again."

"That's the point," Peabody said. "We've got to do something to help keep the Atakapa- Ishak civilization alive, especially since the early settlers had a lot to do with their near-extinction."

"You ain't telling me nothing I don't already know." Boo's voice grew moist with unshed tears. "Ever time I'm out in the swamp I hear them in the wind. They whisper at me, begging me not to forget them. It breaks…my..."

"Why is she still here?" Mouton asked, then he

turned to Boo. "Miss Murphy, I don't mean to offend you, but this is no place for a woman you're age. You'll likely get hurt."

Mili bristled when Mouton turned and stomped off. She excused herself and hurried after him.

Peabody stalled, scratching his chin. "One more thing, Boo."

Boo scrubbed her teeth with her self-made toothpick. "If it's to trail after that man, you can forget it."

He shook his head. "No, if you see anything suspicious, or anyone doing or saying anything would you come tell me?"

"Not sure I would—not sure I wouldn't. Why? What's going on?"

"Nothing, but…"

So, she'd been right to come there looking for Dawg. She just hadn't figured on losing Sasha in the process.

"Day's passing, and soon it'll be dark," Boo said. "I'm gonna call it a day and head home."

"Back up to the house?" Peabody pointed at the trail.

"Just to get my boat. Nope, I'm going home. Ain't no sense in my hanging around here. You guys got it all handled."

"You'll keep our project to yourself, right?"

Boo crossed her heart, gave a Girl Scout salute, and smiled. She hoped he didn't notice the fingers in her salute, which were also crossed. "You don't need me in the way. I wish you luck."

She turned and headed down the trail to the abandoned house to gather a few supplies.

She figured it would take at least an overnight trip—maybe two nights—to get to the spot on the map marked with a big X. The lost silver mine of Wild Azalea Canyon. Maybe if she found it, she could use that information to gain the release of Dawg and Sasha. But what would that do to the swamp?

First things first—she had to save her family—and that included Dawg.

Soon as she got to the abandoned house, she went straight to work looking for a tent or a sleeping bag. Luckily, a musty-smelling bag lay tucked to the back on one of the closet shelves. At least the bag would protect her from the elements. She couldn't find a tent, but since she preferred sleeping under the stars anyway, that didn't worry her none.

Next, she went to the kitchen and filled a brown paper bag with coffee, canned goods--along with a can opener, and a box of kitchen matches just in case she ran out of those she'd brought from home. Satisfied, she headed down to the swamp where her pirogue bobbed in the water, waiting.

Gear loaded, she climbed in and took a seat, her heart pounding with excitement.

Reaching in her pocket, she pulled out the map and took one last look. She'd head up river towards Hardin County. Likely she could get in a few hours before sundown. One thing she didn't plan to do and that was travel at night. She knew the swamps around her place, but she didn't know upriver that well. No sense in taking foolish chances. Just before the sun set, she'd find a place to camp overnight then get an early start the next morning.

She went to the map one more time, trying to burn the directions into her brain.

Then, back again.

"Boo, you might know the swamps better'n anybody else, but you can sit here and study this dang map till the cows come home," she said, "and it ain't gonna get you there." She folded it and returned it to her pocket.

"Might be rough for an old bird like me to take on such a trip, but I got Sasha and Dawg into this, now I gotta get them out."

Out of habit, she whistled for Dawg to follow. Then her heart felt the same as it had the day she found Mama in the garden lying on her back, dead, the cold, damp earth beneath her, a hoe in her hand and a peaceful smile on her face.

But Boo didn't smile—then or now. Somehow she didn't think Dawg was smiling either.

She headed north. At least as north as she could while following a liquid path cut centuries ago by fast-flowing waters seeking its mama, the Gulf of Mexico, and then on to its granny, the Atlantic Ocean. She seldom took her pirogue as far north as Bon Weir, but, heck, she could find her way. Weren't no waterway ever got the best of her, 'specially with Dawg and Sasha at stake. Paddling against the flow made her muscles burn like the Satan heaped hot coals on them instead of on her tongue. Several times, the pain forced her to paddle to the side where the force of the river allowed for a slower pace and an easier breath. When that wasn't enough, she pulled ashore and rested no longer than necessary, She dared not slack her pace else she'd lose what ground she'd made. She needed to get a little further upstream before stopping for the night.

An alligator snapping turtle surfaced near the pirogue, opened its mouth, and stuck out its tongue. The worm-shaped feeler on the end wiggled, hoping to tempt a fish gullible enough to buy its false advertisement. Something told her the turtle wasn't the only one doing false advertising.

She watched it crawl ashore, its heavy head and long, thick shell, and the three ridges of large scales down its back always made her think of a dinosaur. Its usual gray shell was covered solid with bright green algae. Although she couldn't see them now, she knew star-shaped fleshy *eyelashes* surrounded its eyes.

Time alone invited memories from her past to creep

in as she paddled. Likely, the swamp critters she passed had their own folktales about her, same as she had about them. The sound of water lapping against low-hanging tupelo trees created eerie whispers, and the whispers seemed to push the branches against the shore.

In the whispers, a voice pulled her deeper inside, demanding she obey the command for her presence before Ka, her father, and the high chief. Along with the command, the familiar odors of rancid oil and human stench drifted in.

Why had her father ordered her to come? He never bothered with her or any of the other females of the clan—except on certain ceremonial occasions such as when the victorious warriors captured a brave or a swift and strong enemy. Evidently, one of the braves had slain an enemy in combat, stripped the body of the enemy of certain portions of his flesh, leaving the remainder on the field for the scavengers. Without a doubt, the surviving brave had built his fire, dried and smoked the human flesh, and carried it to the camp.

Making her way down the path, the damp sand cool under her smooth bare feet, she soon reached camp. She'd arrived late. Everyone else had already formed a circle around the fire. She tapped the shoulder of the woman in front of her, who let her pass. Others did the same as she made her way to the chief who sat swathed in a ceremonial robe the color of the river that ran red, further north.

He glanced at her, his look a reprimand. Later, she knew, he'd scold her for her tardiness. Now, occupied with chiefly business, he raised his arms above his head, one hand clutching a long spear with a half-circle of feathers fanned out on one side.

"Women with child," he called out, "come, stand before me."

No one came.

Every female in the camp looked at each other,

discomfort clouding their eyes. After the longest delay, a mother nudged her child forward. The obviously pregnant and obviously frightened girl couldn't have seen more than twelve winters. Startled to see that they married off their girls at such a young age, Boo feared the child would be too small to deliver a baby.

As though the bravery of the youngest gave courage to the others, another woman stepped forward, and then another. Last to emerge from the crowd was one too old for childbirth, but whose belly still swelled as if in defiance of the years she'd spent on this earth.

The chief stepped to the oldest first and placed a morsel of the enemy's flesh into her mouth. "May your unborn child gain the valor, strength, and fleetness of our enemy inherent in this morsel of his flesh."

He looked out over the crowd and proclaimed in a loud voice, "Remember, the flesh of another must never be eaten except when our enemy attacks us first. That is the only time we might defend ourselves."

The woman swallowed what was put on her tongue and took her place in line with the other pregnant women and children as the chief went down the line repeating the same process. When he approached the youngest, she threw a desperate look at Parahaia, as if begging to be excused. The look ripped Parahaia's heart. Why couldn't Ka see the poor girl was not well? It was obvious he had never been with child else he'd bring a little more sympathy to these ceremonies. If it were up to her, eating the flesh of the vanquished would be discontinued. She'd begged her father to give up the old ways, but his stubbornness wouldn't allow him to admit times had changed. The poor child must be miserable, for she shivered when the chief placed the flesh on her tongue.

"Swallow it, my child," he said, his words leaving no doubt who was in charge.

The girl forced the flesh down but immediately grabbed her belly, bent at the waist and lost everything she'd eaten—apparently for days.

A stronger wind blew up, and the images and whispers vaporized. In came the welcome fragrance of fresh air, along with the return of Boo's familiar aches and pains.

Strange, Boo thought, startled by what she'd witnessed—or daydreamed about.

But something told her the tribe, along with its smells and customs, hovered nearby, waiting for someone to come along with ears that listened to their stories of so long ago.

But her role in the scene as Parahaia left her as confused as it did the last time it happened. She'd heard tales of time travel, but this was ridiculous.

Chapter Sixteen

Drip, down, cross, drip, down, cross, the paddle eased up, down and back—first on one side and then the other. Boo traversed the bends and curves of the swamp, the sun growing higher and hotter. She was wiping her forehead with her long-sleeved shirt when she spied a sandbar and decided to take a break. Paddling the boat far enough onto the sand to take it out of the current, she rested the paddle across her lap and reached for the thermos of coffee.

No longer hot, but still tolerable, the black, bitter brew worked its magic as she sipped and watched, mesmerized by a water bug gliding across the water's surface, leaving a V-shaped pattern in its wake. The peaceful scene took her mind off the past and landed her smack in the middle of paradise. She felt herself move out of the dream state that had clouded her thoughts the last few miles.

Refreshed, a few minutes later, she maneuvered the

pirogue off the sandbar and plied through the water with barely a ripple or a sound. As she traveled, she noticed a change in foliage and weather. There weren't as many water tupelo and cypress trees. Instead, tall spindly pines pointed to the heavens. The swarms of mosquitoes that had driven her crazy were now few and far between. Native shrubs, brush, and wildflowers also changed along the way to ones more native to the area. While at water's edge, a doe and her fawn both acted like Boo belonged there as much as they did.

The river, 75-100 feet wide, looked isolated, which surprised her. Didn't folks know about this place?

When weariness overtook her, she again looked for another sandbar, and after a brief rest, pushed off and resumed her journey. It didn't take many of those stops before she realized this trip was going to take longer than she'd figured, for paddling in the still waters of a swamp took much less energy than paddling upriver.

Not deterred, she reveled in the beauty around her. At one point, she caught herself about to point out a bunch of yellow primrose to Dawg, and then remembered why she had taken the trip in the first place. She missed him like crazy—missed their chats on their daily jaunts into the swamps. Without him to talk to, she had way too much time to worry.

It pissed her off that folks at the camp knew more than they let on. Something about the whole business didn't sit right with her. Soon as she got Dawg and Sasha back, she'd skedaddle out of there—that is if that ghost woman would let her.

Just as the sun hinted that dusk wasn't far off, a gentle breeze rustled across the tops of the trees and spiraled down the mossy vines. They twisted and sang a song of peace, of peace, and assurance that everything would be okay. The wind's embrace felt like it seeped into her pores and stirred her insides. She sucked in a deep breath, allowing the dampness to fill her lungs with every particle of oxygen available to her. She held that breath as long as she could, hating to let it go, for never before had she felt so strongly that she and the swamp were one entity, with one purpose—but what that purpose was, she hadn't a clue.

Listen, the wind warned. *The swamp is at risk. Don't you feel it? Can't you tell?*

And with the wind, came the same woman who saw Boo naked in the bathtub, the same one who walked through the walls into Boo's bedroom, and who now floated closer, staying connected to the water by the mere hem of her long-tattered dress. The breeze brought the figure nearer, and as it approached, Boo felt a strong sense of oneness with the woman.

But along with the oneness, a sense of danger moved in and settled around Boo's heart. "I don't understand, what do you mean?" Boo didn't know she'd spoken the words until the sound penetrated her brain, and the figure disappeared into the approaching dusk.

She was shaken by yet another visit by this...this...illusion... Boo was certain she was losing her mind. Either that, or she'd spent way too much time on the water. It gave her the creeps to call it a ghost or a sprit, but it sure wasn't flesh and blood.

Eager to set foot on solid earth, Boo paddled ashore, collected her gear and carried it a few feet up from the waterline, then hid the boat under a cluster of bushes. She wasn't taking any chances.

Weary and stiff, every joint ached as she located a good, protected spot to set up camp for the night. Maybe a night's good sleep would help her state of mind.

Mother Nature and her beautiful timing of life and death provided plenty of deadwood, so it didn't take her long to gather kindling and enough larger pieces of firewood to hold her through the night. Scraping aside dry grass and anything that might cause the fire to spread, she built a fire ring with nearby rocks and piled wood in the center. Soon, a flame roared. When satisfied the fire was good to go, she tucked the book of matches in her pocket and proceeded to set up camp.

First task was to fill the blue granite coffee pot with river water, dump in coffee grounds, and put the pot on the fire. Nothing revived her like a fresh pot of hot coffee brewed in pure river water.

Weariness overtook her. She dragged her aching body to a fallen tree trunk and leaned against it, feeling her age more than ever. "Now's the time for a good puff," she said. She pulled her favorite clay pipe out of her pocket, along with a pouch of tobacco, and soon had it filled and smoking. But it didn't bring her near the satisfaction without Sasha bitching at her about it.

Smoke curled around her head while doubt twisted her thoughts. Maybe she shouldn't have taken on this task—and she wouldn't have, she reminded herself, if Dawg and Sasha hadn't gone missing. No way could she have gone on like nothing happened to them.

Her thoughts went to the figure she'd seen a few minutes' earlier. Mama always talked about a swamp spirit she'd heard about but never seen. Why was it, Boo wondered, that she'd never seen it either—before. Why now, and was this the same thing? And why did the thing keep showing up?

As she recalled, the story went that at dusk, after the plants and animals soaked up all the sun's energy they could hold, that's when the swamp spirit drew life from them because they were so full to overflowing. That way, Mama said, people might see the spirit of the swamp if the light was just right. Maybe something was going on that helped the spirit draw a lot of extra energy. Maybe that's what gave her enough power to show herself to Boo. Maybe that's why now. But it still didn't tell her why.

The sizzle and rattle of the coffee pot brought Boo back to the present. Bones aching, she forced her body up and over to the fire, poured a cup of the hot black liquid, and sipped.

Boo could almost hear the tale Mama always recounted to everybody who would listen. "Nobody knows the swamp like my Boo," she'd say. "You know why? She was born smack in the middle of it. Kid wasn't due for another month, so I figured I'd go catch supper. I'd just hooked a big catfish and hauled it into the boat when my water broke. A few minutes later, Boo came out screaming. Even the swamp critters sat up and took notice of the screeching baby."

Since Boo was a child, she could feel when someone was in the swamp doing something they shouldn't. When she'd tell Mama, she'd just nod and say there were two swamp spirits—one embodied—Boo—and one not, who both drew their power from the living, breathing swamp.

Boo never thought much about it until now. How the figure drew closer to her, floating just above the water, the tail of her tattered dress skimming the surface like she had to stay connected to the life or disappear altogether. Yet, the figure had also shown up while Boo soaked in the tub and then came through the wall of her bedroom. Some days must have more power than others, depending on what's going on in the swamp.

A breeze blew in again. Spanish moss dangling from the trees twirled and swayed, adding an eerie feel to the evening. The gentle wind embraced Boo, seeped into her pores, and stirred her insides again. But this time, she knew what was coming. She waited, holding her breath a fraction of a second longer, until…

"All is not well. Trust no one," the voice in the wind whispered again. Then, a stillness fell over the campsite, and whatever energy had been there, moved on.

"Well, dang it. You already told me that before. If you're gonna bug my evenings, least you can do is tell me something different. How many times you plan to warn me without telling me what the heck it is? Reckon

I gotta figure it out by myself."

She strolled the campsite, mumbling. "Keep your eyes and ears open, Boo Murphy. Something's going on around here and it ain't good, but ain't nobody gonna help you.

She looked up at the night sky where limitless stars twinkled. If it weren't for the warning and her missing loved ones, the night would be perfect.

Rested now, hunger came at her full force. She dug in her backpack and came up with a can of chili and heated it at the edge of the fire. After eating every bite and wishing for more, she scrubbed the can clean so as not to attract critters and then put it by the fire.

Needing to get an early start the next morning, she checked for snakes, unrolled an army surplus sleeping bag and crawled in. Soon, her eyelids grew heavy and closed.

Amidst pirates, Indian princesses, and a water buffalo with a clanging bell around its neck, something startled her awake.

"Who's there?" She peered into the dark.

"No worry. It's just me, Shadrach," a deep voice called out. "I ain't gonna harm you. I'm just a passing through on my way home."

A giant of a man clanging a big brass cowbell stepped into the light. His wrinkled black skin glistened in the firelight.

Boo sat up with a start. "Shadrach, you say. Humph. You look to me more like Uncle Remus than any Bible name—and stop ringing that dang bell. The noise 'll raise the dead."

"Sorry, ma'am. I rung my bell so's I wouldn't frighten you."

"Heck fire a mighty. That dang cowbell's what give me a heart attack, not you slipping up out of the dark."

"Ain't rightly slipping, ma'am," he said but stopped clanging the bell.

"You said passing through. Passing through what?" Her mind went to her gun. Thank goodness she'd had the good sense to keep it nearby. "Where's home? I ain't seen no fiery furnace around here." She eased one hand behind her and felt for the rifle.

"No need for that, ma'am." He nodded at her weapon. "I mean no harm. I'm right sorry to be coming up on you like this in the middle of the night. No wonder I scared you. I was just heading to my cabin up there in the woods. But then I seen your fire and figured I best check it out. Been lots of strangers around here lately. Don't want no forest fires raging out of control."

"You seen strangers? Doing what?"

"Oh, this and that, nosing around places their nose ain't got no business going. Say ma'am—is that coffee I smell? Mind if I pour me a cup from that coffee pot? I reckon with it sitting that close to the fire, it'll still be warm enough." He tossed his knapsack to the ground a safe distance away from the fire.

"Help yourself," she said, struggling to her feet. "I reckon I'll have me a cup, too, seeing I'm wide awake now—thanks to you."

"Good, I'm glad you're going to join me." He refilled her tin cup and then looked around for another. Finding none, he picked up the empty chili can, smelled it, and then poured coffee for himself.

"If'n you don't mind me asking, why's a woman out here all on her own this time of night? Ain't always safe, you know—especially for a woman who likely can't defend herself." He gave her the once over. "Then again on second thought—maybe you can."

> Boo returned to her sleeping bag, sat on it crossed-legged, and leaned against the tree. Shadrach stood nearby, propping one foot up on the same tree.

"Helpless, schmelpless. Ain't no man ever got the best of me yet," she said. "Now—tell me why're you herc? I don't believe that cock and bull story about a cabin. I checked out around here before it got dark I didn't see no such thing."

"It's just a half-mile up that trail there." He pointed towards the tree line. "It belongs to me and my two brothers."

"Let me guess. Their names wouldn't be Meshach and Abednego, would they?"

The man's belly shook with laughter, forcing a chuckle out of Boo.

"Matter of fact—that's exactly what their names are. Sounds like you done read the Good Book a time or two."

"Well, not no more. It ain't that I'm ignorant of the Bible. It's just that I never seen much sense re-reading what you've done read time after time after time since no one else is adding anything new to it."

"Well, you never know. You might still learn something new." Shadrach picked up a stick, walked over, and stirred the fire.

"Heck, when I was a kid, my ma made me go down to the Baptist church every summer to what they called Vacation Bible School." Boo stared at the ground, her mind once again traveling back to her childhood. She caught herself doing that a lot lately. "Every day, we had Bible drills, where the teacher would call out a book of the Bible, give chapter and verse, then say go. First kid that found it took a step forward. I was faster'n any kid there. Teacher finally made me sit down so the other kids could win. Since then, I figured there ain't no sense wearing the book out."

"Well, ma'am, I reckon I can't argue with that." The old gentleman's shoulders shook as if he tried to contain his laughter the same way Boo had the day before when Sasha hung onto the dock post.

It seemed like forever ago.

He was silent a moment, slurping the coffee and staring at the fire, now mere embers. "Mind if I put another log on?" He pointed at a stack of dead tree branches Boo had stacked nearby.

"Help yourself."

He rested his makeshift cup on the ground, collected a few pieces of wood, and tossed them into the hot coals. Soon, the fire blazed, lighting up the whole clearing.

Boo felt toasty and dry, and just a mite drowsy.

"Now, I'll tell you who I am and what I'm doing here, then you can return the favor. As I said, my name's Shadrach. And who I am is one of the few remaining Creole Atakapa Indians."

Boo opened her eyes wide. "You don't mean it! Sure enough?"

"Actually, my people called themselves Ishak, meaning *the people*. The French were the ones who started calling us Atakapa, which means flesh-eater, but there's no proof to that. Quite the contrary."

She decided to act ignorant about their reputation and what Ka had explained to her. "You mean you didn't eat people like the old saying goes? That's too bad since folks these days like to think of them as cannibals. Makes it more exciting."

She couldn't help but think of how pleased Sasha would be to learn they weren't—that is, until a horrible thought crossed her mind. What if Ka and his tribe saw her and Sasha as the enemy who attacked first, just by showing up in the area—Dawg, even? That thought almost did her in. But she held her counsel, shook her head to clear away the image, and forced her back straighter.

"Today, our people are all mixed in with the Creoles. Our genes go from light or brown to black. Most of us today don't know our full racial identity." Shadrach stopped, took a deep breath, and then looked Boo in the eye. "Now, it's your turn. Tell an old man what you're doing out here like this all by yourself."

"If I told you, we'd both know." Humor colored the

well-worn phrase, but no way was she going to tell this man anything about herself or her missing family members. It was difficult enough to sit on the sleeping bag and not return to camp and search for Sasha and Dawg. But if she wanted to free them, she needed something to use as a bribe—like knowing the location of that silver mine.

And she had the map. She figured they suspected it was in her possession, but so far, they hadn't tipped their hand. She must be careful, however, that they weren't following her.

Could that be what this Shadrach guy was doing here? Was he one of their cronies?

She took a closer look at the guy.

White hairs, intertwined with tight black curls, glistened in the firelight. He wore faded overalls and a plaid shirt, a color she couldn't fully make out in the half-light, but it looked like shades of green and black.

He saw her scrutinizing him, and said, chuckled. "Well, since you ain't gonna tell me, I reckon I'll have to tell you."

"And just how do you know that, Uncle Remus?"

"Don't mean to be rude, ma'am, but the name's not Remus. It's Shadrach."

Boo's face flamed with heat. "Pardon me, sir. My mama didn't teach me to be rude. It's just that I have a hard time picturing you as some Bible character."

Shadrach's belly bounced with laughter. "Don't look holy enough, eh?"

"No, it's not that, it's just…" Boo grew quiet and sat staring at the fire. Mama would be so ashamed of her behavior, she reminded herself.

But on the other hand, she wasn't sure how far to trust the guy.

Shadrach must have felt the tension, for he stood and looked around him. "I reckon I ought to head on up to the cabin. Sure you don't want to sleep inside? Be a lot safer.

Alligators been known to come ashore at night and get in fights with warthogs."

"You calling me a warthog?"

"No, but I don't know what alligators think."

"What say you visit with me here for a while longer," Boo said, beginning to feel a kinship with the stranger. "Truth is, before you come up, I was spending too much time in my head anyway."

"If you're okay with that, I reckon I can stay a little longer. I mostly toss and turn when I goes to bed myself. Here, let me get a refill." He refilled his coffee can and returned to the tree trunk.

"You're a strange man, Shadrach."

He gave her a hard stare, then shrugged. "Folks tell me that all the time. Truth is, I'm not strange—I just seem to know stuff."

"Like what?"

"Like you're on a secret mission—but you don't want to be."

Boo sat silent for a minute, then said, "I almost asked you how you know, but I figure I don't need to— that you gonna tell me anyway."

Without saying a word, Shadrach picked up a good-sized rock and stepped to Boo, who thought judgment day—or night—wasn't far behind. When he drew back his arm and hurled, all she had time to do was throw her arms over her head and wait for the blow.

Chapter Seventeen

Eyes slammed shut, she waited for the coming blow. But when it thudded behind her and something squalled, she looked up in time to see a bobcat darting off into the woods. Heart running a footrace, but determined to not let it show, she managed to squeak out, "Well, I'll swan—what's wrong with my nose—I usually smell them things before they get that close."

"Sorry, hope I didn't scare you. With that wind coming from the other way, I figured you wouldn't get a whiff. I seen its green eyes glowing behind you. He's probably hoping we got food."

She waved off his concern. "You asked about me. Tell me something about you. How'd you get that name? Was your mama that big a Bible-thumper?"

"Don't recall my mama. By the time she got us three boys born, she'd lost too much blood. Raised by a couple of wet nurses till we could fend for ourselves. Then Pa took us home again."

"You been living out here long?"

"Oh, I come and go. How 'bout you? Do you live nearby?"

Nearby, an owl hooted. The day's warmth finally released its hold on the day, and the air grew cooler. Encouraged, a bird nestled in a nearby tree sang its soft, peaceful chirp of sleep.

"Well, not this exact area." Boo shifted on her blanket and stretched out a leg. "I'm from down river a ways. Know the bayous in that area like the back of my hand." Boo smiled. "Swamp's a powerful place, you know. Seems like at times, I can feel spirits floating above the water."

"From the past?" Shadrach's eyes lit up.

"Yeah, I reckon. Or maybe the future—or from some in-between time I don't know about yet."

"Maybe they do." Shadrach smiled as if he knew something she didn't. "What spirits you seen?"

"Well, once I seen Jean Lafitte. You know, the pirate what fought in the Battle of New Orleans."

"Yeah."

"Lately, I been hearing this woman scream, and then I seen this swamp spirit. She had black hair down to here." Boo indicated her waist.

"What's she telling you?" Shadrach sipped his coffee.

Boo looked up, startled. "I didn't say she was telling me nothing."

"Oh, my mistake. I thought you said she had."

"Well, it seemed like she did—like she wanted me to know something wasn't just right out here—like a warning. You know?"

"Reckon I do," Shadrach said, smiling. "Her name's Parahaia. Usually has a wolf following her."

The sound of the river lapping against the shore registered in Boo's brain, along with the hoot of an owl, and the deep labored breathing of her visitor. He now sat across from her stirring the fire like a Boy Scout intent on earning a new badge. Boo held her breath, afraid to move, afraid to know who Shadrach really was, how he found her, and what the devil he wanted.

But curiosity won out over her fear. "Who'd you say you was?"

"Name's Shadrach."

"You already told me that. I mean who are you really? I said you looked like Uncle Remus, and you sure tell stories as good as him, but something tells me you ain't." Boo stood, paced the clearing, her hands on her hips. She turned to her companion. "You the one told that woman to show up at the foot of my bed in the middle of the night?"

"She ain't no woman."

"Yeah, that's kind of what I thought—she ain't real," Boo said with relief.

"Oh, she's real all right."

"Then tell me how, when she comes around, I feel like I know stuff I ain't known before then."

"You knowed her all your life. Since you came out of your mammy that day she was out in the swamp hunting and fishing. Parahaia walks between worlds, and is sometimes known to take others with her."

Boo choked on her own saliva and went into a coughing fit. Once she recovered, she still didn't know what to ask or say to this man who seemed to know more about her than she did. Oh, she knew about her birth all right, but he'd said *before* that—before her mama delivered her while sitting in the pirogue.

"Parahaia is the spirit of the swamp all rolled into one female entity." Shadrach said, pitching the dregs of his coffee onto the fire. The red-hot coals sizzled.

"Like a ghost, maybe?"

"She ain't a ghost, neither."

"Then what?"

"Well, Boo Murphy, maybe sometimes she's you

and your mama all rolled into one."

"I ain't no spirit. I'm sitting right here on this ground in front of you. I can touch and feel myself. I couldn't feel that woman. I could see right through her. You're a crazy old man. I ain't listening to another word you…wait just a goll-darn minute. How'd you know my name? I never told you that."

He stood as if to go. "Time I call it a night."

"Wait. You can't drop a bomb on me like that and get up and leave. I don't mean to insult you. It's just… What you're telling me don't make a lick of sense."

"Don't have to." He grabbed a rag and collected the old blue granite pot off the fire. After he'd poured himself another can of coffee, he held the pot up to her in question.

"You mean there's still coffee in that pot? Sounds like it's turned into a bottomless pot, like the widow's cruse of oil—in the Bible, don't you know. The one what never run dry."

Shadrach grinned. "Sho must be," he said and laughed. "Sho must be."

She stuck her cup out toward him. "Go ahead, fill mine, too. I need something to clear my head." After he filled it to the brim, she blew on the contents and sipped. "Coffee always has a way of making me think better. Now, let me get this straight—you say that woman I saw and the whole spirit of the swamp are all rolled into one. That I knew her the day I came out of my mama, and then you say she might be my mama."

Shadrach didn't agree or disagree. He just looked her in the eye.

"And I get the idea you think I should help her. How in the world am I supposed to help her, which is helping myself, and she's my mama, long dead and gone?"

"It's complicated, Boo Murphy. Life is simple as all get-out, yet it can also be one of the most complicated, involved, ongoing, endless threads connecting us all together. If you're not ready to retire for the night, there's a story I need to tell you—a story about my people."

Right about then, she'd heard about all the stories she could handle. She figured his story was about the same as she'd heard from Peabody and the chief, but since she wouldn't be able to sleep after what he told her, she might as well pretend he was her mama come to tuck her in. Who knows, the way things were going, maybe he was.

"Shoot. I'm all ears." Boo stretched out, propped herself against the log, and put her hands behind her head. "Go for it."

"My ancestors, the Atakapa-Ishak, they was what folks call nomadic. They followed the wandering herds of bison and hunted them with bow and arrow. Their bows were big—some of them up to four and half, five feet tall. Made them out of hickory. Over the generations, they learned to craft these bows till they was so powerful they could send an arrow clean through a bull bison. But what's different about the Ishak is that they honored the *string* as much as they did the bow and arrow."

"What do you mean, they honored the string?"

"They included it in their name for the weapon. So it wasn't just called a bow and arrow. It was called a te n o n tik—*bow, string, and arrow*. The string on their main hunting bow was triple-twisted sinews. Strong."

Shadrach's eyes lit up as he talked. If Boo hadn't known better, she'd have guessed the man lived during those times.

"When hunting deer, sometimes my people would run the deer to exhaustion rather than slay it with an arrow."

"Why's that?"

"I reckon they enjoyed the challenge. Like it was a sport—good exercise."

"They fished, too, didn't they?" Boo shifted, reached underneath her hips, pulled out a pinecone, and tossed it behind her.

"Oh, yeah. Long before Europeans got here, the Ishak harvested the teeming waters around here. They caught fish by hand, by net, by hooked bone, by wires, or traps, and also by arrow and spear. They harvested saltwater oysters along the coast. They dried and smoked the oysters and shrimp and used them for food and barter."

More than intrigued now, Boo also wondered why Shadrach was spinning such a long history lesson. She didn't dare interrupt him, however, for somewhere in this long tale was her answer, if she were patient enough to wait.

"They traveled by seasons, gathered food, like nuts, berries, herbs, and roots. Then they used food to barter along trade routes of other Indians. These forays led them into what is now southeast Texas and southwest Louisiana. They tramped through forests and more than half a dozen streams looking for roots, berries and nuts. They collected wild grapes, honey, persimmons—stuff like that. Along with food, they also gathered useful plants for making baskets and mats. Plants like sedges and rushes, and medicinal ones to use as remedies."

A look of sadness overtook him. He stretched his arm towards the dark river. "You know, if I walk there and pour the dregs of this coffee into the water, it has an effect. There's always a cause and effect—to everything. You asked me about Parahaia. Look around you. You know how when you ply the swamp, you fret and stew because of all the trash others leave behind?"

"Yeah, it pisses me off. Used to piss off my mama, too. And I've heard the legend about Parahaia looking for her talisman."

"Then, you've likely heard about her promise to watch over the swamp."

"Yeah, heard that, too." Boo slapped a mosquito on her leg. Something about Shadrach's words scared the bejesus out of her. Like there was more to whatever went on in this world—especially in her beloved swamp—than she knew about. But did she want to know that much? Some of it didn't make sense—and the other part— well... Easiest thing to do was to shut down this conversation. She cleared the clog in her throat before she spoke.

"I don't know who you are, or what you're getting at, or why you're making up all these fairy tales, but I changed my mind. I've heard enough for one night. You best be on your way to that cabin you say's out there."

With that, Shadrach stood, picked up his knapsack, and disappeared into the woods.

Startled that he'd left so easily when she'd expected him to delay, she lay thinking about what all he'd said. Even questioned her own sense of knowing. She'd hoped to get a good night's sleep, but that wouldn't happen now. She kept watching for the strange man to return, wondering who he really was—and if he really existed. Maybe she'd dreamed him up to take her mind off of Dawg—Sasha, too, of course.

But instead of Shadrach, something else filled her night—the thought that if evil and negativity had entered her swamp, she and this swamp ghost must help each other. After all, it seemed they were connected by one vital love...the living, breathing, reproducing swamp. The swamp spirit may conjure and haunt the waters around here, but she also drew her powers from it, just like Boo did.

Then, another thought crept in between the stars. If Parahaia really lived at one time and suffered the indignation and threat of encroaching civilization, then, of course, she would want Boo to help her save the swamp from someone or something set on stripping it of its resources. That thought scared her more than any other. She didn't have too many more years left here on this earth, and neither did Dawg or Sasha, for that matter, but generations to come? She shuddered at the thought of what their swamp might look like if greedy treasure seekers started silver mining.

In a way, she guessed she was like Parahaia, for, after all, didn't Boo feel revived every time she plied the waters. Didn't she have to stay connected to her swamp to exist?

Come to think of it, it didn't seem like it was Parahaia speaking to Boo. More like the gentle swamp breeze carried messages between the two. Boo recalled the soft whisper in the wind and along with it, emotions of caution, extreme danger, and at the end, a feeling of compassion, almost like someone hugged her just like her mama used to.

Once again, the breeze seeped into her pores, and stirred her insides, made her feel like as long as she held her breath, she was one with the swamp. Maybe that's what Shadrach meant when he said she and the swamp spirit were one.

But that still didn't explain why Boo's arm and hand had looked like that of a young Indian maiden, or why she kept feeling like she was living in a different time.

She took a deep, cleansing breath, allowing the dampness in the wind to fill her lungs, and once again, every particle of air she breathed seemed alive. She held the breath, hating to let it go.

She felt a connection to the swamp, she always had, but never before like this—never so… It was as if she and the swamp were one entity, with one purpose—but how could she be sure what that purpose was?

Trust no one, came the voice on the breeze.

No one? How could she do that? How could she doubt everyone she knew or came in contact with—folks like Sasha, Durwood, even Shadrach? Of course, she still wasn't sure she trusted him anyway. Some of what he said made sense, then again, some of it sounded so far-fetched nobody would believe it. She still wasn't sure if she did or not.

And did that lack of trust extend to her? She sure wasn't perfect, even stretched the truth now and then to fit her needs—or maybe wants.

She must have slept, for when she opened her eyes, dawn had crept in through the trees and landed smack in her face. She tossed the cover back and pulled to her feet, steadying herself with a hand on the tree trunk.

Wishing she'd made it farther upriver the day before, she didn't take time now to light a fire. Instead, she gulped down the last drop of coffee, still a mite warm from the smoldering embers, and chewed on a piece of beef jerky.

"Looks like no alligator wanted me for their late-night supper," she said, forcing last night's visitor out of her mind.

After a quick cleanup of the campsite, she packed her gear and limped to where she'd stashed the pirogue underneath a couple of large bushes.

When she shoved the branches aside, the boat wasn't there.

Chapter Eighteen

Bumper dragging the ground, Durwood coasted Old Betsy down the mud-rutted driveway and brought her to a stop under the lean-to beside his house. Still worried sick about Boo, he'd checked on her for the third time that day, but she still wasn't home. Sasha wasn't either.

Boo had gone to check on them Indians again. He knew it, but for the life of him, couldn't believe she'd talked Sasha into it. That woman had never gotten any closer to the water than her front yard—and that was two hundred feet away.

What possessed Boo to take such a risk—for both of them? He'd warned her against going out there snooping around. Something sounded mighty fishy about the whole blamed thing. "Damn stubborn woman." He yanked the truck's door handle and shoved hard. It creaked and groaned, but swung open and came to a squeaking stop.

A stiff hip slowed his exit from the vehicle. Using

the doorframe for support, he eased one foot to the ground and then the other. Not bothering to close the door, he headed toward the house to figure out what to do next.

Whiz, his hound, and longtime buddy, crawled from under the steps as he approached. The old dog woofed half-heartedly, as if with the heat and humidity that was all the energy he had to spare. He ambled up to Durwood whining, ears dragging the ground.

"What we gonna do with that woman, Whiz, that's what I gotta figure out. I never seen one so stubborn. She's almost as bad as me." He chuckled and scratched the top of the dog's head. "I might be wrong, but something tells me she's in trouble."

He went inside, made a cup of green tea, then sat at the old drop-leaf table and sipped and thought. By the time he reached the dregs in the bottom of his cup, he'd reached a decision about what to do. Call the sheriff and ask if he'd heard about Indians doing stuff in the swamp. Maybe he'd ask about a dead man, too.

Boo had told him there was a dead body, hadn't she?

He rummaged through his memory, not as sharp as it had once been, until he found a fragment of the conversation. He followed that thread until he got to the part where she'd shrugged it off, saying the man's death was a heart attack or something.

He pushed himself to his feet and shuffled into the sitting room and over to the phone. Lucky for him, the sheriff was in and willing to take his call.

"Sheriff, this is Durwood Davis, out at Indian Lake. You got a minute?"

"Hi, Durwood. Sure I do. What's up?"

Durwood explained his concern about the two missing women.

"How long have they been gone, Durwood?"

"A couple of days, I reckon. That's when I last seen Boo, and she promised me she wouldn't go out there."

"Well, that's not so long, Durwood, especially for Boo. Hold on, though, let me check."

Papers rattled in the background, and then the sheriff came back on the line. "I went over everything for the last couple of weeks and didn't see a thing.

"Humph." A couple of swear words came to mind, but Durwood didn't voice them. He had too much respect for the law and the sheriff to do so.

"I can tell you're worried," the sheriff said. "But, Durwood, you know as well as I do, that woman does exactly what she wants when she wants to do it.

"Boy, don't I know that. Well, what about a report of a dead man?"

The line went quiet.

"Hello? You still there, Sheriff?"

"I'm here. Did you say a dead man?"

"Yep."

"Was someone supposed to call in a report of body?" The sheriff's voice tightened.

Durwood struggled to control his growing impatience. "That's what I'm asking you. Did they?"

"If I had a report of someone dead out there—anywhere—I'd be on it like a June Bug, Durwood, and you know it. We don't have a single report about anything going on out there. A dead body report jumps out at me first thing—because we'd already be on it." The sheriff sounded a little impatient himself. "Chances are, Boo's out there enjoying her swamps, And Sasha's off visiting other kin. If any such report comes in, I'll call and let you know."

"Thank you, sheriff, I'd appreciate it."

"If she doesn't come back, though, call and let us know, and we'll go check."

Somewhat relieved, Durwood hung up and flopped into his wooden rocking chair and rocked, hard. "That's all I can do at this point, boy," he said to Whiz who'd ambled over and laid beside his chair. His eyes fell on an old photo of Boo hanging on the wall holding up her prized forty-two-pound Channel catfish she'd caught on a trotline.

Then, an idea struck him. He straightened his back and cleared his throat.

"Or is it?"

Durwood pulled into the driveway of the white two-story house, climbed out of his truck, and headed across the wrap-around porch to the side entrance of The Third Eye, Sid Smart's private detective business. Her original office across the street from the courthouse had burned to the ground a while ago, and since then, she'd temporarily worked out of her Aunt Annie's recently restored Civil War-era house.

Durwood could depend on Sid to help him make sense out of all this—she'd never failed him yet. Even worked on a case for him. Then later, she'd helped prove Boo hadn't killed Sasha's husband, Zeke when the sheriff thought she had.

He rapped on the door.

No one answered.

He knocked harder and waited. When no one came, he gave up and headed to Ben Hillerman's office on the second floor of the courthouse. Ben, the local district attorney, was also sweet on Sid, if anyone knew her location, he should.

As luck would have it, he pulled into the parking lot just as Ben walked outside. Tall, slender, and dressed in a dark brown suit the same color as his hair, the man looked smashing. Even a man as unstylish as was Durwood, recognized style when he saw it. No wonder Sid liked Ben. The two made a cute couple.

He wished he could say the same about him and

Boo. Dang stubborn woman. He yanked on the door handle and stepped out.

"Ben! Hey, Ben, you got a minute? I need to ask you something."

The weather had grown threatening, and a gust of wind caught Durwood's hat and tossed it across the parking lot. Ben ran and collected it.

"Hey, Durwood. What's happening? Haven't seen you in a while." He stuck out his hand and gave Durwood a firm handshake.

"Looking for Sid. Know where she is?"

"I know where she is, alright, but likely you can't reach her. I've tried a couple of times, but her cell phone's been out of range. She and Annie took off on a road trip across Texas and north into New Mexico to attend a wedding. They should be back in a few days. Why? What's up?"

"Oh, it's Boo, again. Don't know where she is or what the heck she's doing. I wanted Sid to help me check on her. I have her business phone number but not her cell. You have it?"

Ben rattled it off from memory, while Durwood jotted the number down in the palm of his hand.

"Ben, the jury is in! You better hurry," Ben's secretary hollered out the door. Ben rushed off, excusing himself with a wave of his hand. He called back, "Call me later if I can help."

Durwood raced home and shuffled in the door, met by Whiz, ears dragging the ground. "Ain't got time to feed you just yet, boy. Hang on. Let me make this phone call." He dialed and waited.

Sid's cell phone rang.

And rang, and rang, until finally a recorder came on and said the caller was unavailable. He waited a few minutes and tried again. This time, at least he got her voice mail. "Sid, it's Durwood," he said into the phone. Boo's done got herself into a heap a trouble again, I just know it. She's disappeared—her and Sasha too. Even Dawg ain't home. I need you to come help me." He started to hang up, then pulled the phone back to his mouth, "and hurry."

He limped outside to his flat-bottom boat leaning against the side of the house. How far might it get him if he took it out and tried to find the old biddies? One old woman loose in the swamp was one thing—but two?

Boo would be livid with him if he found her, and she was okay, and even more so if she knew he'd called Sid and got her involved—if he ever reached her.

But if she wasn't, she might be mighty glad to see him. Regardless, he had to make sure nothing had happened to her.

"That woman's gonna be the death of me yet," he said to Whiz, who had followed him outside. The hound looked unconcerned—about anything. Not even the fly on his nose.

Durwood had loved Boo for years, but the woman never took his advances seriously. He'd asked her once if she'd been hurt by some guy in the past, or if she just didn't like men.

She'd laughed and kissed him on the cheek. "Sure, I like men. I like you, silly." Then she'd gone back to patting out a pan full of buttermilk biscuits, and the moment had been lost. He'd planned to ask her to marry him that day—even had the ring in his pocket. It lay neglected in his bureau drawer ever since.

That's as far as he ever got—just a kiss on the cheek.

"That woman has more fire in her than the whole passel of other women I know, Whiz. I gotta go see if I can find her—make sure she's okay."

After ensuring there was enough food and water for

Whiz, he went back inside, made a couple of sandwiches, grabbed a bottle of water and a banana, and then tucked it all into the pockets of his hunting jacket.

"Dang, stubborn woman." He collected a box of shells, grabbed his shotgun, and headed outside. He hadn't shot anyone since the Battle of the Bulge in '45, but for Boo, he would.

"Even if she won't give me the time of day, I couldn't live with myself if something happened to her," he mumbled. He'd lost his wife years ago, and then his only son last year in a train accident. Boo was the only person left on this earth that he really cared about. She didn't have to marry him. Just keep living.

"I'm coming, Boo. Hang on." He half jogged half limped to his truck and backed it over to the boat and trailer.

Chapter Nineteen

Panic rumbled through Boo when her pirogue wasn't where she'd left it. Had she tied it tight enough? Had she pulled it high enough ashore? Had she put it somewhere else?

"No, dang it, I know I didn't do none of those things. I ain't never lost a boat yet, and I ain't lost this one. Somebody took it, that's what happened." She scratched around inside the bushes but found not a single slide mark either in or out of the water.

What did that say about her memory? Was she losing it? Was she going smack dab crazy? Sasha had been talking about how old they were both getting. Maybe she was right. Maybe it was time Boo quit all this tomfoolery.

But at that point, she wasn't sure she could, not with a ghost on her heels—not to mention her missing family. Of course, she could turn that over to the sheriff, but…

Puzzled and put out, she returned to the campsite, dropped her gear, and peered up and down the shoreline, looking for what might be a clue of something—anything.

Nothing.

Now, what did she do? She sure couldn't walk her way out, and likely no one would be passing this way for days.

Shadrach.

He'd said his cabin wasn't far.

She looked at the line of trees he'd disappeared into the night before. With little other option, she grabbed her shotgun and started in that direction.

But as soon as she stepped into the thicket, she felt watched, like inquisitive eyes followed her, peering down, asking each other who she was and why she was there. Could it be Shadrach, or whoever took her boat, or maybe just critters keeping an eye on her lest she wander out of her own boundaries and into theirs?

A light rain started pelting the trees and filtering down through the leaves until big drops found the top of her head and rolled down into her eyes. Shoving aside wet shrubs and tree branches, she made her way along a winding trail. After a short walk, she caught a glimpse of what looked like an old miner's shack, hopefully, that of Uncle Remus—no, Shadrach. It wasn't nice of her to call him something he weren't.

He might be called Shadrach, but *what* he was, she still wasn't sure. There was something different about him—something she couldn't quite put her finger on. Maybe he wasn't who he said he was at all. Maybe he was the one the voice in the wind warned her about. And maybe he'd taken her boat to keep her stranded out here.

Following the narrow path, she approached the shack. The door was closed and likely locked, and not a soul in sight. The only sound, other than her feet crunching on pine needles and dried twigs, was the trill of a Mockingbird perched atop a nearby pine tree.

Shoving wiry gray strands of hair out her eyes, she

stepped up on the stoop and rapped on the door. While waiting, she watched behind her in case someone approached.

Nothing. Not a sound. Even the Mockingbird flew off.

And no one opened the door.

Should she try the handle or not?

"What's to lose?" Since obviously no one was home, she pulled on the handle. The hinges squeaked as the door creaked opened. A dank smell slammed her face.

She eased into the room, checking from left to right, and then behind the door. A hint of daylight glowed through one dingy window, leaving the remainder of the room in half-light.

"Anybody home?" she whispered and then felt ridiculous. "Might as well shout, ain't nobody going to hear me," she said, speaking louder.

In the middle of the one-room shack, two rickety chairs sat around an equally rickety table with an unlit kerosene lamp on top and a box of kitchen matches nearby. Careful where she stepped, she shuffled over and lit the lamp. Soon a warm glow filled the room.

An aluminum cot, a faded blanket at one end and a rust-stained feather pillow at the other, stood against the wall.

On the small counter next to the sink, a white cup and saucer looked to have been rinsed and turned upside down to drain dry. On the other side of the sink, a dented teakettle sat on one burner of a two-burner camp stove. An empty pet bowl on the floor looked like it had been licked to the last drop, scooting it off a piece of yellowed newspaper. Nearby, a calico kitten lay curled in a ball sound asleep.

But no Shadrach.

Hopefully, she wasn't in the wrong cabin.

She picked up the kitten's bowl, filled it with water from an old-timey hand water pump at the sink, and returned the bowl to the floor. The kitten didn't budge.

The rain fell heavier, pounding on the split-roof shingles like someone unleashed the power of Toledo Bend Dam in one gigantic bucket drop.

A crack of lightning split the sky. Boo smelled smoke and opened the door just in time to see the top half of a tree crash to the ground, smoke curling from the burnt end.

"Guess I better wait here till it passes," she said, closing the door against the storm. But she'd no sooner shut it and turned her back than it blew open and banged against the inside wall. Whirling around, she was startled to see a dark hulk filling the doorway dressed in denim overalls, flannel shirt, and a big Texas-style ten-gallon hat.

"Oh, it's you." She stared at Shadrach. "You scared me half to death. Didn't your mama teach you to hold onto the door, especially in this kinda weather? The wind like to have knocked it off its hinges."

Shadrach laughed, pearly whites glistening against his black face. Instead of answering, he grabbed the door, latched it tight against the storm, and turned to her, the smile still on his face. "Well! I didn't expect to see you here this morning. If'n I had, I'd cleaned the place up a mite better."

"Know anything about a missing pirogue," she asked without preamble.

"Your boat's gone?"

"Like you had nothing to do with it."

"'Scuse me?"

"I didn't stutter none."

"Wait a minute, woman. Don't you go saying I'm a thief."

"Who else would've taken it? Ain't no one else around excepting you and me."

"Leastwise, anyone you knows of, you mean." He sauntered to the hotplate, shook the teakettle a couple of times, refilled it with water, and put it on to boil. "I'm going to act like you didn't accuse me of being a thief, okay?"

Although he didn't look at her as he crossed to the table and pulled out a chair, Boo felt the energy in the room shift to one more pleasant than it had been just a couple minutes ago.

"Here, sit yourself down," he said.

A man hadn't held her chair in more years than she could remember. Not since the boat captain. She smiled, remembering how he'd hold the chair and wait for her to bend. He'd slide it underneath her, and then rub her shoulder a minute before he took his own seat. Old Spice, that's what he wore. She could almost smell it now.

She *did* smell it now!

"That Old Spice you wearing?" she asked, fearing for her sanity. What was it that kept jerking her back to the past—and some of it way beyond her years.

Shadrach chuckled. "Yep, put a little extra splash on this morning, hoping you'd come to call. Ain't often a lady-friend visits."

Boo puffed her chest. "Humph, I ain't no lady. Never been, and don't intend to start now. Leave that to my cousin, Sasha. She does it good enough for the both of us."

Sasha's name quickened inside Boo. She shifted, cleared her throat, and blinked away the possibility of a tear.

"You're a mighty good-looking woman, though, Boo Murphy."

She ignored his smooth-talking words.

"How come you don't let people inside?" Shadrach asked heading to a shelf on the other side of the room where he pulled down a glass jar and unscrewed the lid. "You drink tea, I reckon," he called over his shoulder.

"Depends on what kind a tea you making. Don't recognize what you got in your jar."

"Sassafras. You drunk it before, ain't you? It's good for what ails you."

"What ails me is some thief took my boat, dang it. You sure it weren't you who took and hid it?"

"What if I did?"

He spoke so softly she wasn't sure she'd heard him right. "What's that you said?"

Shadrach turned and repeated the question, a slow smile spreading across his face. Even in the dim light, his teeth shined.

Dancing with the devil, that's what I'm a doing. Boo shoved her chair back, stood, and headed for the door, but she'd taken no more than a couple of steps than Shadrach lunged and grabbed her arm.

"Listen to me, Boo Murphy. Sit down here and listen."

She hesitated a long moment, then felt her eyes drawn to his.

She sat.

A high-pitched whistle from the teakettle called Shadrach to the stove. He motioned Boo to stay put. "Wait just a minute. Let me get our tea. You look like you could use a little relaxing concoction. Besides, you sound a mite congested after that night sleeping on the ground. This be good for you." He poured their tea while he talked, brought the mugs to the table, and sat across from her.

At first, they both didn't say anything, just sipped their tea.

Anxious to get on her way, Boo felt like she had ants in her pants. She squirmed and glanced out the window just as something flashed by.

She tensed her nerves on high alert. Had she seen someone, or imagined it? She looked back at the window and saw the movement again. Like a shadow passing the window. She forced herself to sit still, moving only the muscles it took to speak. "Somebody's out there."

Shadrach looked up. "Here? Outside here?"

"Don't move. They passed the window a couple a times. I seen them."

"No one knows this place. Must just be a random hunter or something."

"Or your partner in sin—whoever took my pirogue."

"I didn't *take* it Boo, I just hid it 'cause I needed to slow you down. We gotta talk before you hightail it out of here, heading off into what I figure might be an ambush."

"Likely story."

"You heard me."

"Shush! Be still." Boo said when she saw another movement outside. "They don't know we seen them. You mess it up, and we'll never find out. I'll leave by the back door, and when I give a whistle, you come out the front." She picked up the shotgun she'd propped against the wall when she'd come in while Shadrach kept up his attempt to convince her no one was outside.

"Time for talking's passed, Shadrach. Get your butt up and help me catch them. Move." Easing out back, she inspected the yard. When she saw no one covering the rear, she slipped around the cabin, gave a whippoorwill signal to Shadrach, and peeked around in time to see him stomp outside in all his glory. Pissed her off royally.

"Don't waste a bullet, Boo." He held his hand out to her. "There ain't no one here excepting you and me."

"Then who's that standing right there next to you?" she asked and fired a warning shot above the head of the shadowy figure.

Chapter Twenty

Boo had no intention of shooting the figure that stood before her, but she wasn't going to back down until she got to the bottom of the situation. She squinted at the apparition beside Shadrach. "She's the spitting image of the woman I seen floating across the swamp at me."

Shadrach stepped over and pushed Boo's shotgun aside. "She don't just look like the same woman you saw, she is her. You might not believe it, and even if you do, you might not like it. But you and her are just alike. You both talk swamp."

"Get outta the way, Shadrach, my aim ain't what it used to be. This 'un can't be the same as the one I seen. This 'un's on dry ground. Ain't no water for a half-mile or so. You said the one I seen had to stay connected to the water." Boo stepped around him and again raised the shotgun to her shoulder.

Shadrach bowed. "Have it your way, Boo. Shoot."

She did—a warning shot over the woman's head.

The woman didn't flinch, just kept smiling at Boo.

"Told you you'd waste a bullet." This time, Shadrach took the gun out of Boo's hands and led her to the doorstep. "You better sit yourself here and catch your breath before you make a fool of yourself. Ain't no way you can hurt her anyway, so you might's well give that up."

"None of this makes any sense," Boo said, parking her bottom on the steps, and then scooting over to make room for Shadrach, who joined her.

"You think you and she can't be from a previous lifetime 'cause that don't make sense to you. But I'm here to tell you, just because it don't make sense, and just because you can't see all them spirits walking amongst you don't mean they ain't here. And it don't mean when they've soaked up enough of the day's energy, and they have a real need to do so, they can ease over to dry ground while their energy lasts."

"If that's so, then why can't I see them all the time, and not just now?

"Only some people can see them, and even then, the person has to be ready. You just went through a big shock, losing your dog and Sasha that way. I can't see her, but I figured it'd be her outside since I been sensing her here ever since I met you the other night."

"You mean you really can't see her?"

"That's what I mean, Boo." He sighed as if weary of trying to explain. "But my guides tell me she's here. Look, you know the swamp. Heck, it's almost like you *are* the swamp. Think about it. You're more at home in the bayou spending time with swamp critters, than you are on dry land, with humans. It's like you have one thing you love, and that's to be out here. She's the same as you, only difference is, she lived here a lo-o-o-n-g time ago. She's felt at one with you all these years. You must have felt her spirit, even if you didn't know what it was."

Memories flashed through her mind, memories of

her early years, and how she'd always felt more at home there than she did anywhere on earth. How she had no interest in friends and family, preferring to be with the swamp critters. And yes, she whispered to the swamp, and it, to her. In truth, she'd always felt something she didn't understand, only accepted. But she'd never seen a spirit before now. Maybe she'd spent so much time out here that she lost her grip on reality. Made her wonder if all this was a figment of her imagination.

On the other hand, maybe it wasn't. She had always depended on what she knew about the bayous, but she never thought about who her teacher might be. Now she knew why, and why she depended on the lessons. But why had the spirit of the swamp chosen now to show herself? Could it be because of the threat of silver exploration and strip mining?

Danger. That's what it must be. The swamp spirit knows the swamp's in trouble. Heck, she'd felt it herself, but she'd been so blinded by her own pleasure of being out here that she ignored that little voice inside her head saying all is not well.

That's why—all is *not* well. Something was indeed wrong. Perhaps she hadn't been listening to the swamp as well as she should. How many signs had she missed—signs she'd ignored because of indulging her own pleasure in spending time fishing and hunting—and just being on the bayous.

"Okay," she said to Shadrach. "I get it. But tell me, does this spirit have a name? Is the same one I saw coming at me from across the waters?"

Shadrach smiled and clasped her hands in his. "She's the same—Parahaia."

"Humph." Boo paused and let that sink in. "That's the name of the woman standing at the end of my bed one night. Can swamp spirits come into your dreams and talk to you?"

"Perhaps, or perhaps it's your subconscious telling

you what you've been ignoring and not listening to."

That name Parahaia haunted Boo. The woman in her dream, that's where she'd heard it first. That girl, Taka, the one she'd seen in the Atakapa camp had called Boo that, and then in the village when she'd been ordered to tell their story—whatever that meant.

Oh, yes, and Taka dragged her to meet her father.

As if Boo wasn't confused enough, Shadrach's next words caused more.

"Ever heard of an avatar?" He picked up a stick and started scratching in the dirt.

"No, but have you ever heard a spirit ghost out here what sounds like a panther?"

He gave her a strange look. "Why?"

"Because sometimes I hear her. Like she's… Never mind. I was just wondering."

They both sat in silence a few seconds, then Boo recalled his question. "By the way, what the heck's an avatar?

"An avatar is a bridge between us and the spirit world. They have special abilities."

"Like what?"

"They can go back and forth between here and the spirit world. Maybe that's what you've seen. Most avatars come from India, but not Parahaia. She is thought to have been the swamp come to earth in human form."

Boo chose to keep her opinion about such nonsense to herself.

"The sad thing is, while Parahaia could command the earth, the air, fire, and water, there was one thing she couldn't command. Yellow Fever—brought here by the white man. She came down with the sickness.

"Yeah, I heard all about that fairy tale. By the way, got any idea what that talisman looked like?"

"Legend is, it's a smooth stone, smaller than a man's hand. It had a tiny but perfect hole in the middle. On full moon nights, and when held over one eye, the tiny hole grew large enough to hold the entire moon."

Magic? Boo thought. Heck, she and Sasha used to do that with empty toilet paper roles.

She leaned her head against the support post and sighed, hoping Shadrach got the message.

He didn't.

"Okay, you do believe we got a soul, don't you? That there's more to life after we die?"

"I reckon. Sasha says—at least she used to—that there is. So for arguments sake, let's just say I do."

"Good enough. Now, let's go a little further. I'm here to tell you that it ain't just after that we got a life. It's also before."

"Whoa, wait just a cotton-picking minute. You're taking this too far."

"Humor me, Boo." He held his hand out at her.

She sucked through her teeth and crossed her arms over her chest. "Take me for a fool. That's what you do."

He chuckled. "You don't have to believe what I'm about to tell you, but one thing's for sure. I'm smart enough to not take you for a fool."

But even if you listen, you don't have to believe a word I say."

"I'm listening." She stared straight ahead, refusing to give him the pleasure of believing she bought a single word he said.

Evidently, he bought it, for she felt him relax against the other supporting post. Shadrach went on, acting like he hadn't heard her. "Here's what I know for sure. We come into this world with a set of lessons to learn in this lifetime. We can learn them or not, but if we don't, we will likely get a chance to learn them the next time around.

"You mean to tell me you believe we have more than one life?"

"Don't have a clue about that. I'm just telling you what makes sense to me. 'Cause if I have lessons to learn in this life, it behooves me to learn them —just in case I come around again in another one. I sure don't want to work on these same lessons all over again."

"Well, I reckon I don't want to either."

He sat in silence a few minutes as if letting that sink in before going on with his story.

"The way I see it is that one of the lessons you came here to work on was how to get along with other people— how to take a risk and let them get close…"

He stopped as if waiting for that to sink in before continuing.

"Humph. Seems I still got work to do on that one." She figured he'd say, you think? But he didn't.

"Another lesson is not to isolate yourself. Enjoy the swamp, but share that joy with others. Speak up for nature's glory. Defend it. Protect it."

"Is that all?" Boo asked, growing a mite defensive.

"It's up to you to figure these out, Boo. I just made a guess. Likely, Parahaia showing herself to you is a part of those lessons, or she wouldn't be doing so. My guess is, she figures you, of all people, will help her save the swamp from destruction."

Boo laughed. "And her a high priestess. You'd think she could find someone more worthy of her time."

Shadrach tapped Boo on the forearm. "No telling. Maybe you were one, too, if there is such a thing as previous lifetimes. I got a feeling your soul's Atakapa."

Boo jumped to her feet. "So if she lived that long ago, how come I can still see her?"

"Remember, she can walk between worlds, and evidently take you with her as she desires—at least in your mind."

"You don't know what the heck you're talking about, Shadrach. Telling lies like that, I wouldn't go around any more fiery furnaces if I was you."

Shadrach ignored her pun. He just stared at the ground.

"I'm going to act like you ain't told me all that crazy stuff about her." Boo looked to where the woman had been standing, but she wasn't there anymore. "Where'd she go? I don't see her now."

Shadrach motioned to the bushes, and the amorphous looking woman approached, clad in the same long muted green dress billowing behind her, a mane of dark hair blew in the wind.

She looked Boo up and down.

"Who are you? What do you want from me?" Boo said, returning the once over.

The woman—ghost—avatar or whatever she was—didn't speak, she just stared at Boo, a gentle smile playing about her lips.

"I'm not real sure I believe who you are—but okay, I'll bite. What do you want from me?" Boo said, then stood quietly waiting.

Thoughts began to form in Boo's brain, although she didn't see Parahaia's lips move.

You love the swamp. You are in tune with it, and sense when it is off-balance. It is now, due to greed and selfishness. I am here to assist you.

"Assist me? How about a little protection?" The conversation—weird as it was and as weird as it made Boo feel, talking to a ghost—hadn't helped clear Boo's confusion.

You seek the lost silver mines of Wild Azalea Canyon.

"Yeah, I'm trying to find the silver mines all right, but not for me, to help me save Dawg and Sasha. I just hope they're not dead already."

"Not likely just yet," Shadrach said, as the figure faded.

Chapter Twenty-One

Boat and trailer hitched to his pickup, Durwood stopped by the store for food and supplies. Soon he and his truck and trailer rattled down the road to Boo and Sasha's.

He'd worried over Boo for a long time, but he'd never been so afraid for her as he felt now. Seems like the woman just wouldn't slow down, take anyone's advice, or take rational measures for her own safety. She did exactly what she wanted, when, and gave the devil the boot if he argued.

For the life of him, Durwood couldn't figure out why he hung around. She never gave him the least bit of encouragement—quite the contrary. Any attention he gave her came only swith his own insistence. Yeah, she liked his company, okay—sometimes. But she always backed off when he tried to get close.

He'd been widowed so many years now, he barely remembered what it was like to be married. If it weren't for his old faithful coon dog, Whiz, he'd have never made it. The critter brought lots of company. But snuggling up in bed with a hound was a far cry from snuggling with a warm, round body of a woman. Sometimes he wondered why he bothered with Boo and didn't find another woman who might want his company on a regular basis. Not that he needed to get married. Too late to worry about those details, but just…

Sasha came to mind. Ever since her husband died, she'd cut him the flirty eye. But he wasn't sure he could handle all that primping and fixing up she had to do. Yeah, she liked to go to church and all that stuff, which wasn't for him, but he could tolerate her going. She was a good cook, that's for sure. He'd tasted some of her leftovers Boo had brought home and shared when he stopped by unannounced.

But no, Sasha wasn't his kind of woman—the kind who liked to do things. Not those afraid to get their hands dirty. Besides, he wasn't sure he could afford to keep Sasha in lipstick, much less all the other fancy clothes she wore trying to outdo all the other women at church.

Arriving at Boo's, Durwood went inside, thankful the stubborn woman refused to lock a door or window, saying, instead, if anybody wanted what she had, they were welcome to it.

Straight to the phone, he dialed Sid's number again. This time, she didn't answer, but at least he could leave a voice mail. "Sid, I need you. Boo's missing, and I don't know what's happened to her. She's lost out in the swamp or something—her and Sasha. Come quick…" he choked on the words and rang off.

Straight outside, he collected his gear, launched the boat, and paddled off.

"I just wish Sid would call me back—and that I had some idea where to look," he mumbled. Boo had mentioned something about some kind of little peninsula or something. But if she'd never seen it before, he wondered how in the world he expected to find it. He'd fished and hunted in this area, but he didn't know it like Boo.

After a couple hours and nothing, Durwood started feeling sorry he hadn't asked Boo more questions about the location. But he had to find her before it was too late.

Chapter Twenty-Two

Sid dusted off her beige slacks and white shirt and then ran both hands through her close-cropped white hair, all while keeping an eye on a highway with no tow truck in sight. Annie stood next to her, watching as well, along with the mangy dog that looked as if he wanted them to make the wedding too. At least the odor emanating from him had subsided somewhat. Decent food in his belly must have contributed to that.

She checked her cell phone again and found yet another message from Durwood, one that, combined with Boo's earlier message, scared the daylights out of her. Boo was in serious trouble, Durwood was in a panic, and here she was, stuck in a New Mexico ghost town with a broken-down car and a wedding in Santa Fe the next morning. The pressure in her chest tightened its grip.

She dialed his number and waited. She hadn't talked with either of them in a long while. The day before she and Annie left town, she'd started to call and check in on them but got distracted. For some reason, she felt a certain responsibility for them. Perhaps because she'd worked on cases for both of them—she certainly hoped that wasn't going to be a pattern for her. After all, when she'd left Sam, her Baptist preacher husband—ex-husband—she'd given up being responsible for the whole world. Baptist preacher's wives carry a heavy load, and it was a hard habit to break.

The phone finally started ringing.

She'd been wondering how Durwood and Boo had been getting along. Or rather how he was getting along with her. From what Sid could tell, Boo could take him or leave him—or any other man for that matter. As independent and ornery cuss of a woman she'd ever seen. Only a serious situation would push Boo to ask for help.

Durwood answered on the fifth ring. "Hello, this is Durwood Davis…"

"Hey, Durwood, it's Sid. You called and…"

"I'm not here right now. Leave a message."

The beep ricocheted off her eardrums. She always had been a caring person, but the depth of her concern over the old couple surprised even her. Something was dreadfully wrong, and here she sat twiddling her thumbs.

She turned back to Annie. "Looks like we're going to spend the night in a ghost town. We have a choice," she said, watching the sun sink below the horizon. "We can sleep in the car, or take the travel blankets into the abandoned hotel and sleep on the floor."

She hadn't seen the old man since earlier that day and wondered if he'd been a figment of her imagination, or if he indeed lived somewhere nearby.

"I don't know about you," Annie said, "but my old body needs to be prone while I sleep. Much as I hate sleeping on a dusty floor, I think I'd rather try that than curl up in the car."

"Back seat wouldn't be too bad. I can take the front."

"Not sleeping back there where the mutt was. No telling what he left behind. I'd be scratching all night. Soon as we can take the time, I'm heading to a car wash."

The multi-mixed breed, whose name, Sid had learned, was Paint—because of his color and pattern, gave Annie an indignant look as if he couldn't be blamed for the current situation. Sid understood that feeling. "Then let's grab a couple bottles of water and the blankets and get settled in for the night. I'll leave a note here on the windshield for the tow truck driver telling him where we are."

Exhausted, wishing for a non-existent cool shower to wash off the day's sweat and grime, but thankful they'd brought bottled water, they collected enough for the night, along with a bag of snacks.

Her back turned to Annie, Sid double-checked her handbag for the Glock she kept tucked inside then led the way to the half-standing hotel.

As they approached, a faint light glowed from inside.

The weather-beaten porch groaned as they tromped across it and through the swinging doors of the old lobby cum saloon. The flame from a kerosene lamp flickered on a rickety table. The same old man Sid had met earlier was settling down for the night amidst a pile of torn, filthy-looking rags. Sid asked if they could join him. She explained they'd hoped the tow truck would have arrived, but…

"Yep. Them tow trucks from Ft. Sumner come when they gets a mind to, and not before. Likely, it'll be here at daylight. But if'n you asking me if you can sleep here tonight—far as I care, 'tis fine. Course I can't speak for the spirits that hang around after dark."

Sid choked, but Annie laughed, saying, "Won't bother me none. I don't buy into that junk New Age stuff."

"Ain't nothing *New Age* about it." He kept his back

to her as he talked, kneeling to straighten his pile of rags, much like a dog nesting for the night. "Fact is, ain't nothing new about what some folks call New Age. Old stuff. Been around for centuries."

Recovered from her choking fit, Sid took a step closer to the old man. "Excuse me, Mr... What did you say your name was?"

"Folks call me Mary."

"Mary?"

"My mama wanted a girl real bad."

"Okay... Ma... Sid struggled with the name. Needless to say, it didn't fit a bedraggled old man living alone in the desert. "So, what do you mean—spirits—plural—as in more than one?"

"Sometimes."

The feeling of a spirit walking across her grave made Sid shiver.

Meanwhile, Annie settled inside her makeshift bedroll, and by the time she closed her eyes, started snoring.

Mary turned off the lamp and squirmed around on his pallet. She did the same, then lay staring at the ceiling—or where she figured it to be—for the longest time. Moonlight through the windows created weird shadows dancing on the walls.

Sid's mind went to her earlier messages from Durwood and Boo. She wouldn't have been that alarmed with Durwood's concern. He always panicked when it came to Boo's welfare.

However, Boo's message gave Sid chill bumps. It had bounced around in the back of her mind ever since that brief episode of 'one bar' cell phone service.

Boo and Annie were each quite a handful. Put them together, and one never knew what might happen. They each gave Sid a run for her money in the contest of orneriness. Annie came out on top in a variety of categories, while Boo topped her own list.

They'd met the first time when Durwood had almost kidnapped Sid and forced her to go with him to talk to Boo. Taken aback at first, by the old woman's tough shell, she'd gotten past the outward appearance.

Sid had been raised first by her mother, and then by her preacher-husband, Sam—preacher-ex-husband, she reminded herself—of the importance of a woman always looking her best outfitted in the full regalia of make-up, perfect every-hair-in-place hairdo. Only after she'd left that world did she learn she didn't have all the answers, and in fact, didn't even know the questions.

At last, she'd learned neither did anyone else, even those who thought they did—like Sam.

Okay, she didn't need to spend the night thinking about him. Ben was a much better subject. His sweet smile ran through her thoughts. She wondered what he was doing tonight, and if he had tried to reach her. If so, did he pace the floor when he couldn't?

As much as she cared for him, she insisted on making her own decisions about what she did and where she went—as did he—which drove him nuts. Lately, it seemed he wanted to wrap her in a security blanket and hold her so tight she couldn't breathe. Until he got over that and proved he had, she'd stay single.

The cause of his worry might well be the risks on her life with a couple of her cases, but that went with the territory. The threat of death also made her feel alive for the first time in her life. Playing it safe tucked away in a world set apart from any risks, she'd learned, carried many more risks—for her, at least.

Sleep not forthcoming, for either Sid or Mary—she heard him still squirming and talking to himself—she decided to pick up the conversation where they'd left off—likely the reason she wasn't sleeping. After all, when one watches for spirits, it takes at least one eye open.

"Mary, can I ask you something?"

"You just did, but I'll give you two."

She chuckled at the man's humor. "You said *spirits*, as in more than one—sometimes. What did you mean by that, and how many?"

He flipped over on his side and faced her. "Depends on them. Shadows of a half a dozen or more have been spotted waltzing in the empty rooms upstairs on the second floor where the restaurant used to be. They can be spotted on nights of heavy rain and lots of cloud to ground lightning bolts."

When a desert storm crashed overhead a few minutes later, Sid gave up on sleep and spent the rest of the night trying to stay dry, watching for spirits—and listening to Annie's snore.

Chapter Twenty-Three

Shadows changed directions as the big bright ball inched across the sky. Its warmth induced Shadrach to relax his head back against the post, and soon Boo heard a soft snore.

Good, now was the time to try to figure out what it all meant—all these stories he'd fed her. Stories she still hadn't accepted as the truth. How could she…so far-fetched…

Her thoughts didn't get far, however, before a weary blackness tempted her eyes to close, and she let them have their way.

What crazy world had she walked into, and how'd she get out of it?

Aware of the rise and fall of her heavy chest, she sucked in a few deep breaths to clear out the tightness and waited for her heartbeat to return to normal.

Startled awake some time later, she opened her eyes to find Shadrach wasn't there. No one was—unless you count a mangy, half-starved wolf with a swollen underbelly of engorged teats. The critter stood in the middle of the yard looking at her.

"Hey, girl. You looking for food or something?"

The wolf cocked her head at Boo and whined.

"Don't put me on your menu. I'm a tough old bird—dry and tasteless—no matter salted or not."

Help me in her eyes, the wolf took a couple halting steps Boo's way.

"Where's your babies? You lose them or something?"

The wolf glanced back over her shoulder, turned around, and headed that way, then stopped and turned again to Boo.

"You got something to show me?"

The wolf repeated the step and the glance.

And again.

Short on energy, and reluctant to move, Boo forced herself to up and took a couple steps toward the wolf. When she did, the wolf took off into the woods, checking to see if Boo followed. Before long, the critter stopped, whined, looked at Boo, and then down to the remains of two newborn wolf cubs.

"Ah, honey. Something got your babies, didn't they? I'm so sorry." An urge to pet the wild critter gave way to reason. Instead, she softened her voice and said. "You got aching boobs, don't you? Here, first, let's bury your babies so critters won't bother them, then let's go to the cabin." She scraped a hole in the sand with a dried tree branch while she talked. "I'll draw some cool water, and you can lay in it. Them teats 'll dry up after a couple of days. Maybe I can find a few sage leaves to make you some tea to drink. Mama used to say that was good to dry up a woman's milk."

After a proper burial, Boo and the wolf made their way to the cabin. The critter waited while Boo went inside, filled a blue granite roasting pan with cool water, and sat it on the porch.

The wolf inched up, sniffed, walked off, came back, and sniffed again. Then, she moved to the long end of the roaster, straddled it, and submerged her aching teats into wet bliss, shivering as if heaven had descended to earth and surrounded her with glory.

While the animal soaked her teats, Boo went inside, found a can of Spam on a shelf, opened it, and dumped it on the porch.

The half-starved critter gobbled it and licked the rough boards clean of grease.

Oozing gratitude for the now-eased pain of an empty belly and swollen teats, the dripping wet wolf ducked her head, schlepped over, and rubbed her head on Boo's leg. A couple minutes later, the creature positioned herself on top of Boo's feet, eased her body to the ground and closed her eyes. In less time than it took Boo to wonder how long she'd have to sit still while the lactating, cub-less creature slept, the wolf snored.

With nothing to do but wait, Boo rested her head on the post again and dozed. How much time passed, she couldn't guess, but when she roused, her back ached like a son-of-a-gun. She shifted, slow like. The wolf stirred, then leapt up, hackles raised.

"It's okay, girl. We're friends, remember?"

In all her born days, Boo had never seen a wolf wag its tail, but this one did.

"Ain't you gonna go back to where you came from?"

The wolf kept rubbing her head on Boo's leg like she might rub all day and still not get tired.

"Go." Boo pointed. "You belong out in the wild, not here with some old lady."

The wolf kept rubbing.

"Well, okay, then. If you're gonna stay with me, I reckon I better call you something." She rubbed her chin, thinking of Dawg, and wondered what he would do if she ever found him, and he saw she'd adopted a wolf. Would he be jealous? Think she'd replaced him with another?

"Well, I reckon we'll just have to deal with that when the time comes. That is if I ever see Dawg again." She rubbed her fingers in the coarse gray hair of the animal's head. "If'n I do find Dawg, and you're still around, the two of you'll have to get along. You know that, don't you?"

The wolf looked her in the eye and whined agreement.

"Okay, let's see." She scratched her head and thought a minute. "I reckon Wouf will do just fine. And since you ain't got no babies to feed, we need to get you dried up. Let's go find some sage leaves, and I'll make you some of that tea I promised. A few days drinking that'll take care of that milk supply."

Off through the woods they went, Boo in front, and Wouf on her heels. The image of the cubs burned in Boo's memory. Her heart hurt for their mama. "I'm sure sorry you lost them babies," she said.

Wouf ducked her head as if she understood the intent of the words that matched her grief.

"I know it's tough to lose someone you love," Boo said, wondering if she should tell Wouf about Dawg and Sasha. For all she knew, Wouf might already know about them. Animals were sensitive that way. Besides, to keep talking about it just piled on the grief. Too much at one time could break a body. Grief, held together by grit and determination, still threatened to crumble her heart to pieces.

The two made their way through the woods, unintentionally scaring rabbits and a covey of quail that bustled off.

When she found a sage bush, Boo filled her pockets with the herb, and the two returned to the cabin. Boo kept her eyes peeled for the see-through woman and Shadrach, but didn't see either one. Sure enough, she found the cabin empty once again. Wouf plopped on the stoop while Boo went inside and made a big dish of sage tea, blew on it until it reached drinking temperature, and set the container on the porch. Wouf hunkered down and inched closer, stuck her nose in the bowl and sniffed and sniffled. She gave Boo a look that said, "You really don't expect me to drink this, do you?"

Boo scooted the bowl closer. "Drink it. Come on, every drop. I made it weak enough you should be able to get it down. Don't want to start with too strong, it might make you sick." She nudged the bowl closer still. "Go head, do as I say."

Wouf dipped her long pink tongue into the tea, and then, as if the taste itself told her of its benefits, she lapped up the liquid, gagged a couple of times, then returned to lying on her side where the breeze could cool her hot teats.

"Good girl. I know it tastes terrible, but it's good for you. It'll dry up that milk in no time. Give it a day or so, and you'll feel much better."

Wouf looked at Boo, her eyes glistening with moisture.

If only Boo's problems could be fixed with a bowl of sage tea.

With little else to do but wait for Shadrach, she pulled one of the kitchen chairs outside, sat, and leaned against the porch rail, wishing she hadn't given up dipping snuff.

"No sense in getting in a big hurry," she said, half to herself and half to Wouf. The pirogue was gone, and so were Shadrach and the invisible woman, added to the disappearance of Sasha and Dawg.

A bluebird chirped in a nearby pine tree, while a mockingbird taunted a brown squirrel that scampered up a tree and into his hole. Her eyelids grew heavy and closed. Somewhere in the deep recesses of her brain, she heard Wouf growl, deep, menacing, but try as she might,

Boo couldn't open her eyes, couldn't move. Instead, she felt like something outside her body pulled her to a place she wasn't sure she wanted to go. Her last conscious thought before she got there was, oh, no, here we go again.

A young woman—where'd she come from—appeared, her back to Boo. Where was she going? Boo rose fearing she'd lose sight of her, or…

The figure led the way down a long dirt road running alongside the river.

Boo hurried to keep up. "Don't walk so fast," she called out to the retreating back. Something about the figure looked familiar. Although Boo couldn't come up with her name, she knew it as certain as she did her own… If she could just remember…

Birds twittered overhead while a huge grasshopper leapt across the path and off into the bushes. Somewhere far off, a commotion of some kind broke the peaceful silence—maybe an animal breaking through the bushes, or a dead tree falling in the woods.

Following along behind the young woman, it seemed they walked for hours, yet Boo had grown neither breathless nor weary.

The young woman kept looking behind as if to assure herself that Boo still followed her through the pine forests, rock canyons, and thickets of wild azaleas, which seemed out of season to Boo, for she knew they usually bloomed in March, and here it was early June.

Determined drumming overhead made Boo stop and follow the sound. A woodpecker drilled the tree trunk looking for insects. He must have heard her, for he stopped, looked down, and gave a wild laugh.

The delay almost made Boo lose track. Soon as she took the next turn, the young woman would be out of sight. Boo glued her eyes to the retreating back and increased her speed until she'd made up the ground she'd lost.

Boo feared the young figure would never stop walking, but at last, she did—right in front of what looked to be the entrance to an old, abandoned mineshaft.

That's when she turned around to face Boo, delight on her face—a face Boo recognized as her own—many years ago.

Chapter Twenty-Four

Durwood loved to hunt and fish, but heretofore, he always did so at Adams Bayou. He wasn't that familiar with where Boo went fishing. Often he'd tried to go out with her, but she always refused. Said she didn't want anybody else with her. That he *jawed* too much. All that talking would scare away the fish. He suspected she just wanted to be alone. Now him, he liked to fish, but he also liked being out in nature with others who liked it, too. He'd had enough being alone.

But, in the bigger scheme of things, he'd rather have his times with Boo, even if she did keep him at arm's length, than being with someone he didn't like as much, but all the time. Guess a man couldn't have everything.

Speaking of Boo, where was she, and how in the world did he find her out here in this endless jungle of swamp, bayou, and wilderness? His back and arms ached from the hours of paddling. If he didn't find her soon, he'd be forced to find a place to pull ashore for the night.

What kind of night that would be, he could only guess. He'd packed all the provisions to do so but still didn't look forward to it. Sleeping on the ground certainly wasn't his idea of comfort—not with these old bones. He remembered the time when such adventure thrilled his soul, but old age caught up with him.

That's what he liked about being with Boo. She made him feel young, as giddy as a schoolboy. One thing he couldn't convince her of, though and that was he didn't want to change her—except for maybe not being so standoffish with him. Lord a mercy, women can drive a man crazy.

She liked the attention he gave her, but no way would she let on that she did. He'd seen her looking out the window at him the other day when he'd driven up, then acted like she didn't care if he came or not. She didn't fool him—not for one minute.

But where was she? And where was Sid?

He looked up to see the sun setting behind what he figured was Andrine's house. Boo had told him about the old voodoo woman, said lots of people did like her, that she scared them. But her and Boo'd been friends for a long time. Maybe he should stop by and ask if she'd seen Boo.

Drawing closer, he made out a figure on the steps leading up to the screened-in front porch. By the time he tied up, he guessed it to be Andrine. He got out and headed toward her. "Hey, you Andrine? Sorry to bother you, but—"

"You ain't bothering me none. I'm sitting out here waiting for you, ain't I?"

"How do you know who I am, or why I come?"

"You're the one what's sweet on Boo, ain't you?"

Durwood choked and sputtered.

"Never mind about that now," she said, patting the step beside her. "Here, sit and rest a spell."

He eased down, stretching his long legs out in front.

Before he could ask, she answered the question uppermost in his mind.

"You're right to worry about Boo. I don't feel good about some of the people I sense around her. They're not all bad, but she ain't sure which ones is and which ones ain't."

Durwood's hands began to shake. He squeezed them into fists and pounded his thighs. "I feel so dang helpless when it comes to that woman. I warned her about coming out here, but noooo, she's gonna do what she's gonna do."

The two sat in silence a long moment, looking out over the still waters of the bayou. Night birds were coming in to roost, and not far away, a hoot owl called to the setting sun.

"Boo's one of them people one bubble off-center anyway. You gotta take her as she is, or not take her at all—walk the other way. She's got this...this... attitude that I call flat stubborn bullheadedness." Durwood sniffed and wiped his nose with his sleeve. "I've tried to call Sid Smart to see if she could help me find her, but I can't find her either. Some days, I just don't understand the world."

At first, Andrine chuckled, but then she grew serious. "I'm glad you're looking for Boo. I get the feeling she's either in trouble or soon going to be. Of course, God help the man who gets in between her and what she wants."

Despite his concern, or perhaps because of it, he laughed. For he knew the truth in that statement more than most.

"It'll soon be dark," she said. "Best you sleep here and leave at first light."

Durwood looked at the woman, wondering if he dare enter the sanctuary of her home. He'd heard tales of things going on inside that place, and his yellowed old toenails were already curled enough. He didn't go in for all this hocus-pocus, and he sure didn't want to conjure up the dead.

"Aw, come on, Durwood. I won't eat you. Can't promise a ghost won't show up, but I can promise I'll wake you at dawn so you can get going."

She stood, held him by the arms, and helped him rise to his feet, and the two went inside.

Just before the screen door banged behind them, Durwood took one last look back so as not to miss his last chance to see the real world.

Andrine pulled on his arm. "Oh, come on. It ain't that bad. I don't eat tough old men." She snickered under her breath, but not so quiet as to keep him from knowing he amused her.

"Yeah, just the young, good-looking ones, I guess." But just as the words came out his mouth, and from a cloudless sky, a bolt of lightning struck the house, and the acrid smell of smoke filled the room.

Chapter Twenty-Five

Sid and Annie pulled into the parking lot of old mission just as the church bells rang, announcing the gathering. Couples walked arm in arm up the steps and through the doors, now swung wide in invitation.

Sid awakened to see Annie smoothing out the skirt of her fluffy, hot pink bridesmaid dress and straightening the puff sleeves. Great! Just what she needed to see first thing in the morning—a hundred and seventy pound, big-bellied, redheaded Bridsemaid Barbie.

"Shame on you, Sidra Smart, for thinking such uncharitable thoughts," she admonished herself.

In contrast to Annie's sunshiney attitude, Sid felt like she'd been on a binge-drinking crime spree instead of on the floor of a ghost-riddled house counting the ghosts that waltzed by. She still wasn't sure if she'd dreamed them, or if they'd tripped across the floor for real.

The tow truck had been waiting for them by the time

they returned to the car. Within a few minutes, the Spanish-speaking-only man loaded them in the cab, attached the wench to the car, and off they went—east.

Indeed it had been the timing belt. Instead of losing time awaiting the repair, Sid rented a car, and off they went—to the infernal wedding.

Now that they'd arrived, Sid could breathe. She could also check her messages. While Annie walked down the aisle, Sid sat near the back and listened to Durwood's message again. Something in his voice—something she'd never heard before—made her want to hurry home and check on them. Boo might be okay—but Durwood wouldn't be until he found her. That's the part that worried Sid. He wasn't as strong a man as Boo was a woman.

The crowd stood when the wedding march began, and once the bride passed her row, Sid slipped outside and called Ben.

Wouldn't you know, he was in court—and not worried about Sid—according to what he'd told his secretary, but she reported noticing a new worry line across his forehead.

The music quieted, and the priest started repeating familiar vows. Sid wondered if the groom knew how long—or short—forever could be—and how many marriages his bride had to have expunged from church records before his wedding could take place.

According to Annie, the bride had not a single *obey* bone in her body—for that matter, neither did Annie. Hopefully, the priest wouldn't use that word and make the bride lie all over again.

At least there wasn't to be much of a reception, within a couple of hours, they could be back on the road toward Fort Sumner. The mechanic promised he'd have the Olds ready later that day.

She tried dialing Durwood's house again, but he didn't answer.

Neither did Boo when she tried her number.
Sasha didn't either.
Okay, now she was really worried.

Chapter Twenty-Six

Boo stared into the face of the young woman she'd followed, the one who looked exactly like her—fifty years ago. She ran her fingers across her own face, hoping she hadn't herself walked into that other world never to return. The wrinkles and sagging skin assured her she had not.

Yes, her skin had once been that firm and smooth, but that was a long time ago. Not now. Now her face showed the signs of too many days outdoors. Sasha would add, and too few nights without moisturizer.

No, the figure wasn't Boo, but why did she look like Boo had at that age?

Boo swept a look around. The afternoon sun had lessened its hold, and shadows moved across the area.

The young woman pointed to a heavy brush, then looked at Boo and smiled.

Heart in her throat, Boo blurted, "What? Is that a cave?"

The woman smiled bigger and gave a slight, almost imperceptible nod.

"The lost silver mine?" Boo thought of the map in her pocket and pulled it out, compared the two, and indeed realized the similarities. She looked up at the figure standing at the mouth of the cave.

The woman's countenance hadn't changed. Nor had her expression.

Now, what should Boo do? She had the map, but she had been so consumed following the woman, she'd paid no attention to the trail. She had no idea the path they'd taken, not to mention how to get to Shadrach's cabin? Not to mention finding the Atakapa settlement again. And now, with night approaching, this person wanted her to go inside a dark cave.

Indecision rode high on her shoulders. Considering her options out loud, she said, "To tell you the truth, I'm as lost as a goose. I been so preoccupied following you, I ain't paid no attention to where we was going. I'm not sure I can find my way back. That's hard to admit for a tracker. I reckon I'd find it—that is if I live long enough. But, I dang sure can't walk that far tonight, and if'n I could, which way would I go?"

She hadn't realized Wouf had been following them. But now that she'd stopped, she caught a whiff of the now-familiar odor behind her. She turned. Wouf stood with her head ducked, eyes on alert, and her tail just as still as her flattened ears.

"What do you think about this, girl? Do you know this woman?" Boo turned to point and realized the maiden was gone. She looked at Wouf, who now added a growl deep in her throat.

"You still see her, don't you, girl?"

Wouf bared her teeth and continued to growl.

"What. You don't think we should check out the mine?"

Wouf grabbed Boo's sleeve, dug her paws into the

dirt, and pulled.

"Dang it, lemme go, Wouf." Boo pulled back.In the midst of the tussle, the young woman reappeared between them.

Wouf let go with a tiny yelp.

Now that the woman had Boo's undivided attention, she ,crooked her finger, floated through the scrub brush and disappeared into the darkened entrance.

"I'm gonna follow her inside a ways," Boo said to Wouf. "But I don't want you to come.

You've got problems enough with them swollen teats. You stay here and rest. I'll be back soon."

Boo found a thick stick, built a torch and lit it from the matches still tucked in her top pocket. By the time she stepped inside the cave, however, the figure was nowhere to be seen—or had simply vaporized, which seemed to be the going thing lately. The smell of wet earth, combined with that of stale, musty air sent Boo into a sneezing fit, and the echo bounced back at her.

After her eyes adjusted, an orb of light appeared a few feet in front of her and moved deeper into the pitch-black tunnel. Boo followed, telling herself that she was too old to do this sort of stuff. But something—or someone—made her feel nineteen again.

The deeper she went, the more slippery and uneven the path became, and the more erratic grew the path of the orb. Sometimes she saw it for a few minutes, then it darted off and disappeared. Then, later, it would show itself again. When she reached an unusally wet, slippery area of the cave floor, she put her free hand on the cold, damp wall and slowed her pace. All along, she kept telling herself that she was a fool to be in a pitch black cave following some *thing* who'd gone so far ahead she doubted she'd ever catch up.

The enclosed blackness caused time and distance to disappear.

With no idea how long she'd been in the cave, she

told herself just a little further. At any minute, something might make sense. She'd find something—a pile of bones or maybe complete skeletons—prospectors who gave up the ghost on their quest for the riches in a strange new world. Or maybe those treasures Peabody wanted.

She'd just decided this was the most ridiculous thing she'd ever done in her life—which was really saying something—when the guiding orb shot off much like the girl had. Total darkness. The puny glow from the torch was all the light she had, and it reflected off of what looked like a piece of glass on the cave floor in front of her. Steadying the beam on the object, she realized it was a shard from a very old bottle—evidently a wine bottle. Moving the beam around the area, she saw other pieces— scattered as if someone had thrown the bottle against the cave wall.

That's when she saw the skeleton, leaning against the wall. A piece of yellowed paper lay near what looked like finger bones.

Then her torch fizziled out.

Water dripped somewhere off in the distance.

"You're a silly old fool," she said, needing to hear a human voice more than anything. "Now you really got yourself in a pickle. You can make your way out, or sit down next to that feller and die. Problem is, you ain't got a bottle of wine like he did, to ease the pain."

Wait. A skeleton in a cave and a bottle of wine. The journal—one name had never been added to the list. Maybe because that guy was him and dead men don't talk.

Then her mind went to the kegs of Mexican silver. Could the old guy have been looking for them? But with a bottle of wine in his pocket?

Eager now, inspired by her find, she eased along, fearful she might trip, break a hip and end up a skeleton herself, she jumped when her foot hit something that wasn't there before—she'd swear it wasn't. A rock, perhaps, but she didn't dare bend to check for fear of losing her balance. If she fell, she'd lose all sense of direction and never know which way was out.

Apprehension grew. Which way was out? She was certain she hadn't veered off the path. Her fingers tapped across the jagged wall until something with lots of legs scampered over her arm. Boo couldn't help but think of how Sasha would've yelled to high heaven. Screaming wasn't something Boo did, but she sure was tempted this time.

Soon, she spotted a pinprick of light ahead of her. Wanting so much to hurry, yet knowing if she fell and broke her hip she'd die before anyone found her, she forced herself to go slow and easy.

The pinprick of light grew larger as she moved until soon, the mouth of the cave came into view. She increased her speed, still taking care not to trip and at last limped into the bright moonlit night. Wouf had fallen asleep but awakened by Boo's exit, the animal leapt up and ran circles around her. Boo reached for a low hanging tree branch for support and eased her sore body to the ground. Soon, she'd stretched out on the grass, so weary she thought she'd die. Wouf crept up, curled up beside her, and the critter's warm soft body eased Boo into an exhausted sleep. The next thing Boo knew, the bright morning sun struck her in the eye, and her hip hurt like hell.

Why had the young woman led her here in the first place?

An image of a bear's bloody paw flashed across her mind. She'd never seen a real bear trap, only photos and movies of them, but the image made her wonder if she'd gotten herself caught in one. The problem was if she'd been led here as a trap, who set it and why?

Chapter Twenty-Seven

More than anything, Boo wanted to go back inside the cave to follow the lines etched into the rock and hopefully find the kegs of silver, but she was smart enough to know it wasn't safe for her to try that again. Especially alone, and without any equipment like a compass, headlamps, maybe a pickax—and drinking water.

"Time to head to Shadrach's cabin." She patted Wouf on the rump. "I reckon you can find it better'n me. Let's head that direction. Maybe after we rest up, we can talk Shadrach into coming with us and helping us search the cave. I got a feeling this is the one Peabody and Mouton's looking for, but we sure ain't gonna tell them what we found. They want it, they can well find it on their own. Besides, we got the map."

Wouf lifted her nose and sniffed the air. She circled the ground a couple of times sniffing it, too. Her bearings straight, the animal looked up at Boo and then started a slow walk, as if she knew Boo needed time to work out the kinks from sleeping on the ground.

Along the way, they spotted a bush of ripe late-season blackberries sparkling with morning dew. They sat and ate their bellies full while they rested, then took off again. Boo got the distinct impression that Wouf slowed her own pace for Boo's benefit, for every few minutes she stopped, as if tired, then, after Boo's breathing slowed to normal, Wouf was ready to go again.

The pattern continued until Boo caught a glimpse of the dilapidated cabin through a stand of trees. Relief washed over her. As they drew closer, and she saw Shadrach on the doorstep, she almost peed her pants. She'd never been so glad to see anyone in her life. It wasn't like her to feel so lost and without a better sense of direction.

Shadrach smiled when she walked up. "I was a hoping you'd make it here last night before dark. When you didn't, I lay awake worrying about you all night long."

"That makes two of us." Boo shook her head. "I ain't never felt so discombobulated in my life. I feel like either I'm living in a crazy world, or I'm the one taking everybody else there."

Shadrach seemed to ignore her words. "Who's that you got with you?"

"A mama what lost her babies. Look at them teats. They're better, but she still has a way to go."

"Then I guess she's the one what drunk the sage tea. I found the dregs in the kitchen. Wondered why you made that."

"Well, you seem to know everything else around here, I'm surprised you didn't know that." Boo's words sounded sarcastic, and she felt bad after she'd said them.

"Ain't you the testy one," Shadrach said, chuckling so his belly shook.

"Don't mean to be. Just weary as all get out. Weary

and confused and hungry." She pulled the map out of her pocket. "Here, look at this map I found."

"That can wait. Right now, let's go inside, and I'll scramble you some eggs.

Boo allowed him to hold her chair for her while she bent her stiff knees and eased into it. Then, she watched as he scrambled the eggs and delivered the food to her. She did not have to be invited to partake.

While she ate, scarfed it down would be more like it, he studied the map she'd found. "Where'd you get this?"

In between chewing and swallowing, Boo explained that she'd taken the map from the Dead-Man room—the same map Peabody and Mouton wanted—but didn't know she had—at least, she didn't think they did.

"You'd make a mistake to think that. Maybe they do," Shadrach said.

"Could be. I gotta think maybe they do, that's for sure. That might be why they took Sasha and Dawg."

"What?"

"Hang on." She went on to explain how she also saw Mili under the tarp with Dead-Man and how maggots crawled in and out of her body, only to see her alive later. How first Dawg disappeared from her house, and then what happened to Sasha. The whole mess came spewing out.

He listened without saying a word, waiting until she was spent. All the while she talked, however, deep thinking lines etched his face.

Once she finished, he let out a great breath of air that sounded more like a whoosh than it did a sigh. "Land a goshen, woman, you sure carry around a heap of trouble. No wonder you called me to come help."

Boo leaned back in her own chair, irritation crawling under her collar. "Call you? I never done no such thing. I ain't never asked a living soul for help. I can take care of my self, thank you very much."

"If'n you don't mind me saying, it sure don't look like it."

"Humpf."

"How come you such an ornery old woman? You never let folks in."

"'Cause when I do, they always want more'n I can give."

"Like the lighthouse keeper did?"

Boo's mouth dropped open. "How do you know about him?"

"I been around a long time. Seen lots of things, heard lots of things."

"Long time, huh? I'm seventy-four, beat you can't beat that." She pulled her mouth into a smug grin.

"How old you think I am?" He picked up a stick and drew a lighthouse in the dirt.

"Not seventy-four, that's for sure." She peered at him, her eyes half-closed. "I'll say not a day more'n seventy."

"Would you believe one hundred and twenty tomorrow?"

"Get outta here. You can't be."

"Will be tomorrow."

"That means you was born in 1891."

"Good math. Yep, I celebrated my tenth birthday in Galveston, the same day as the great Galveston Hurricane. Two thousand people died that day, along with my whole family there visiting relatives."

"Then how come you look so young?" Boo chuckled. "Not that seventy-one is young, but..."

"I know what you mean. One of these days, I might tell you—that is if you don't figure it out yourself. But we were talking about the lighthouse worker. Ah, what was his name? It's on the tip of my tongue."

"Oh, him. I forget it myself." Boo tried to hide the emotions the mere mention of Henry resurrected in her heart, but she doubted she had. She'd loved Henry. Lord, she'd loved that man. He'd touched her in places she never let another man touch—before and since. The memories of him set her afire even now. A shiver ran up her spine just thinking about the man.

But lighthouses were in his blood, and swamps and bayous were in hers.

Her cheeks grew hot. She shifted and looked at Shadrach, who hadn't taken his eyes off her the whole time she'd been remembering Henry. Something told her he knew exactly where she'd gone with her thoughts. She had the feeling he'd taken her there on purpose.

"It ain't good for folks to be alone." Shadrach drew a second circle in the dirt, connecting the two until they became a figure eight. "We're social creatures. We need each other."

"Don't need nobody." Boo puffed out her chest.

"Well, it seems to me if you want to find your dog and your cousin, you'll need somebody to help you. Ain't that the reason you're here?"

"Okay, Mr. Smarty Pants, since you think you know everything, I have a question. You half-way explained Parahaia, but why in the world are all these other Indian folks showing up like they know me, but I don't know them. Heck, I don't know if they're real or all in my head."

"Just because they're in your head, that don't mean they ain't real, Boo Murphy."

Both stared at the other for the longest time until Shadrach broke the silence. "Seems to me, they got something to say you need to hear."

"All I want is Dawg and Sasha back. That's why I'm here in the first place. They ain't said nothing that makes that happen."

"You sure 'bout that? Seems to me, you're the one who brung them Indians here. It sure ain't me—I don't need to talk to them folks. I ain't the one with a problem."

Boo's mind went ninety to nothing. What the devil

was this man talking about? "All I know is, I want to get home where I belong."

"With your family?"

"If I got any family left. Looks like I lost them all."

"Did you ever have them? Seems to me all you had was Dawg, and now he's gone."

"What about Sasha?"

"Didn't know you cared much one way or the other about her."

"'Course I cared...care. It's just that she's...

"Irritating?"

"Well, yeah. But don't you go preaching to me, old man."

He held his hands up in defense. "I ain't no preacher, that's for sure. Been in enough fiery furnaces for a lifetime. Tell you what, I'll help you find your pirogue and you can head to that Indian camp and show them that map. Maybe then they'll give you back Sasha and Dawg and tell you what's going on. It's for sure I ain't helped you none."

"All right, smarty pants. I get the message. Now—you gonna help me find my pirogue or not?"

"Come on, let's go." He stood, put her plate in the sink, then took her arm and ushered her out the door.

The three of them, Shadrach, Boo, and Wouf headed down to the river and started a more organized, detailed search of the bank.

Unsuccessful in their pursuit, Shadrach's irritation became evident to Boo. "You look like you lost something and can't find it," she said grinning.

"Oh, hush, you nosy old woman. I hid your boat for your own good, and you know it. If'n I hadn't, no telling what trouble you might've gotten yourself into. Lord knows you're in enough already."

Boo couldn't argue with that.

They kept looking, but Wouf found the pirogue—smelled it out and led the others there, and before long, the three made their way downriver. Boo took her place in the back of the boat, Shadrach took the front seat, and Wouf, Dawg's.

Their passage downriver, instead of against the flow, made the going easier. Boo paddled until her arms gave out, then Shadrach picked up the task, and on they went.

While they traveled, Boo made small talk, fearful if she didn't, either she'd start thinking about the lighthouse keeper—or Shadrach would bring up the topic again. "So, Shadrach," she said to his hunched-over back. "Tell me how your mammy happened to call you that Bible name?"

"My mama didn't." He snorted and laughed until his shoulders shook. "To tell you the truth, my mama wanted to name me Remus, but Papa wouldn't let her."

"Get out! Well, I'll swan, no wonder you're up there snorting through your nose."

"Honest truth. Papa was a preacher. He always loved to do a sermon on the book of Daniel—that was his favorite. Guess that's why I always played with fire when I was a kid."

The chit chat continued until Wouf looked behind them and set off an alarm with a deep growl in her throat.

"What is it, girl?" Boo shifted and turned to look. She saw another boat heading their way that grew larger as she watched. "Looks like somebody's following us."

Shadrach pulled the paddles in long enough to take a quick glance back. "Uh, oh. I could pull behind that stand of bushes and let them pass. Or, if you want, I could slow down and see who it is and what they want. 'Course they might want us."

"That's what I'm thinking—they just might," Boo said. "It's for sure they're going faster than us. Hear that outboard?" She looked around them, then pointed. "Over there around that cut-out, pull in there, and we'll hide till they pass. We got a couple of minutes. Hurry."

Taking advantage of his massive arms, Shadrach poured on the steam, and within a couple of minutes, rounded the edge of the cut-out and maneuvered the pirogue full-circle. Boo held aside the overhanging bush while Shadrach eased underneath. Wouf splashed to shore and stood silently, but with her hackles raised, fire dancing in her eyes.

Boo and Shadrach also stayed quiet as they watched the boat grow larger and then stop just yards away from where they'd hidden.

Three men were in the motor launch—two in the rear and one upfront at the wheel. Boo didn't recognize the driver, but the other two were Peabody and Tarek, Mili's brother. They were so close Boo could hear them mumbling.

"Where'd they go? They were right here," Peabody said, irritation coloring his voice. The man at the wheel slowed the motor and put it in idle. When he did, the launch drifted their way. Boo held her breath, irritated that she'd believed Peabody when he'd said they didn't have anyone who knew these waters. Looked to her like this man knew it quite well. So why'd they want her? Did they suspect she had the map like Shadrach suggested? A flock of quail chose that minute to flush from the bushes near where they were hidden. Boo held her breath.

The boatman, a hunter for sure, heard the quail and looked their way, then shielded his eyes with his hands and squinted. "Hey," he said, his voice secretive but with volume enough that Boo could understand. "Looks like we found what we're looking for."

"Where?" Peabody asked.

The boatman pointed right at them. "Look right there. See? There in those bushes. I think the covey of quail flushed out more than hunters. They also flushed out the hunted."

"Move the boat closer," Tarek ordered. And as he recognized what he looked at said, "Okay, Boo, we know you're in there. Come on out."

Boo glanced at Wouf, still onshore, and whispered. "You stay there, girl like you're not a part of us. I'll come back and get you when I can. Just hang around this area. I'll find you."

Wouf looked at her with sad eyes, ducked her head, and then turned and walked off.

"And if I can't get back, you'll be fine on your own now."

Wouf gave a low whine, but slinked further ashore, hiding in a stand of azalea bushes.

"You, too, Shadrach. Ain't no sense in you going. They ain't seen you in here cause of them dark clothes and your dark skin."

Shadrach eased into the water and waded toward the shadows. Boo had expected a little disagreement or at least a goodbye, but before she knew it, he had disappeared—just like before.

"I'm coming." Boo picked up the oars and paddled the boat out.

"Well, finally, your highness leaves her hiding place," Peabody said, sneering.

"Don't get your panties in a ruffle. I ain't hiding. I was resting and just dozed off when I heard your boat coming. Weren't sure who it was, so I just stayed put. What the heck you doing here? I thought you didn't know these waters."

"I don't, but he does." Peabody threw his thumb in the direction of the boatman. "When you didn't come back, we figured we better come find you. You've been gone so long, we weren't sure what happened to you. Where have you been? Did you find the mine?"

"How would I find the mine? I ain't found nothing. Flat nothing. Nothing but a hard time and a waste of that. I doubt there is any lost silver mines around here." She glanced at him to see if he knew she lied, that she indeed had found what she suspected was the mine they wanted, but what the hey.

"We know you took the map, Boo. You're the only one who could. If you want to see your sister and your dog, you better hand it to me."

"Even if I did, you ain't never gonna find it."

"So, you have been there—just like I thought."

"All I did was look around inside. Oh hells bells, Peabody, tell me what's going on. You ain't told me the whole story, that's for sure."

"Give us the map, or take us to it, and we'll give you Sasha and the dog."

"You strike a tough bargain—not sure which one I'd rather have, the map, or—"

"Where's the map, Boo?" Tarek asked.

"I hid it back at the house."

"Okay, you follow us there," Peabody ordered, "and we'll give you Sasha and your dog in exchange for you showing us where you hid the map."

Boo crossed her fingers behind her, knowing the action would keep the lie she was about to tell from counting against her promise. "I'll come all right, but I ain't following you. It's hard enough for an old woman to ply these waters, let alone try to keep up with a motor launch. And I dang sure ain't tying my boat to yours. That'll tear it to pieces. Tell you what, I'll get the map and meet you at the camp."

"Can we trust you to do that? Remember, we have your family."

"I don't go back on my word. Besides, I've had enough of you." At least the last part of that sentence wasn't a lie.

But she'd never been so entertained in all her life.

Peabody and Tarek mumbled something about not having enough gas to follow her, then Peabody said, "All right. We're going on ahead. But you see that you get that map and bring it straight to us. If you don't, it's not just your flesh we'll soon be eating."

"Yeah, yeah. So what if I don't? You gonna grind my bones to make your bread?"

"Something like that." He roared with laughter as the driver shifted the boat into gear and accelerated off.

The pirogue rocked in the wake of the other boat while Boo sat cogitating, trying to make sense of what she'd learned the last few days. For sure, she wasn't heading straight to get the map and take it to them—for one, she still had it in her pocket. Two, she still had questions she didn't have answers to, not yet, at least. Long as she had the map, Peabody wasn't going to hurt her family.

Curious as a cat, Mama always called Boo. And along with that, she never failed to warn Boo that it would get the best of her one of these days.

What was it about mamas that made their voices live in your head forever?

She'd go to the Atakapa camp, all right, but not straight away. First, she had another stop to make.

Chapter Twenty-Eight

Boo paddled through the deepest, darkest part of the swamp, determined to reach Andrine's house before the sun went down—and that wasn't far off. Something just didn't add up about this whole mess, and time was running out on a chance to save Dawg and Sasha. Andrine was the only person Boo trusted to help her make sense of everything. All she'd been getting were pieces of information, and she couldn't even believe those.

But as she grew closer to Andrine's, she caught a glimpse of two men in a flatbottom boat pushing off from her house. "Not another one," she said under her breath, wondering who it swas and what they had to do with Andrine.

Their backs had been to her, so she felt certain they hadn't seen her yet. She manuvered closer to shore and hid behind Spanish moss dangling from cypress and tupelo trees. Curly gray ends of the moss dragged and swayed with each ripple and wave.

The first person she recognized as the boat passed was Ka, the Atkapa chief. He sat up front peering out over the water, a satisfied smile on his face. Another man, someone she didn't recognize, sat behind the chief paddling.

Boo held her breath and didn't move a muscle when an alligator slid off the bank and disturbed a group of water moccasins that swam through the murky water in every direction. After a couple of minutes, the other pirogue eased on down the river with barely a ripple. When she felt they'd gone far enough that they couldn't see or hear her, she eased out into the middle of the waterway.

Since Andrine's house was the only thing out here, they must have been visiting with her. Boo had known the woman many years, even been out here a few times to sit and chat. She'd never had her cards read or had any spells cast, but she knew the woman to be as honest as the day was long. Brutally honest.

So what in the world could the chief be needing from her? Surely she didn't read his cards.

Supported by posts, Andrine's house squatted in the middle of the bayou as if it grew there along with the trees. She steered the pirogue to a small dock in front of the house, and by the time she'd tied up, a dark-skinned woman dressed in a long, full dark skirt and long white peasant top headed out the front screen door and down the steps, trailed by what looked to be a German Shepherd. Dozens of multi-colored beads around Andrine's neck swayed back and forth as she walked. Long, black hair curled around her face and down her back.

By the time Boo tied up, Andrine stood waiting, hands on her hips.

"That's some dog you got there," Boo called out, hands covering her eyes to shut out a bright ray of sunlight arrowing through the trees. But when the animal stepped from around Andrine and Boo got a closer look, she saw it wasn't a German Shepard at all.

It was Wouf, tail wagging.

"Where in the world did you find Wouf? I had to leave her miles upstream."

"Somehow, I knew she had a connection to you. Wasn't quite sure how, but I expected you'd show up sooner or later." Andrine reached down and rubbed the wolf's head.

Wouf's whole body shimmied in anticipation, and despite her own stiff joints, Boo felt like she shimmied, too. She climbed out of the boat faster than usual. "I can't believe my own eyes," she exclaimed. "I was afeared I'd never see you again, girl." She tried to kneel to hug the animal, but her knees refused the effort. So she held Wouf by the chin and looked in her eyes. "I sure am glad to see you. You okay? How's them teats?" Boo inspected them and said, "Oh, they look much better."

Andrine interrupted the reunion with, "I get the feeling you and the wolf coming here is not a social visit—guess that means I don't have to put on the tea kettle." Andrine smiled, showing off a mouth full of pearly whites glistening against her dark skin.

"You got that right. Those two men I passed? I figure they been here to see you, too. That worries me more'n a little. But I sure could use a cup of tea."

"What's going on, Boo? I never seen you so jumpy before."

"Let's go inside, I'll fill you in, then you can tell me what I should do."

"You know I won't do that. But maybe I can shed some light on whatever's going on." The two headed up the walk, Wouf at Boo's side.

"As you might have guessed, this here's Wouf. She came to me for help the other day after she'd lost a litter of pups. I could say I adopted her, but it's more like the other way 'round."

"Wolves carry powerful medicine, but I guess you know that. Long's you got her, or she's got you, you can be sure spirit's gonna be there."

Boo chuckled. "Well, that's for dang sure. They been haunting me to beat sixty. Ain't never called on you for nothing, but right now, I need somebody to help me make sense out of what's going on—'cause I sure can't do it by myself. Figured you was the one I needed to talk to."

"I is such," Andrine said, bowing deeply.

Humility never had been one of her strong suits.

"What can I do you for?" She asked, taking Boo's arm.

"There's these people got Sasha and Dawg. I need to find out what's going on and what they really want from me. First, they said they wanted me to guide them through the swamp and help them find a silver mine. But now... " Boo shook her head. "Seems all of that was a baldface lie. First, they know where the mine is, and second—"

"Don't say nothing else." Andrine held her hand up to halt Boo's words. "If I know too much, sometimes it keeps me from paying attention to what's in the cards 'cause I try to read stuff into them. Come on up, lets take a look at the cards—see what they say."

When the two went inside, the strong odor of burned wood filled Boo's nostrils. She rubbed them, and said, "Dang, Andrine, smells like your house is on fire."

"It ain't now, thanks to a kindly old gentleman who helped me put out the fire the other night after lightning struck it."

Her smile told Boo she didn't get the whole story, but she let it drop.

Windows on either side of a sparsely furnished front room let in a soft glow of energy left at days end. A kerosene lamp, already lit for the evening, sat on a table next to an old, dilapidated rocking chair. Other than that, a couple of rickey side chairs and a single bed in the corner filled most of the room. In the middle of the rear wall a doorway revealed what looked to be a tiny kitchen.

Andrine led the way to the window on the left to a small square table covered with a spotless, white crocheted table cloth which hung almost to the floor. A violet-colored candle sat in the middle on—of all things—a silver charger. Two chairs were tucked under the table on both sides.

"I already lit the candle. I had a feeling someone was on their way. Sit." She pointed to the chair on the left while she pulled out the other and sat.

A deck of over-sized black cards lay in front of Andrine, who picked them up and started shuffling. "As long as I knowed you, Boo, you ain't never come for a card reading. I'm feeling you ain't sure you're gonna buy into anythin' I say. I just want you to know that's okay. Don't mean any of this ain't right." She shuffled the cards. "'Course, don't mean it is, neither. You the only one can judge that."

Boo nodded.

"Now, you got a problem, and you looking for answers how to handle it."

What sounded like a question was more a statement of fact.

"That's about it. There's these people..."

"People that—what?"

"And then there's this woman I'm seeing. Somehow I get the feeling she's from way long ago, but then, sometimes, she looks like me when I was young. It's like she's telling me something without moving her lips."

Andrine spoke up. "Sounds to me like you've met Parahaia, the spirit of the swamp."

"That's what Shadrach said."

Andrine looked at Boo, her eyebrows raised in question, then, "We'll get to him in a minute. Right now, let's talk about Parahaia. At one time, she really lived—tens of thousands of years ago. Legend goes..."

Andrine told Boo the story of the seventh daughter of a seventh daughter. How the birth had been fast and painless. How, afterwards, her mama stood and held the infant up to the fullest, biggest, brightest moon she'd ever seen. When the moonlight fell on that newborn, the whole sky lit up like daylight. Most often, shamans were men, but on occasion a woman would rise to the top. That very night the shaman, who was also her father, declared her name to be Parahaia, the future shaman.

How she grew to be a young woman with a strong heart for her people and with an inate wisdom of the swamps no one had ever seen before. Often she stood, arms lifted to the heavens, calling in the wisdom of the ages.

Of how, when she died, she claimed the swamp as her and her daughter's permanent abode for all eternity.

"In physical form," Andrine said, "she could do only so much good. But as spirit, she and her daughter watch the goings-on in the swamp and work to keep nature's balance to this very day."

"Then, I guess that means Parahaia had lots of time to grow her power," Boo said, her mind racing.

"Yep. Like I said, some believe she's been here since the beginning of time, just not in human form. Then, she live here, die here, and pass to what she be before she come. Likely has a special time of day when she can draw the most energy from her swamp. Energy to harness enough power so some folk can see her." Andrine looked up. "Folk like you, Boo Murphy."

Boo squirmed in her chair. She'd been in the swamps all her life herself, so why did this swamp spirit choose now to show herself to Boo? What was it about now, and about Boo that she chose her? Or had she been the one that Boo had felt watching her all these years—almost like a protective interest.

Andrine continued. "That time is probably just at dusk after the sun's put all its power into what lives out here—like plants and animals. They soak up as much sun from the day as they can, and they're full up to the top. So then, after Parahaia draws enough of it, she has enough power to show herself to who she wants. Some say she can take physical form for brief periods of time. That her spirit might even dwell in animals."

Boo's mind went to Wouf and wondered.

"And there's this Shadrach guy who comes and goes that I ain't quite figured out yet," she said. "I always thought I was a pretty good figurer, but—"

"Shh, say no more." Andrine stacked the deck of cards on the table and asked Boo to shuffle one more time and cut them. After she'd done so, Andrine picked them up and started turning them face up. She must have turned twelve or so, and in some kind of order that must've made sense to her. It sure didn't to Boo.

Each card had a different woman on it. Weird looking women from other parts of the world and all decked out in god-awful dress. Boo began to regret coming. This was nonsense. What did these cards have to do with her? She looked for answers, not dress-up playtime.

One by one, Andrine went through all the cards, summing up Boo's life while she sat with her mouth open, wondering how the woman knew so much about her past. She mentioned something about one of Boo's ancestors and then said it was Boo, not an ancestor—as if Boo had lived more than one lifetime. Hogwash was the word that came to Boo's mind, but something stopped her short of saying it.

"There's a man in your life—someone who comes by to see you."

"Yeah." Boo thought of Durwood.

"He fond of you."

"Yeah, wants to marry me, but I ain't marrying

nobody."

"I don't see marriage here." She flipped the edge of a card as if studying it closer. "He does make an impact on you, however. You think he's a bother."

"He is."

Andrine smiled. "We'll see. He's looking for—"

"For a wife, yeah, I know—but I didn't come here to talk about him. Let's move on."

Andrine looked up at Boo, a smirk spread across her face. "Whatever you say." She studied the cards and added, "There's people you know who ain't who they say they are."

Boo perked up. "You can say that again."

Andrine tapped a card. "See this snake curled up at the bottom?"

"I see it."

"The snake says be on the alert. Don't believe everything they say."

"What I want to know is, is my cousin alive—and my dog. Cause if they are, I'll move hell and high water to find them. If they ain't, no sense in me going on with them people."

Andrine sat silently for a couple of minutes, studied the cards, flipped the edge of one. "I see deception. The thing is, you'll wanna be careful when you try to figure out who lies and who tells the truth."

"I think I know."

Andrine lifted another card. "Not so sure—maybe, maybe not.

"What the heck does that mean?"

"It means it may not be the person you have in mind. Listen to your wolf, she carries powerful medicine."

"How so?"

"She adopted you as family, didn't she?"

"For sure." Boo glanced out the screen door. Wouf sat on the front porch, watching, ears raised as if on high alert.

"Wolves protect. Their sense of family is strong."

Boo remembered the animal's grief over the loss of her cubs.

"They live by rules and rituals. Wolf spirit is freedom and wildness. Their rule is survival. Each pack has its role in the group. Alpha male and alpha female. One's in charge of the group, and they all follow that guidance. They make firm attachments, and their hearing is a hundred times greater than ours. They make quick decisions. If this wolf come into your life, it means its time for you to take a different path, go a new direction, take a journey."

"What does any of this have to do with me right now?"

Andrine picked up the cards, collecting them into a deck. "What did you expect? Me to tell you to chop off the neck of a chicken and drink its blood?"

"Well... sort of."

Andrine smiled. "Nice to see you, Miss Boo. You come, again." She stood, blew out the candle, went to the screen door and opened it.

"I guess that's my signal to leave."

"If you feel so."

"I don't feel so. I just need help. Something other than that mumbo jumbo."

"Like what?"

"Like who the world is this man who says his name is Shadrach."

"I can't tell you that. You've got to figure it out for ya self."

"If I knew how to do that, I wouldn't a come seen some woman what does magic. Heck, you don't do magic, you're just a card reader."

Andrine smiled. "Say what you want. I say, be careful."

"But—"

"Okay, here it is..."

Andrine dropped that sentence into the black void of Boo's thoughts and then grew silent.

Saying not a word, Boo turned, marched to the chair where she'd been, sat, and stared at Andrine. After a few minutes silence, Boo grunted and said, "Okay, Andrine, I'm listening. Talk at me."

"I can't tell you about that visitor you seen in the boat what came to see me right before you. That wouldn't be right. But I can tell you, watch out. Things ain't as they seem. Not real sure about intent, but I do know theys looking out for they own self."

"What can you tell me about Dawg and Sasha? Are they alive or dead? Cause if they're dead, I can just tell them people to forget the whole deal and go home."

"I don't get the feeling they's passed to the other side."

Boo gave a sigh of relief. "Okay, good. What else?"

"Here, let's look at these other cards. They my favorite," Andrine said, as she pulled out a different deck of cards. "Here, shuffle and cut them twice, then turn the top card."

A card that read Page of Cups stared Boo in the face. "You know I don't really believe in this stuff, don't you?"

The sound of Andrine gritting her teeth traveled across the table. "You want my help or not?"

"Yeah, but can't you do it some way other than pulling a card?"

Andrine shoved her chair away from the table, stood, and stomped to the front door. "You can just leave, *Miss Aster*. Right now. Walk out this door and don't come back. I won't entertain folks in my home what dishonors me."

Boo shoved her chair back. "I thought you were a friend in time of need, but I guess I was wrong about that." She started to the door again, but Wouf stood just outside the screen like she had before, but this time, a deep growl filled Wouf's throat.

"What is it?" Boo argued with the animal.

Wouf held her stiff-legged stance, blocking Boo's way.

"So, you're siding with her, huh? Well, you can just live here with her, then. I'm leaving." She pushed her way past Wouf and headed down to the dock, smoke coming out of her nose—or at least she felt that hot.

But when she reached the pirogue and saw Dawg's favorite rawhide gnaw toy in the bottom, her heart melted. Andrine had said both Dawg and Sasha were still alive. She guessed she could hang onto that hope and put up with a little more of Andrine's nonsense. She ducked her head in shame and headed up to the house again. Wouf stood watching her the whole way.

Instead of knocking, this time she opened the screen and marched in. "Okay, okay. Go ahead, tell me what Page of Cups says."

Andrine took Boo's shoulders and looked her square in the eye. "This is serious business, Boo Murphy. Don't put your loved ones at risk by your stubborn, closed-minded attitude about things you don't understand. This ain't black magic. It's just a way for folks to tap into what they already know, deep inside they selves. God works in all kinds of ways and uses all kinds of mediums. I know you ain't much on church, but I never knowed you to shake your fist in the face of The Almighty."

"Quit your preaching and read the dang card." Once again, Boo flopped in the chair where she'd sat earlier.

Andrine took her chair as well, picked up the card, studied it then chuckled. "You ain't gonna like what I tell you—but what else is new? You pulling this card says there's a love affair in the works."

"A what?" Durwood flitted through her thoughts again, but she made sure he went all the way through and out the other side.

Andrine laughed. "I never knew you had it in you.

Here you always push everybody away—even me, and we been friends for years. But this card ain't about friendship as much as it is about love."

"What the heck does that have to do with me finding Dawg and Sasha?"

"Let's pull another card and see. Cut the deck again."

Boo turned over the top card and put it on the table between them.

"King of Pentacles. Hmm. There's someone you might consult, somebody you trust.

"Well, I reckon that's you. Humpf. Okay, give me another one."

Andrine turned another card, the sight of which startled Boo.

"Why's that lightning striking that stone tower?" she asked, "and why are two people falling off? Is that Sasha and Dawg?"

"Could be. Only you know for sure. But I will tell you this. The Tower's a card in the Major Arcana. That means it's a card you don't want to mess with by ignoring. So my guess is, yes, you got serious risk here."

"Okay, talk to me." Boo scooted her chair closer to the table.

"Well, first, you need to remember they build towers on solid foundations and can be rebuilt should they crumble. You're strong, Boo Murphy, and whatever the outcome, you'll be fine. Actually, you'll be stronger than before."

"But you said they hadn't passed this life. That means they ain't dead yet. I might can still save them."

Andrine drew another card and turned it over. Eight colorful wands were arranged on the card.

"Expect the unexpected," Andrine said, with a smile on her face. "Your life's 'bout to get very busy. Nothing's gonna happen like you expect. Around every corner there's a surprise waiting for you."

"I ain't much for surprises. I hope at least they'll be good ones."

"Some will, but not all of them. Remember, some folks ain't what they tell you they is. But this is the time to grab that gold ring, or it'll slip out of your fingers."

"Gold ring my eye! This stuff ain't helping me a bit."

"I can't do it all, Boo. Dang it, you gotta work with me. I'm just giving it as I see it. You're the one who's gotta fill in the details."

Boo's patience with the whole process grew thin.

"Okay, one more," she said, ready to get on her way.

Andrine turned the next card. "*The Fool*, reversed."

Boo slammed her hands on the table. "I ain't no fool!"

"Fool reversed, I said," Andrine laughed. "Give me a chance here, okay? *The Fool* is the first card in the Major Arcana. You've had two in it now. Remember? If you notice, the other cards had numbers on them. This is the only one what doesn't. It can be at the beginning, or the end, or anywhere in between. *The Fool* is a card of starting over." Andrine threw her hands up in abandon. "It says, enjoy the journey."

"Okay, one more." Intrigued now, Boo scooted her chair closer to the table.

Andrine drew a card, looked at it, and roared with laughter before showing it. When she did, Boo saw three cups on a table surrounded by colorful drapes.

"There's gonna be a wedding," Andrine grabbed her belly and roared again. And my guess is, it's yours!"

"You're kidding me."

"Well, only a little bit. Three of Cups hints of a birth or a wedding, but it can also foretell about success in a project."

"Like finding Sasha and Dawg? If so, I'll take that one." It may not have been, but for the first time, Boo noticed she'd switched from putting Dawg's name first, to that of Sasha. Maybe she really did love the old girl. If that was the case, she needed to get busy finding both of them. She shoved her chair back and stood. "Okay, I think I'm seeing what you're saying. You give me what the cards say, but I have to make the information fit me."

"Exactly. You cut the cards, so it's what they call your subconscious telling your conscious mind. As I said, cards ain't magic—like lots of folks what're scared of them think. They ain't against God or Jesus or any other holy being. Cards just help you tap into what you know on the inside."

"Okay, I think I know what to do now. I'm gonna find those two and bring them home if its the last thing I do."

"At least the last thing you do before you get married."

"But there sure aint' gonna be no dang wedding!"

She headed out the door, leaving Andrine balled over with uproarious laughter.

No sooner had she hit the front steps than she realized night had fallen. Hating to go inside and face the woman again, she had little choice but to do so. She grabbed her sleeping bag from the pirogue and went inside, prepared for a long, ridiculous evening.

Chapter Twenty-Nine

The next morning, while Andrine still snored, Boo rolled up her sleeping bag and slipped out before daybreak. She found Wouf in the pirogue, waiting. More determined than ever to find Sasha and Dawg and be done with the whole mess, Boo climbed in herself, and off they went.

She hadn't gone far when a creepy feeling crawled up her spine and settled at the base of her neck. She glanced at Wouf, whose hackles stood on end.

"I get the feeling someone's watching us, girl. Wonder if it's the chieftan what just left Andrine's last night. Could've been, he saw us and waited all this time for us to leave." She slowed her speed and watched, eyes pealed for the slightest movement, sound, or smell.

A shot rang out from her left.

She ducked, yelling for Wouf to do the same, and then heard a yelp and saw the animal crumple to the bottom of the boat.

Panic squeezed her chest. "Not Wouf, too. Criminy,

what do these people want with me?" She rowed to shore expecting more shots to follow.

None did. Instead, everything went quiet except for the ripples of water lapping the shore. She sloshed to the bank and pulled the pirogue under a stand of bushes and went to Wouf. The critter's eyes gleamed in pain, but the bullet had merely pierced her shoulder and gone all the way through with little bleeding.

Relieved, Boo grabbed a handful of healing herbs, spit on it enough to make a pack, and covered the wound. "This'll help it heal. You stay here. I'm gonna sneak around and see who's up to this nonsense. I'll come for you. Promise."

Wouf whined.

"But if I don't, get back, you'll know what to do for yourself." She kissed the wolf's head, grabbed her shotgun, and sneaked through the bushes. When she found no one, only an empty casing on the ground, she wondered if perhaps the shot was a hunter, accidentally taking aim at any innocent wild critter. Maybe.

Regardless, she had to be sure. Shoving aside brush and overgrowth, she peered behind trees and outcroppings of rock. A sound behind her made her spin, but just as she did, instant pain and blackness consumed her. Vaguely aware of falling...

Pain, bad pain, head, stiff, aching were the feelings and thoughts that came to Boo as consciousness slowly returned. Then came the realization she was way too old for this kind of life.

When she opened her eyes and looked around, she realized someone must have transported her to this place, and it looked awfully familiar.

The cot, the table, and chairs, the sink...the pet bowl

on the floor...

Shadrach. She was in Shadrach's cabin. She sat up faster than the pain allowed and immediately crashed to the cot. When the pain eased, she looked around, realized she was alone, and started up again, slower this time.

So far so good. After the room stopped whirling, she swung her feet to the rough plank floor and tested her ability to stand. Taking her time, she hobbled her way to the door holding onto what support she found along the way.

She reached for the door handle and pulled, but the door, swollen from humidity wouldn't budge. She went to the window and looked out but saw no one. She banged on the thick glass to test its strength. Breakable, she thought, but not without a chair or something heavy. She tried to pick up one of the two chairs but lacked the strength. "In a minute," she mumbled. "Once I get my strength , I think I can break out of here."

She stumbled to the cot and lay down, hoping the room would stop spinning. Her head burned like fire. She felt the back of it and came up with a hand covered in half-dried blood. She looked down at her shirt and found dried blood.

She hadn't been too sure about Shadrach. Suspecting all along that his motives weren't pure, now she knew they weren't. The guy must be in cahoots with Peabody and the rest of them. But she never would a figured him to shoot an innocent wolf.

Then she realized the bullet hadn't been intended for Wouf. Maybe it had her name on it. That's it. *Shadrach meant to shoot me, but he ain't a good shot.*

Then why didn't he just shoot her from behind, instead of hitting her on the head and transporting her all the way upriver to his place? The whole thing just didn't make sense.

She must have dozed, because the light from the window had grown dark when the sound of someone yanking on the door awakened her.

Boo tried to sit up, but decided against it and lay still as a mouse, eyes closed.

The door creaked open, but Boo dared not look. She had to give whoever it was time to check on her and get busy building a fire or something. Then she'd slip out.

The sound of someone lighting the lantern and boots scuffing across the floor was almost more than she could resist, but she slowed her breathing more and lay still.

That is until cold, rough fingers touched her throat and said, "S'what I thought. You're playing possum. You can open your eyes, Boo. Thank goodness you're awake."

When she did, Shadrach stood over her, his black face glistening from the lit candle in his hands.

She eased her legs off the cot and raised to a sitting position. "I should've known you wasn't who you said you was. I figured you was in cahoots with the other folks from the start. You just play dumb. But you ain't. As I said, you look like Uncle Remus, and you's smart as him, telling them Brer Rabbit stories to the kids. Like the stories you been telling me."

"I was a feared you'd think that. But, I swear to you Boo. Believe me or not. I didn't hit you. It looked like you was unlucky enough to be standing in the wrong place at the wrong time. A tree toppled, and one of the branches must've grazed your head on its way down."

"Well, I don't believe you. So there."

"Have it your way, honey. Least that careless hunter didn't shoot you like he did the wolf. Dumb guy thought he was about to be attacked by the critter."

"Don't give me that hogwash. T'was you. I know. Why're my wrists and ankles red and raw looking."

"'Cause I had to tie you on a pole to drag you here. You ain't so light, you know." He chuckled. "Now, don't be put off by that. I know women folk get sensitive about their weight."

"Oh, hell's bells, that stuff ain't never bothered me."

A movement slashed across the window and then scuffling sounds on the door stoop.

"Shhh, listen."

The door handle rattled, but Shadrach had locked it behind him when he entered. He eased over, put his ear to the door, and listened. Without saying a word, he cracked the door and slipped outside.

More shuffling.

Boo held her breath when the door flung wide. Wouf bounded in and made a beeline to her side. Right behind the critter, Durwood stumbled in, his arm twisted behind his back and held by Shadrach.

"Ouch, ouch, easy, mister. I ain't about to do nobody any harm. Look at me, I'm just an old codger."

"Durwood? What the bejesus you doing here?" Boo tried to get to her feet, but dizziness stalled the motion.

"I'm out trying to find you."

"But how did you..."

About that time, another wild animal bounded into the room behind the others.

"Dawg?! Where'd you come from?" Boo jumped up but had to steady herself. Meanwhile, Dawg bounded across the room. The two collapsed into each other and sunk to the floor. Sobs racked Boo's body, but this time, she didn't care who saw her cry.

"I found you by following these two critters!" Durwood said, wiping his eyes on his shirt sleeve.

"But how? Where?"

Durwood explained how he had the feeling Boo was in trouble and took off into the swamp on his own, even stopped by Andrine's, who told him she'd seen Boo and the direction he might take to find her. A day later, and lost himself, he stumbled on Dawg, half-starved to death but sniffing the ground as if following a trail. "I caught a couple of fish for us, cooked them over the fire, and we was both ready to take off again. Then yesterday, we come upon this wolf," he said, pointing. "They both must've smelt you on the other because they went wild sniffiing on each other. I figured I might's well follow the two of them 'cause they got better noses than me. Then today, we seen this guy here dragging you by the armpits. His pulling you across the bayou caused them to lose your scent for a while, or we'd a been here before this guy walked back in. But I see now we're all his hostages."

"Hostages?" Shadrach spewed spittle. Like Durwood, he wiped his mouth with his sleeve and continued on. "Where do you get off that? I'm on her side, too!"

Boo saw the look on Durwood's face and knew the green-eyed monster surfaced behind his own eyes, but before she could explain, Durwood yanked his arm loose and whirled around to face Shadrach. "Don't tell me I got a little competition."

"I'm Boo's friend. I ain't competition."

"Whew, that's a relief. But..."

"If the two of you will shut your trap and let me catch you up on what I know, maybe we can find Sasha."

"Sasha?" Durwood looked from Shadrach to Boo. "What do you mean, find Sasha?"

Forcing more patience from herself than she thought was even in there, Boo explained. "These people did have Sasha and Dawg both. Guess Dawg got away. Knowing him, he likely chewed through the ropes." She rubbed his head and found a wound still healing. "So that's where they hit you, eh boy?" He licked Boo's face all over. "I'm glad to see you, too," she said, laughing until her sides hurt.

"Will somebody tell me what's going on?" Durwood stood in the middle of the floor looking as lost as a goose.

Boo recounted the tale from start to finish. Throughout the telling, she noticed the lines in

Durwood's face growing deeper.

When she finished, he hung his head. "I warned you about going out there around them people, Missy."

Boo waved him off. "Lotta notice I give what you tell me."

"Well, you dang well should care. Scares the beejeebies out of me, knowing you're out here by yourself getting into all kinds of trouble."

While Durwood complained, Boo saw Wouf ease in beside Dawg, who shifted to make room. Worrying about how the two might get along, much less live together, was a waste of Boo's time. Maybe critters weren't as jealous as men.

Wouf and Dawg stood looking at each other as if they both thought all three of the humans had gone slap crazy. Which sent Boo into a peal of laughter, and was soon joined by Shadrach and Durwood.

"I got my boat down by the river, and your's, too, Boo. When we ran up on the wolf here, she was sitting in it like she expected you to come back any minute. When you didn't, I just tied it to mine and towed it. Let's get out of here at first light."

"I don't know where you two're going, but I'm heading to the Atakapa camp to settle up with Peabody and get Sasha. Ain't going home without her."

"I sure ain't letting you go by yourself." Durwood said. "Shadrach, you going?"

"At this point, I'm in this up to my ears," Shadrach said. "So, you're not leaving me behind. I gotta see this through to the end."

No sooner had they reached the river than Wouf and Dawg headed straight to Boo's boat and jumped in, claiming their places first, Dawg as front guard and Wouf bringing up the rear.

Boo needn't have worried about the two getting along, for it seemed they communicated at a deeper level than humans, each understanding the needs and rights of the other without argument, without diatribe, and without a fight. Contrary to the two men who shuffled back and forth trying to figure out who went with Boo and who went in Durwood's boat. Shadrach had moved toward Boo's vessel, but before he could get in, Durwood bustled over and took him by the elbow. "Come on, Shadrach, you ride with me."

"You think she'll be okay by herself? Don't you think one of us should go with her?" Shadrach gave Boo a knowing smile but followed Durwood. The two flat-bottom boats soon plied the water, Boo in front, the men following her.

The closer they got to the Atakapa camp, the higher the panic built in Boo's chest. What if she got there and found Sasha's dead body. Which made her wonder about the dead man in the house—that Rafe Nations guy, Peabody said his name was. Humph, at this point, she doubted any and everything the man told her.

But when they got to the Atakapa campsite, there was nothing left, not a scrap of paper, not a half-burned piece of wood. It was if no one had ever been there. Even the ground had been swept clean of anything that might indicate there had ever been a soul there, much less a whole tribe of people.

"What's going on?" Durwood said. "You sure this is the right place? Are you sure you're sure? Maybe you made a wrong turn somewhere. It don't look like nobody's ever been here before—at least in a very long time."

"I'm going check the house. At least, I know it'll still be there." She took off down the path she'd taken earlier, the others trailing behind.

Bursting out into the open field, the house stood right where she expected. Thank goodness that hadn't vaporized. Boo hurried to the structure and went underneath to check the tarp where she'd seen the bodies of Dead-Man and Mili.

Expecting to be overcome with stench, she covered her nose and mouth with her hands and then lifted the tarp.

Nothing. No one. Clean as a whistle. Not even a drop of blood.

"I guess the sheriff came and got them." Boo almost dropped her drawers when she looked up to see a headless man coming through the bushes toward them.

"What's that?" she said, pointing.

Durwood looked up and immediately grabbed her arm. "Good lord almighty."

Shadrach followed their gaze and whispered. "That's your Dead-Man. The Atakapa call him Cakta'Lko—human skin desirer. They believe after a man dies, he desires the skin of another and walks around looking for it. See, he's not headless, his head's just dropped forward on his chest."

The weird-looking figure turned and walked into the woods, leaving Boo shaken. Durwood didn't look too stable either, but he found his voice before she did. "You poor baby, you've been through so much. Let's go over here and sit down. We'll go home and get this all figured out."

"Speak for yourself. I'm not leaving here till I find Sasha. If you want to, you go right ahead, but I'm not stopping."

"I'm not saying forget her, but you can't stay out here forever."

"Who says I can't?"

"Tell her, Shadrach. Tell her she needs to give this up."

Shadrach cleared his throat as he stepped forward. "I'm leaving now. There's something I need to go tend to. Take care."

Before Boo or Durwood could say a word, Shadrach turned the corner of the house and was gone.

Now, if she could just get Durwood out of her hair,

she might be able to do something worthwhile. Aha, get him to go for help.

"Durwood, I need you to go get the sheriff. I should've got you to do that a long time ago."

For the longest time, Boo felt his eyes boring into hers, but she dang sure wasn't gonna give in and look at him.

"I don't feel right leaving you here, Boo. Knowing you, you'll get in all kinds of trouble."

"No, I won't. I promise I'll wait right here till you get back."

"I don't know…"

"Hurry," she said, giving his a shove.

"I worry about you," he said, taking her hand. "I hate leaving you here, but I guess somebody's got to go get the sheriff and see if he can help us find Sasha."

"I'll be okay," she said. "I've got Dawg and Wouf with me."

"I know, but you're so dang stubborn." He looked pitiful, made her feel a little guilty for a minute, but she shoved that feeling down into her gut. No way could she let him know what she planned to do, or he wouldn't leave.

He hoped she'd change her mind, she knew that, but he climbed in, took off without a backward look.

She watched as his back grew smaller and smaller. After she lost sight of him, she rubbed the heads of Wouf and Dawg standing on either side of her. "Well, it's just the three of us now. That is unless Parahaia shows up again. These days, I never can tell."

An overwhelming sense of being alone washed over her. She felt just like she had the day she'd walked off from the lighthouse keeper. How would her life have been different had she married him and moved into the lighthouse?

In her mind's eye, she saw the two of them standing along the gulf shore, both young and so much in love it hurt, but saying goodbye all the same. Even today, she could smell and taste the salty air blowing in her face, feel the wind whipping her skirt around her legs, saying goodbye to love so long ago, but still only yesterday.

He'd said he couldn't give up the lighthouse because he saved lives. Without him, people would die on the jetties, die in the eddies, die on the shoals. He loved her all right, but not more than he loved saving lives. Saving lives saves futures, future families...

And she couldn't leave the swamp, she'd told him, "because as weird as it might sound, I *am* the swamp." Without it, she'd always felt like she wouldn't exist.

Water was water, but mingle salt and fresh, and it grew brackish, where no plant could live or grow. When they were together at the lighthouse, she always felt brackish. Maybe he'd felt the same way when he'd visited her.

And why was it that every time Durwood came around, she started thinking about her first love?

Dawg and Wouf sat on their haunches, staring up at her. When they saw her looking, they wagged their tails, and Dawg barked.

"Okay, you're right. Let's look around here one more time, then we'll head to the house and try to get a good night's sleep."

After several minutes combing through the area and finding nothing, she began to think maybe she'd imagined the whole camp, much like she'd believed Shadrach was one hundred and twenty years old. Like she'd imagined seeing her hand look like that of a young woman, like seeing a woman floating across the water, like seeing a dead man…wait…no… Sasha saw his body, too. Then, there was Mili?

If she wasn't losing her senses, then why had she seen Mili with maggots crawling all over her, then seen her later, back at camp? And who the heck was Shadrach, anyway?

And what happened to Sasha? Who had her? Where? She looked at Dawg, rubbed his head. He whined and moved in closer. "I just wish you could talk—tell me what you know, like where were you? Did you see Sasha?" He whined, looked behind him, and barked.

Chapter Thirty

As if her thoughts created reality, she saw Mili coming toward her from the trail that led to the house. She looked much the worse for wear. Dirt and grass stains smeared her clothes like she'd wallowed with a bunch of wild pigs. Her face was bruised and muddy. By the time she reached Boo, she was breathless.

"Boo, you're…in…danger. Go away…cousin…"

"Where is Sasha?" Boo grabbed Mili's elbow and led her to a felled tree. "Sit here, catch your breath, then tell me where Sasha is."

When her breath eased, Mili grabbed Boo's hand and squeezed. "I know you thought that was me under the tarp. They wanted you to think that."

"Then who was it?"

"One of our pregnant women here. She died in childbirth. They took my dress and—"

"Okay, young lady, it's time for you to spill the beans. What in the world's going on here? Where's my cousin, and who should I believe?"

"I'm not right sure, but I do know they took her.

"Okay, then, tell me where everybody's gone and why they'd leave?"

"Mouton threatened to kill them if they didn't."

"I thought they were here to build a new nation."

"That's not exactly true."

"Then what the heck is?"

"First off, I was duped. Yes, I'm an anthropologist, as my credentials show, and yes, my people and I came here and set up camp, but not to recreate a return to the old ways. The old ways are dead and gone. No one today wants to live the way of our ancestors. We just don't want to lose our identity. We want our story told. We want people to remember and respect us."

"Then how did Peabody convince them to come? He told me this was your project. Now you're telling me it was his?"

"We didn't come to find a silver mine. My people came because they were duped into thinking that if we helped Peabody find the mine, he would help us find a precious possession that belonged to our ancestors and perhaps was left in the silver mine long ago. Since he and his people aren't interested in finding it, my people left. But to keep them from talking, he's holding the chief captive. We came to find something lost long ago, but we didn't come here to find a silver mine. We don't care about something like that—but that's all he wants."

"Then, why?"

"Records show our people have been in this area at least since the 1500s when Spanish explorers came ashore. Our people have been called cannibal, thanks to the Choctaw, who told the French we ate people. That's not true, and we want to clear our name of that awful imagine we've lived with since then. But there's this talisman—"

"But I saw..." Boo stopped before she said

something that convinced Mili she was the crazy one—that she'd seen the chief feeding flesh to pregnant women.

Instead, she changed the subject. "But Mili, I did find the mine. I just haven't told anybody yet."

"You what?" Mili grabbed her arm just as Peabody burst through the bushes, a pistol in his hand.

"Thanks, Mili. You're a stupid flake, but you handled that really well," he said.

Boo glared at Mili, but at the same time stuck her hand behind her and motioned to Dawg and Wouf to back off into the woods, and heard them do as instructed.

"No, Boo, I didn't. He's lying. He didn't put me up to this—that's the truth."

"Well, let's put it this way. You're dumb enough to be followed and not even know it. How else would we all be here getting exactly what we want—of course, that doesn't include you, Miss Murphy. But you'll get over it. Now, let's get going. The one and same Miss Boo Murphy is going to take us to said mine."

"Be a cold day in hell the day I do anything for you, you lying cheating…"

"Be my guest." Peabody bowed and opened his arm out to her. "Call me what you want, however, climb in your boat while you can do so under your own strength. Delay much longer it'll be too late for your sister, and you won't be able to. That goes for you too, Mili."

He insisted he take the rear seat—Boo's place—and ordered Boo in the middle and Mili upfront. Boo chaffed against the fact that Peabody still called Sasha her sister—but she figured in the bigger scheme of things, the most important thing was to rescue Sasha—not whether Sasha was her sister, or a second cousin once removed.

Not accustomed to paddling from the middle, Boo struggled to get the boat turned and out into the middle of the water, but in time, the three traveled the swamp as night approached.

An hour or so later, a sudden bubble of light floated their way, then exploded right before it reached them. Boo didn't flinch, for she knew the omen, seen it many a time, and knew if someone didn't break the spell by plunging a knife in the ground, somebody was going to die, and soon.

"What the hell was that," Peabody yelled.

"It's called *Feu follet.* Some say its souls escaping purgatory, come for prayers," Boo said, glad he couldn't see the smirk on her face. "Others think it's evil and means somebody's about to die."

"Well, it sure isn't going to be me." Peabody shifted in the seat behind her.

A slight breeze picked up and scattered the clouds. Under different circumstances, Boo would be in heaven, but instead, her mind centered on Durwood, thankful he'd had the good sense to go get help. She wondered how long it might take, and if Dawg and Wouf could help them find her. But if they did, it might be too late.

Which was okay. She'd had a long, full life. The only regret might be that she'd never let anyone in—not since the lighthouse worker. That pain had been one she never wanted to feel again. But she sure would like to save Sasha first. All this had been Boo's fault. Sasha hadn't asked for any of it.

An unexpected nausea and weakness overtook Boo, and she slowed the paddling. When Peabody didn't complain, she knew the cool evening, and the hypnotic movement through the water had caused him to nod off. Even Mili's chin rested on her chest.

She recalled how Mama used to tell her that some beings are so strong in spirit before they die, that they take their spiritual power with them and get stronger. Then, they grow stronger quicker because a physical body doesn't tie them down. They can also suck energy from whatever is around them and use it to power themselves. Maybe a spirit just sucked some energy from her.

Maybe Parahaia.

Maybe Boo wasn't alone after all.

Later, Boo dozed herself, and only knew she'd gone to sleep when light pierced through the Spanish moss dangling from the trees overhead. She opened her eyes to realize she'd run aground a sandbar, and the boat sat motionless—for how long, she had no idea. The other two evidently still slept since neither of them had complained. Not wanting to raise the ire of Peabody, she eased the boat off the sandbar without looking back and soon had it in the middle of the river as the red ball crept higher.

Mili roused and looked over her shoulder. "Where are we?"

"Couple hours away," Boo whispered. "You getting hungry? Think he'd mind if we stopped? I'm sure needing a strong cup of black joe."

Boo turned to check with Peabody, but he no longer sat behind them—asleep or otherwise. Instead, he drifted face down in the current, an arrow sticking out his back. She knew then he wouldn't mind.

Chapter Thirty-One

Without a word, the two women hustled the boat to shore. Shivering from the cool morning air, not to mention the shock of seeing Peabody floating downriver, they collected pieces of dry wood and soon had a fire going and a pot of coffee boiling. Boo never went anywhere without a waterproof bag of essentials she kept in the bottom of the pirogue, including her old blue granite coffee pot and a tin of coffee.

Soon, they huddled around the fire, their hands cupped around the warm tin cups. Mili took one sip of the hot, black liquid and choked, making Boo chuckle. "Mama always did say my coffee would make hair grow on a woman's chest."

"Just what I always wanted, a hairy chest."

Boo waited a couple of minutes then jumped on the subject filling her head with confusion. "You gotta tell me what's going on. Tell me what I don't know—but should've known from the start."

"I don't know where to begin…" Mili rubbed her free hand down the side of her thigh as if stalling long enough to decide what to tell—or what to tell first."

"Okay, then I'll get it started. First off, what do you think we should do with the body? Go get it? Bury it? Take it in to the authorities? What?"

"I know what I'd like to do with it—feed it to the alligators." Mili avoided eye contact with Boo.

"I reckon that's gonna happen anyway." Boo peered downriver but no longer saw the body. "Likely they already got 'im. But what bothers me is you in cahoots with those two."

Mili put her cup beside her and buried her face in her hands and broke into sobs.

Boo slurped her coffee while the woman got the crying out of her system, wiped her eyes, and glanced at Boo. "We started out that way, but after Mouton came on board, it quickly disintegrated into another whole scenario."

"The bald-headed one?" Boo asked, wanting to make sure she heard correctly.

"That's the one. Sounds like I'm not the only one who doesn't trust him."

"The guy gives me the willies."

Mili gave a little laugh of understanding. "He does me, too. Anyway, after he came on board, the whole plan quickly disintegrated from helping our people to some get-rich-quick scheme. Mouton convinced Peabody there was money to be made by tricking my people and holding them hostage."

"Hostage? Where? How?"

"The plan was to gather those willing to replicate an Atakapa camp, stay out there for a couple weeks as an experiment, get the media involved, and try to raise funds to establish a foundation to fund research for our work.

"You mean to keep you working."

Mile ignored the implication. "We gathered a group

together—the ones you saw there earlier."

"Where are they now?"

"You mean right now—since Peabody lost control of the project?"

"I mean right now. Are they okay?"

"I think so, although Mouton is still controlling them—what they say, what they do. Earlier, he convinced the people to stay a little longer to make the whole project look up and above board. But, after you showed up and he was convinced you had the map, he didn't need them anymore. He sent them packing with strict instructions not to mention anything about the project to anyone—with the threat that should they do so, he'd make sure there wasn't a drop of Atakapa blood left in anybody living—that he'd even kill Ka, their high chief."

"So, you think Mouton's the one what shot and killed Peabody? Then why didn't he shoot us, too?"

"You saw that arrow in him, didn't you? That's one of his. I've seen them in his hut back at camp. My guess is he didn't shoot us because he's following us to the mine."

"Where does Tarek fit into all this?"

"My brother? He's being held captive with our father, the chief. They're both under lock and key to make sure I do what they say."

"Why you?"

"I'm the one who knows what we're looking for."

"The silver mines?"

"The silver mines, yes, but also the talisman."

"What talisman?"

"A talisman that our ancestors believed protected our people from sickness. We want it for our museum, but Mouton wants it for the price it would likely bring from collectors."

Mili grew quiet, and the silence grew longer.

"I'm still listening," Boo said, trying to sound

patient.

"Okay, Boo, here's the bottom line for me and my people," Mili scooted closer. "The original plan—the reason why so many people were willing to put themselves through the ordeal of living like we have been, is this. We are a proud people, and for centuries, the story has been twisted that our ancestors were cannibals."

"Yep, I heard that, too."

"They get the Atakapa-Ishak tribes mixed up with the Karankawa, who lived along the Texas coastal bend between Galveston and Corpus Christi. They were cannibals. The Atakapa-Ishak was not. That's not to say our ancestors might at one time have eaten a piece of flesh from their enemy in the belief that act would give them power over their enemy should they return in another life. But not cannibalism—we didn't eat people for food or for spite. Contrary to many of the other tribes who came on and off the scene over the centuries, our ancestors were peace-loving, friendly people."

Mili paused, stared at Boo for a couple of seconds, then turned her attention to the fire. "But for generations, the missing talisman seems to have taken the heart out of our people. That, and the fact we have never been recognized as a legitimate tribe by the U.S. government; therefore, we lost any chance for land in which to rebuild our nation. I think if we could somehow find that talisman—if it even still exists—I think our people would at least feel like we reclaimed something that belongs to us—and stolen by the early explorers."

"Humph. Not sure how a talisman's gonna give you all that, but I'm guessing you think it might be in the old silver mine. Right?"

"Legend is that the tribe kept it there so the Spaniards wouldn't get it—but they did, anyway."

Boo remembered the legend about the Yellow Fever epidemic Shadrach told her earlier.

"Our ancestors really weren't much into icons or things of that nature. They were a very primitive bunch of people. We've found very little art, drawings, and artifacts. They lived quite simply. Their pottery and the like wasn't decorative—simple utilitarian. So, if they had any such item, it would be easy to overlook. And if we don't find it in the mines, we don't have any idea where else to look."

"Mines, shmines," Boo said. "Tell me one thing—is Sasha dead or alive? I gotta know once and for all."

"I don't know for sure, but if she's alive, my guess is she's being kept in an old slave shack out at Deweyville—same place where they have Ka and Tarek."

"Is she hurt?"

"Don't know, but I figure our chance in saving her gets better if we give Mouton what he wants—the whereabouts of the mine. Let's go get proof we know where the mine is, and I know of no better proof than that talisman."

"Okay, another question. I could've sworn I saw you dead under that tarp."

"That's what they wanted you to think. Remember the woman you saw at the camp that first day? She went into early childbirth, and right after the baby was born, she hemorrhaged to death. They put her in my dress and stashed her there with Rafe, hoping to scare you off, then fed both of them to the alligators."

"Okay, that's enough. Let's see if I can find that mine again."

"Again?"

Boo pulled the map out of her pocket.

"So it was you that took it. I wondered." Mili said, a big grin spreading across the face.

The two dowsed the fire and headed out.

Chapter Thirty-Two

As they made their way upriver, Boo flirted with the idea of asking Mili about Parahaia, but it took her several tries before she finally got the question out of her mouth. "You know anything about a swamp spirit floating along just above the water, especially at dusk?"

Mili half-turned and looked over her shoulder. "I've heard about her, especially in the swamps around Orange, but I've never seen her. Some say they've felt her when goosebumps ran down their arms—things like that. You know, like when you feel something or someone watching? Our people believe she's an entity that keeps the swamp in balance. Been here from the beginning of time and gets really upset when people do things that mess up. Why? Have you seen her?"

"Yeah, and she keeps on showing up."

Mili's eyes got bigger. "If that's so, I rather suspect she's pretty upset."

"You mean about the storm we just had?" Boo

asked.

"Not that so much as something people do—like damming up portions of the river or leaving their trash behind."

"Or how about raping the earth's resources by strip mining silver?"

"That could do it, yes. Why?"

"Let's just say she has a way of letting me know she's here. This might sound crazy, but it's like she's trying to get me to do her work for her. Like she's disembodied, so needs a body to do stuff. That makes sense?"

"Perfect sense." Mili spoke with her back to Boo, shielding her eyes with the side of her hand, watching ahead of them. "She's not the only spirit out here, either. I've also heard tales of folks seeing an old black man who frequents the swamps, helping people who need it. Don't know if he's real or not."

"Look like Uncle Remus?"

"That's what I've heard, yes. Why, you see him, too?" She gave a quick glance over her shoulder then straightened forward.

"Yeah, but I'm not the only one."

"Oh, of course. Your cousin, Sasha."

Boo didn't confirm or deny—just let Mili assume she was correct. It had been Durwood, but something stopped her from bringing his name into the conversation. The fact that he'd gone to bring help just might need to be kept secret. She still didn't trust anyone.

"I'm not real sure I believe all those tales." Mili glanced back again. "But who knows?" she said with a shrug. "These days, there's not much I wouldn't believe."

"Who knows, for sure," Boo said, smiling to herself.

Soon, the area along the swamp looked familiar, so Boo slowed her paddling and eased along slower until she spotted where she'd tied up before. "This is it, I reckon. Time to get out and go explore a cave. It's really not a mine, you know. The Indians and Spaniards didn't turn it into a true working mine. Looks to me like they just went in and dug out the ore."

The two secured the pirogue, and just as they walked off, Boo remembered the emergency flares she'd stashed in her boat years ago—the same ones she'd wished for the last time she'd gone inside the cave. "Hold on just a minute, I gotta get something."

Back at the boat, she rummaged through her stash and came up with a handful of orange distress flares she kept in the boat in case she got in trouble. Guess this situation counted as one.

Hoping the humidity hadn't gotten to them, she tucked them into her pocket and rejoined Mili.

After a long, rough sweaty walk across boulders and through overgrowth, the two slipping and tripping and twisting their ankles, Boo located the mouth of the cave and pulled aside the brush.

"This is it. Here, I'll light a flare and lead the way. One thing about that map, though, is see that line going past the black X?"

"I didn't have enough light last time, but I think that will lead us through the cave. Keep track while we go."

"Okay, yeah, I see it here." Mili traced her fingers along the curving line.

"Good, let's see what we can find." She pulled one of the flares from her pocket, lit it, and the two stepped into musty blackness. The only sound, other than their breathing, was an occasional drip. The floor of the cave was anything but level and the two held onto each other as they made their way along the rough, slippery terrain.

"I hope we can find our way out of here," Mili said, her voice shaky.

"Hope so, too. I did the other day, so I reckon we can this time, too. Keep an eye on the line, and how many turns we make. We don't want to run out of light."

Boo wasn't ready to mention the skeleton and the

broken wine bottle.

They walked for the longest time, Mili, giving instruction on where to turn according to the lines on the map Boo had given her as they walked in. But they found nothing that looked like a talisman. At times, a little light filtered in from somewhere, which helped them see their surroundings a little clearer.

In time, the dampness did a number on Boo's joints. They ached to beat sixty. She'd stop to rest, but that just made it harder to get going again.

Weary, Boo pulled another flare out of her pocket. "If we don't find the talisman soon, we're going to have to give up. We're about out of flares, and we ain't found nothing. If we leave right now, we're still likely to have dark on the way out." She lit another flare.

To her surprise, the light revealed a large room where water dripped from the ceiling, leaving the whole floor wet and slippery.

What startled her more than the size of the room, however, was the cave wall. Something about it rang a bell. She plowed her hand deep into the pocket of her overalls. Her fingers clasped a rough, hard object—the piece of ore that had rolled off the shell midden and landed at her feet that night back at the house. After extracting it from her pocket, she looked from the ore to the cave, then crossed the room and held it up to the wall.

A perfect match.

Boo looked at Mili. Wow, too many pieces of the puzzle were coming together to doubt either Shadrach or Parahaia.

Mili whispered, but still her voice echoed back at them. "This is awesome. Look at that high ceiling—those lines on the walls. They're elementary—quite simple, really, nothing distinguishable, not like some of the ancient cave drawings, for sure. But look at this one." She pointed to a wavy, horizontal line with something underneath, and then a rustic looking figure coming up through the wavy lines that reminded Boo of water.

Mili traced the etchings as if hypnotized by what they might represent. "This room must have been a holy place of some kind, Boo. Whoever drew this…" Her voice broke. She cleared her throat and started again. "My ancestors believed they came from the sea—this confirms it—at least it does to me. Wow." She looked around the room. "They must have seen this cave as special—a gift from the gods."

They moved around the room, holding onto each other for stability, checking every nook and cranny until the flare died, and the room went pitch black. "I have a couple more left. We need to start back, or we'll be in here forever." Boo lit another flare and headed back the way they'd come, but Mili caught her arm and pulled her to a pile of rocks.

"Just a little longer, Boo. Let me check this right quick." She started removing rocks from the stack. "My people buried their chiefs in shell mounds. Maybe they used the same process to hide a talisman."

"Well, we'll need to hurry." Boo joined in the search and tossed a couple of rocks aside. The rumble echoed through the tunnel.

A sudden scream from Mili sent a chill over Boo. She looked up to see Mouton stepping from behind a rock formation, a flashlight in one hand, a gun in the other, and behind him, a stack of collapsing wooden kegs, silver spilling out.

Mili's scream echoed back at them. Boo came closer to messing in her pants than she ever had in her life.

"Good afternoon, ladies. Glad to see you finally made it. Welcome to the soon-to-be Mouton Silver Mine. As you can see, I found the kegs, so that should give me enough money to excavate and rebuild."

Boo stared at the man, hardly believing her eyes. Here she'd met the man maybe once or twice, and now it seemed he'd been at the root of the scheme all this time.

"So you're the one been following us. How'd you get ahead?"

"When you have eyes like a bat, it's easy to slip around two slowpoke women. Figured if I gave you enough rope, you'd… Problem is I didn't know you could be a real pain in the rear. I knew Ka had gone to see that voodoo woman. Figured he'd be onto us pretty quick, so I had to move quickly."

"So, let me guess. You're the one who shot Peabody."

Mouton smiled. "I wield a mighty bow, arrow, and string—better shot than I thought. Too bad no one was around to see it. Guess I'll have to thank my ancestors for that. Must be in my DNA."

"Why didn't you shoot us, too?"

"I still needed you to lead me here. No hurry. We've got plenty of time."

"Time for what?" Boo wasn't done. She wanted to know the whole story, and the more she stalled and fed his ego, the better.

"I have someone I thought you might want to see." He took a step behind the outcropping and pulled on something.

That something was Durwood with a gag in his mouth and his hands tied behind his back.

Boo's heart felt like it hit her knees before it quit falling. What had she done?

But she sure wasn't going to let this guy know how she felt. No sense in giving him more ammunition. "Pffft, makes me no never mind," she spouted. "He's just an old busy-body fool anyway."

The pain on Durwood's face almost made her take back what she'd said, but she steeled her nerves, knowing if he had any chance for survival, she must stay strong—or at least act like it. "So you've been the one calling the shots all along," she said, glaring at Mouton. "I never would've guessed. Didn't think you was smart enough—

mean enough, maybe, but—"

"That's the beauty of looking stupid. No one did. They all thought me a stooge, mindless, brainless. Looks can be deceiving. You ought to know." His course laughter set off another echo that bounced off the walls.

What about the chief? Where is he? Mili asked. "And my brother, Tarek? What did you do with them?"

"They're not dead, if that's what you mean, but they will be if I don't get back before alligator feeding time— if you catch my drift."

Boo looked at Mili. "So you and Peabody started all this just for the silver, and look what it got you."

"No, Boo. Remember, I told you what my intent was. I thought Peabody was working for the same reason. After all, he is—was—Ishak just like me."

Mouton mocked her. "Somehow they had a problem with being thought of as a cannibal. Can't imagine why. Shoot. If I get hungry, I just might eat this young thing— or maybe I won't wait until she's dead…" He sneered at Mili, leaving no doubt what he meant.

Anxious to find out if Durwood had made any contact with the authorities, Boo got his attention and mouthed the word *sheriff*, questioning in her eyes. He locked eyes with her and gave a slight shake of his head. Just enough so she knew they were on their own.

"Now, the two of you," Mouton said, pointing to Boo and Mili, "put those rocks back like you found them."

"Why? You're gonna tear it all up, anyway," Boo said, derision coating her words.

He threw his head back and laughed, adding, "That's certainly my intent, missy, it's certainly my intent. But in the meantime, you do what I say, or Durwood here will be sorry." He yanked Durwood's arm, making him stagger.

Stuffing her anger, she turned and started replacing the rocks, soon joined by Mili.

But as they did, Boo's hand grasped something that felt different than the other rocks. Smaller, smoother, thinner, flatter, with a hole in the middle. When Mouton looked the other way, Boo dropped it in the top pocket of her overalls.

After they finished, Mouton shoved Durwood and pointed back toward the entrance. "Okay, get going. It's a cinch I can't kill all of you and leave you here to be found once we start excavations."

The beam from his flashlight bounced off the walls as they walked, spotlighting, for Boo, at least, veins of copper ore that likely included silver. So this was indeed the same mine Peabody wanted. That's all this area needed, excavations that dug, ripped, and destroyed. No wonder Parahaia needed help. Well, Boo would dang well give it to her. People might think Boo was a cold, hard, uncaring person—and maybe she was--but she dang sure was no quitter.

Once outside, Mouton herded Boo, Mili, and Durwood to where he'd anchored his motorboat. He shoved Durwood, still bound and gagged, in front, Mili and Boo on the middle seat while he sat in back and drove.

Boo's concern for Durwood grew with each mile they traveled. He'd grown more pale and listless, like he'd lost the energy to live.

They traveled for a ways when, without warning, Mouton steered the boat to shore and forced them all out. "Follow that trail up ahead."

The three did as they were told, Boo on one side of Durwood and Mili on the other, offering what support they could. By now, Boo wasn't sure how much longer she could go, and Durwood was on his last leg, for sure. None of them had eaten for hours, with almost nothing to drink, not to mention a weariness that penetrated the very marrow of her bones. Again, she asked herself how she'd let her passion—her curiosity—get her into such a fix.

Not just her, but others as well. She didn't feel accountable for Mili, but she still felt sorry for her and her people. They had nothing to do with Mouton's evil ways.

After a lengthy tromp through the woods, a large, dilapidated building came into view. A building that looked like if enough people pushed, the whole thing would collapse to the ground. Large cracks between the weathered boards allowed snakes, bugs, and hopefully, a little light inside. Mouton herded them straight for the door, then signaled them to halt while he lifted the two by four barring the door. Once opened, he shoved them into the dark, dank stinky room. But a beam of sunlight streaked through the cracks, spotlighting Sasha, Ka, and Tarek sitting on the dirt floor, backs to each other, hands tied behind their backs. Tape covered their mouths and bound their knees to their chest. Sasha sagged forward like she might be out of it, and Ka wasn't far behind. But not Tarek, his eye's flamed with anger.

"Move!" Mouton said, shoving them deeper inside.

But as he shoved, a sudden chill wrapped Boo in a heightened state of alert.

Fall back against him. The words formed in her head.

She did, hoping he'd either catch her or at least break her fall. A broken hip, and she might as well say her Hail Marys.

It was at that instant that a blurry streak, followed by another, launched through the door, leapt on Mouton and wrestled him to the ground amidst growls, bites, yelps, and flailing legs.

Before Boo could get to her feet, Wouf and Dawg had Mouton under submission, one at his jugular, the other holding onto his groin, while his gun slid across the dirt floor toward Durwood.

"Durwood, do something!" she yelled. "Kick it!"

He tried. But when he did, he stumbled and fell on

his face.

"Hold him there," Boo yelled to Wouf and Dawg, and clambered over to the gun and forced her stiff, aching fingers around the cold, hard metal. Never in her life had anything felt as good as did that gun.

The critters held Mouton while Boo untied Durwood and helped him to his feet. He eased the tape from his mouth while Boo untied Tarek, who grabbed the gun from Boo and hurried to Mouton.

Boo's knees wobbled. Her thoughts went from, *Oh lord—we're all dead meat* to, *so this is how I'm going to die.*

But before the critters could let go of their hold on Mouton, Tarek raised the gun over his head and brought it down on Mouton's head. *Whack!*

When Mouton didn't move, Boo looked at Tarek. "He's not dead, is he?"

He checked Mouton's pulse. "No, he's not dead, but he'll have one doozy of a headache in the morning." he said, laughing. "Or at least I hope he does." He faced Boo, looked her square in the eye then bowed deeply. "I really have to hand it to you, Ms. Murphy. You're quite a woman. I figured you were that first day we met on the trail, but I had no idea how much. You have certainly earned my respect and the respect of my people. We will forever be grateful. A man might pull the wool over another's eyes, but often it takes a woman to see through him."

Boo's cheeks felt hot. She put her hands up to feel, for she never remembered having blushed before.

Mili leaned over and whispered in Boo's ear, "let's just forget about that cave. I think our people and our world is better off leaving it like it is—undiscovered."

Boo rushed over to check on Sasha, who had finally roused from her stupor enough to hoarsely yell, "Get me loose from here…where's my lipstick?"

Chapter Thirty-Three

Boo sat on the edge of Sasha's bed wiping her cousin's forehead with a cool washrag. Sid came in from the kitchen with two mugs of warm chicken broth. "Okay, you two. Now's the time for you to let someone else take care of you for once in your life. Here, drink this and don't put it down until you've drained it dry."

Boo took a sip of hers and then studied Sid. "I'm still trying to figure out how in the world you hooked up with the sheriff's deputies just as they were coming to get us."

Sid chuckled. "That was the easy part. Just getting home from New Mexico was the hardest." She recounted her road adventure with Annie, timing belts, Beetle Bailey, ghosts, and all. The three women laughed so hard they had to hold their bellies in pain.

After Sid recovered enough to speak, she continued. "I was doing my dead level best to get back here and help you guys any way I could. Turns out, you didn't need me. By the time I wheeled into the parking lot of the

Sherriff's office, your friend Tarek had arrived, told what happened, and they were loading up to go. I got in the cruiser and wouldn't get out. They had two choices—take me with them or arrest me." She nudged the bottom of Boo's mug and tilted it up. "Drink."

Sasha grabbed Boo's hand. "I never been prouder of you, sweetheart. For once in my life, I was glad you didn't act like a lady. And I ain't never going to complain about Dawg again.

"You and your critters make quite a team," Sid said. "Before I know it, you're going to put me out of business."

The sheriff's deputies transported them home, where EMS awaited their arrival.

They each received IV drips and had insect bites, cuts, and scrapes cleaned and medicated. Before EMS left, they encouraged them to check with their personnel physicians the following day.

Again, Boo submerged the cloth into the dishpan of cool water, wrung it out, and wiped Sasha's face. "I'm so sorry. I shouldn't have gotten you into all that."

Sasha put her hand on Boo's. "You had no idea that was going on, honey. It's okay. Just don't ever ask me to go out there again, okay?"

Boo sputtered with laughter. "Not to worry. I dang sure won't."

"She sure won't," Durwood said, "'cause she ain't going out there no more. That is if I got something to do with it." Durwood had gone outside to feed and water Dawg and Wouf and now slipped in without their noticing. He moved behind Boo, his hand resting on her shoulder.

"Now wait just a goll darn minute." Boo shoved his hand off. "I never said I ain't going again. 'Course I'm going. Ain't the swamp's fault people do what they do." Besides, she still intended to go back and find the skeleton of the man she suspected was A Phillips.

Nothing there of value, but her mind wouldn't ease until she solved that mystery. Poor guy likely crawled in there, drank his wine, and waited for death. Life was lonely when a body lost everyone who mattered.

Boo hadn't seen Parahaia again, but now she knew when the floating figure appeared, she needed Boo's help.

"Now you all get," Sasha ordered. "I'm going take a nap, then I'm going to get down on my knees and thank the good lord I made it out of alive—that we all did."

"Ain't you supposed to get down on your knees and do that before you sleep," Boo said as she and Durwood headed toward the front door.

"I would, but I'm just too dang tired. I figure it's okay to do it backward this one time in my life."

"I reckon so, sweetheart. You take a rest. I'll cook you some food and bring it over later."

"I'll stay here with Sasha a little while longer," Sid said. "The two of you need a little time alone. I'll check on you before I head home."

By the time Boo and Durwood eased out the front door, a soft snore already issued from Sasha's bed. Sid rattled dishes in the kitchen.

The two crossed the yard, Boo expected him to head to his truck and go home, but he didn't. Instead, he followed her inside, sat on the divan, and waited. For what, Boo wasn't sure.

"Don't know if I told you or not, Boo, but thank you for saving my life. I thought I was gonna save yours, but…"

"No biggie." Boo waved her hand in dismissal.

"I reckon you don't need me," he said, sadness coating his voice. "I'll leave you alone." He rose and headed to the door.

"Oh hell's bells, Durwood. I never said I didn't *want* you."

He stopped in his tracks and looked over his

shoulder, his face a question mark.

Boo smiled at him. "Wanna help me cook for Sasha?"

"Gonna make them biscuits?" He smiled.

"Thought I would."

"If you'll loan me your iron skillet, I'll fry up a mean pile of bacon while you make them biscuits. That okay?"

"Sure, come on." She hooked her arm through his, and they went toward the kitchen. He sure didn't smell like Old Spice, or any other kind of aftershave for that matter, especially since he hadn't shaved in several days, and all because of her. But something about him smelled—well…not so bad…really, not so bad at all.

An hour later, they delivered the food, and Durwood and Boo returned to clean the kitchen.

After he'd dried the last dish, he hung the dishtowel on a hook and prepared to leave. "Know you don't like fussing over, so I ain't. But one day soon, I'd like you to tell me the whole story. I know there's more to it than what you told the sheriff—'specially 'cause you didn't mention that Shadrach fellow to the deputy, or tell where you found that wolf hanging around outside with Dawg."

Boo ignored the comment until he turned and headed to his truck, shoulders slumped and feet dragging.

She hurried to the door and called after him, "Hey, want to come for Sunday dinner?"

He turned, a bright, toothy smile spreading across his face, and took a couple steps her way. "You ain't never asked me for Sunday dinner before."

"Well, don't get used to it," she said, crinkling her eyes at him. "Besides, I ain't told you about the talisman I found in the mine, either. Don't forget to remind me on Sunday." She smiled and patted her pocket.

"I won't forget, that's for dang sure." He climbed in his truck and headed out of the yard. It backfired while Boo stood watching it turn onto the road.

"Maybe he ain't so bad after all." She walked to

Dawg and Wouf who lay on the ground watching her every move.

"Don't say a word." She shook her finger at both of them.

Eyebrows raised, they cut their gaze up to hers.

"And don't play innocent with me."

Each ducked their head and covered their eyes with their paws.

"That's better." Exhausted, she plopped on the steps and allowed events of the last few days to traipse through her thoughts.

But when she did, a familiar figure headed through the shadows created by a low-hanging moon.

Shadrach.

"You did real good, Boo," he said, laughter in his voice. "And you're learning those lessons, I see. I like that you suggested to the sheriff that the Mexican pieces of silver be turn over to the remaining Atakapa tribe. That'll help them rebuild their heritage."

She made room for him beside her on the steps. "Least I could do. The way you kept appearing and disappearing, I should've known you'd show up after everything was over. You got some explaining to do, mister."

"Let me guess. You want to know how I knew all that about Parahaia, and your connection to her."

"That, and how in the world you've lived so many years—unless you're lying."

"I'll have you know I don't lie, Ms. Murphy." He puffed out his chest.

It was Boo's turn to chuckle.

"Not sure I should tell you this—or anybody else, even—since it ain't likely to do you no good, but here it is." Shadrach cleared his throat and sat up straighter. "I must've been fifty—maybe sixty. One day I went out to gather firewood for my cookstove when I come across this weird-looking pine tree full of odd-looking pinecones. I'd never seen cones like that before and ain't seen any since."

"How'd they look?" Boo glanced at him to see if he was *pulling her leg*, but he looked as serious as the day had been long.

"Like some freak of nature or something. They had a kind of coiled shape. You know—like two long, narrow snakes corkscrewing around each other."

"Know what kind of pine tree it was?"

"Best I could figure, a deformed long-leaf yellow pine. Anyway, as I was saying, I gathered a few cones, took them home and dumped them next to the cookstove, thinking they'd make a good fire. A few days later, I noticed a handful of pine nuts had fallen out on the stone hearth. I tossed a few in my mouth and chewed, thinking little of it."

"Pine nuts, you say." Boo fidgeted on the porch step, wondering what he'd come up with next.

"After a few days, I noticed my arthritis felt better and better—I didn't ache so much."

"So you figured the pine nuts did it?"

"No, not for a while. But I kept nibbling on them because they were tasty, and every day, I felt younger and younger. I could walk farther, and I ate better. Then, when I looked in the mirror one day and noticed my hair had stopped turning white, that's when it come to me— the pine nuts."

"Likely story. Now tell me how old you are, really."

"Believe it or not, Boo. That's the God's honest truth."

"Okay, then answer me this. How come you show up and disappear so fast? Did them pine nuts give you special powers or something?"

Shadrach stood as if to go, evidently changed his mind, and resumed his seat on the step. "I feared you'd ask me that question. I ain't got no answer for it though. I ain't got no idea how that happens. I just know it do."

"And you ain't gonna show me the tree or the pine nuts, are you?"

He shook his head. "Can't. After I figured out it was the pine nuts, I kept going out there every year collecting the cones. Then one day, I went like I always did, and to my horror, a bunch of men stood around the fallen tree. They'd sawed it, and all the other trees around it, down and was loading them on a big pulpwood truck. Bulldozers had already cleared the land around the area. Weren't a pinecone left. What might've been on the ground was now buried under the mud and muck. I scavenged and found a few the bulldozer missed. Nuts from them held me up until a few years ago."

"So you're aging again. That means you're gonna get older and finally die like everybody else?"

Shadrach laughed. "Looks like it."

"So how come you didn't plant any of them pine nuts?"

"I did, but they never sprouted."

"Well, did you ever go back out there and see if any tree might've grown back where they cut that one down?"

"'Course I did. Never found nothing."

"Hmmm. Okay, but how does all that tie into you knowing so much about me and Parahaia?"

"I dream a lot, Boo."

Boo snorted. Then, she remembered her own dreams. She wanted to ask him about all the times she'd gone back in time and felt like she actually *was* Parahaia. Who knew, maybe she was.

But if she told anyone, the men in white jackets might come lock her up in an Alzheimer's Unit.

Maybe she'd just act like none of it happened— although, it wouldn't be so bad to erase a few years.

"So," Shadrach said, "you going to talk to Mili? I heard she was wanting to come see you. To thank you proper like."

"Sure I am. I got something in my pocket here that rightly belongs to her and the others. I was going to give it to her before I left the shack, but the sheriff come up and told everybody not to move—and it slipped outta my mind."

"Good. I hoped you'd give it to her."

"How'd you know I had the talisman?" She laughed and waved her hand at him. "Oh, never mind, don't answer that—you already have."

Even in the dark, she could see he looked as spent as she felt. "We both could use a cup of coffee. How about I go put on a pot?"

"Coffee sounds good."

Boo went inside and soon had a fresh pot of the black brew. Mugs filled and ready, she collected them, nudged the screen door open with her hip, and headed out. Only then did she realize Shadrach was gone.

"Should've known he'd be gone. Guess I'll never see him again." She sat the mugs on the top step and eased down to the lower one.

"Wouf, I'm still trying to figure out how you happened to show up out of nowhere just when we needed you. Specially since wolves been extinct around here for a long time. I got me a hunch, though." She looked Wouf straight in the eyes for a moment. "Yep, I got me a hunch, all right. You're Parahaia, ain't you?"

Wouf returned her stare without moving. Then the animal winked at her.

Boo couldn't believe it. *Animals can't wink!* She closed her eyes and shook her head. "I'm too dang tired to think about that right now. I'll think about it tomorrow."

She looked up to see Sid walking across the yard toward her. She turned, collected the still-steaming mugs, and when Sid got closer, handed one of them to her. "Here. I made us coffee." No way was she telling Sid she poured the second cup for Shadrach—a man who appeared and disappeared in the blink of an eye. Folks already thought she was crazy.

"Coffee smells good," Sid took the mug and sat on the step next to Boo. "I likely won't sleep anyway." She took a sip then put her free arm around Boo's shoulder. "I'm sorry you and Sasha had to go through all that, and especially sorry I was so far away."

"Ain't your fault. I did it to myself. What makes me so ashamed is, I did it to Sasha. Scares me how close I come to losing her and Dawg because of my dang bullheadedness."

Sid laughed. "You got spunk, woman, I'll give you that. I guess you're ready to take it easy for a few days."

"Not a chance. I'll be heading into the swamp tomorrow morning at first light —maybe even earlier."

"You're kidding!" Sid shook her head. "What in the world for?"

"I'll be looking for a very special kind of pine tree growing a very special kind of pinecone. One of 'em used to grow out there—I know that for sure. I figger since one did, there's got to be another one somewhere. I was sitting here thinking about asking you to go with me. If we find it, it can change both our lives forever. But I ain't gonna tell you any more unless you say you'll go." Boo grinned, raised her mug and held it toward Sid's.

"Well, Boo Murphy, you're sure pulling out the *big guns*." Sid clicked her mug against Boo's. "You know I can't resist a good mystery."